Chasing Marian

Chasing Marian

The Most Anticipated Feel-Good Novel of 2022

by

Amy Heydenrych   Qarnita Loxton   Pamela Power   Gail Schimmel

with fictional guest appearances by Marian Keyes & Himself

MACMILLAN

First published in 2022
by Pan Macmillan South Africa
Private Bag X19
Northlands
2116
Johannesburg
South Africa

www.panmacmillan.co.za

ISBN 978-1-77010-760-1
e-ISBN 978-1-77010-761-8

This book is a work of fiction. It is based on a wide range of personal experiences and observations. Names, characters, businesses, places, events and incidents are either the products of the authors' imaginations or used in a fictitious manner. Any resemblance to actual persons, living or dead, or actual events is purely coincidental.

Editing and proofreading by Nicola Rijsdijk and Jane Bowman
Design and typesetting by Nyx Design
Cover design by Ayanda Phasha

Printed by **novus print**, a division of Novus Holdings

Jess

People notice a woman who drinks alone in public. I suppose they say things. Or at the very least, they wonder. Is she lonely, depressed, friendless? Or simply overconfident, carefree, celebratory? I'm guessing it's always one or the other.

The other day, *I* might have been the one to make a remark to whoever I was with.

Watch to see if she ordered a glass or a bottle.

Does she sip or does she gulp? Is she waiting for someone? Does that make it okay? Or does she just keep on drinking, sitting there on her own? There's something deliciously rebellious about a woman doing that, I think, swirling the crisp dry rosé in its pleasingly bulbous glass.

'Can I top up your wine, ma'am?'

'Please.' I smile at the waitress in her neat white uniform and red lipstick as she fishes the translucent Babylonstoren bottle out of its nest of ice. 'Keep going, keep going, and … stop.' The elegant glass is filled to the brim – it's more like a bowl of wine. I clutch it with both hands to avoid spilling.

A woman I guess to be in her seventies – wearing a sheer, leopard-print shirt, a shock of white hair and dewy skin testament to medical science – taps the leg of my table with her cane.

'A woman after my own heart,' she says. 'You've figured out what matters long before I did.'

I wonder what she means. Is wine what matters? Or being comfortable enough to sit at a beautifully set table in a crowded restaurant and not feel awkward? Or maybe that most radical indulgence: a mother-of-two taking time out for her own enjoyment? Before I can ask, she sidles up to a table in the corner of the smoking section, where her three equally preened friends are waiting for her with a game of bridge, and a gin and tonic heavy with garnish.

I twirl my spaghetti puttanesca onto my fork and take another sip of rosé. Lean back and watch the shifting tides of people floating through Ta-shas. Nestled in the heart of Hyde Park Corner, it provides a temporary escape to a carefully manufactured fake-Paris. Outside, Johannesburg rages on with its power cuts, complicated history and oppressive heat, but in Ta-shas, with its muted blush décor and gentle lighting, the café is suspended in a blissful golden hour. It's one of those places that's always full, usually with folk who come day after day and order the same thing. At a marble table in the centre sits the middle-aged lawyer, always with the front button of his shirt loosened, his tie flopped to one side as he loudly proclaims the fine details of sensitive, high-stakes cases on his mobile phone. His hair looks as if it's held in place by its own power supply. There's the personal trainer who comes straight from her sessions at the private gym nearby to 'enjoy' spinach and scrambled egg whites, and there's the dia-mond-encrusted retired couple who eat every meal at the café, but move to a different table over the course of the day. In between, there's the reliable throng of battle-taut mothers in imported yoga pants, and self-important men in suits, more on their cellphones than at the table.

I have opinions about every table. I make up stories. So of course I wonder what stories these strangers could make up about me. Here I am, the sun pushing through the skylight, casting a golden spotlight on my blissful set-up — a seemingly bottomless bowl of pasta, a bottle of rosé on ice and the latest novel by Marian Keyes — my first I've read by her, in fact. I'm a few chapters in. I laugh out loud at some of the lines (not discreetly into freshly manicured hands like some of my 'ladylike' peers would do).

I am either serenely blessed or raving mad. There is no in-between.

This anonymity is addictive — I drink it up faster than the wine. In my sweeping block-printed maxi dress, sparkling gold sandals and mass of unmanageable black curls, I could be a tourist exploring Johannesburg for the first time, or a high-powered executive grabbing some 'me-time' after acing an important presentation. I am all too aware that privilege floats around my every gesture, a too-strong, too-expensive perfume, but I'm in a room where everybody else is wearing it too.

Another woman walks past my table, round about my age, so late thirties-ish. 'Sorry, I just have to tell you that your hair is incredible. Are those natural curls?'

'They are,' I say. 'I only just chucked out the straightener and started embracing them.'

'Well –' she waves her hand – 'your hair, all of it, looks stunning.'

'Thank you,' I demur. Although I feel completely different on the inside, I am approached often with compliments on the woman I present to the world. Beauty has a strange ability to hide the truth.

To everyone else at this restaurant, I am a woman who has my priorities straight, a woman with an enviable life, who has the time to read during the day.

I am absolutely not a woman whose husband has just left her.

And there's more.

A vaguely interested passer-by who cares to notice my eager slurping would never guess that the pasta in front of me is my first tentative foray after over ten years of stoking a fear of gluten, and that I haven't had a sip of alcohol in almost the same period. That through a gradual gaslighting process involving sketchy online testimonies and social media influencers half my size, I'd convinced myself that gluten disturbed my Gut Microbiome – an elusive, consistently moody fairy queen with an ever-growing list of demands. If only I could please the Gut Microbiome, I would magically be transformed back into my early twenties, pre-childbirth body with its pre-motherhood confidence. As for alcohol, I stopped drinking when the hangover began to outweigh the brief respite of the night before. Besides, my husband – possibly soon to be ex-husband – Joe, didn't quite approve of Unhinged-dancing-in-the-kitchen-to-punk Jess. He preferred Quietly-stirring-macaroni-cheese-while-picking-on-a-salad Jess.

Another sip of wine. Another mouthful of pasta.

The grey-suited men come and go, rushing through the time on their hands. I notice that my Gut Microbiome has not voiced her discontent, and my head actually feels lighter. There's no headache in sight.

I love this wine. I love this book. Marian gets me like nobody else. She feels like a powerful ally in uncharted territory. Yet I find that I've been reading over the same sentence for the past ten minutes. Suddenly my setting feels forced, stale.

The pasta's turning cold. I gulp the wine.

I can only mask the cracks with humour and high living for so long. Very soon, those close to my orbit will begin to guess that I'm going through A Time.

I pick up my phone, alive with notifications. I check WhatsApp. Fifteen unread messages, the bulk from my four-year-old's preschool moms' group. There's an update from the class mom on the Valentine's Day picnic, and someone advertising the babysitting services of their nanny. As per usual, Kelly, the group's most enthusiastic contributor, has shared details of her four year old's vast intelligence:

'Madigan woke up this morning and said, "What a bootiful time to be alive, Mummy." A wonderful message we could all do with today xxx'

Strangely, the great orator has never graced us with her musings – the most I've heard from her is a muffled grunt. Not that I begrudge the child, just the pressure mothers feel to persistently frame their children. Willow, my four-year-old, is my second child. Hannah, my eldest, is twelve going on twenty-five, and I know by now that no matter how hard you try, there are no prizes for 'best child' or 'best effort'. Childhood, much like life, follows its own course. Sometimes I wish I was a better mother to them, but I comfort myself saying at least I'm not the worst.

I scan through the predictable coos and sunny emojis.

'How lovely, Kelly!'

'Clever girl!'

'What a lovely girlie and what a lucky mummy …'

I itch to say, 'Nobody gives a shit, Kelly.' Instead, I promptly leave the WhatsApp group. Does nobody else notice this shit? Does nobody else want to call out the airs and affectations and burn the whole system down?

Another WhatsApp group lights up. It's the organising committee for a charity fundraising gala to aid the victims of gender-based violence in

South Africa. It's a cause I'm passionate about, but I still shake my head at the fact that I'm at an age where I'm called upon to arrange such events. Isn't there a responsible grown-up out there to call the shots?

Oh.

The item up for discussion is the person to deliver the keynote address. The rest of the committee are plumping for a cricketer, or a manly South African thriller writer of the kind that is trotted out every time the privileged classes need entertaining.

The light in the café has deepened into a luminous rust. It's time to relieve the nanny of wild Willow, and check in with Hannah on her maths homework. As I settle the bill and make to leave, I am suddenly struck by the most brilliant idea.

What if Marian Keyes was to deliver the keynote? I'd heard via the grapevine that she might be coming to South Africa for some literary festivals – I think the charity event is around the same time. She's charming, feminist and – if I managed to convince her to speak – would have major clout with the high net-worth individuals we're trying to woo. 'Individuals!' It appears that when your bank account reaches a certain number you're automatically promoted from 'person' to 'individual'.

Joe is an individual. I remain but a person.

Still, it's a brilliant cause, and with a name like Marian Keyes on the tickets, we could make a massive difference in the lives of those who need it. Are my intentions completely altruistic, though? The charity is Joe's baby, something he's nurtured for several years since becoming an executive at the investment bank. It has raised a modest amount each year, but nothing like what we could achieve selling tickets for Marian's address. What a delicious, squelchy slap in the face that would be for him! Remind him of the mover and shaker I once was, that I used to think I was as attractive as everybody else does, that I used to mean something to him.

Then there's the matter of Beverly, the event's treasurer and, I highly suspect, my dear husband's lover. In my experience, Beverlies fall into two distinct categories, Beverly or Bev, and she is most certainly the former. Beverly is an earnest literary sort, the kind who writes lengthy reviews about 'real literature' on Facebook book groups and publicly poo-poos anything vaguely entertaining. She wears Trenery to my Country Road, and her style could be described as 'classic'. It seems she would much rather titter politely at the damp jokes of an ageing, private-schooled South African male than laugh in solidarity with another woman. I must say, I'm more than a little surprised by his choice.

Dammit. The thought of Beverly – with her sensible, wiry bob and penchant for picking invisible lint off my dress – has soured my pleasant afternoon. It's funny the difference fifteen years in a marriage can make. I pine for the university-sweetheart Joe I married in my early twenties, who used to laugh with me at my paranoid observations; now I'm wondering if he's lying next to Beverly as she carefully unclips the press studs of her flannel pyjamas. Everyone thought that after getting married so young it would all go up in flames. Not with a bang, but a whimper more like.

Having left Tashas, I nip in to Woolies to get some groceries. Scowling at the script running through my brain, I pick up a rotisserie chicken and some salad for myself and the girls. Wait. Back to the chilled section. Switch salad for oven chips. Throw a tub of ice cream into the trolley.

The girls are aware Joe is gone, in an abstract sense. They know he is elsewhere but then again, this is not unusual. He often travels or works late over dinner time, or is completely hypnotised by the vortex of his phone. The collapse of his fund has only caused him to retreat further into himself, to a restless, dark place where I can't reach him. Still, a common absence doesn't make it less noticeable. He's the only one who actually understands Hannah's maths homework and can read Willow *The Gruffalo* with all the different voices.

A strange, desolate feeling tumbles through me as I drive home, park my car in the garage, and see the empty space next to mine. As defiant as I am, as much as I've grown to resent the way he doesn't see me and as much as I hate the less-than-surreptitious execution of his unsexy affair, our house in Sandhurst still holds the ideal of our marriage. The couple we were when we first moved in. How big and grown-up its modular design felt, the great steel electric gate, the proper sprawling garden. The ivy we once planted now covers the front façade; the rose bushes have grown into one another while we have, I fear, grown apart.

Enough.

I grab the groceries and bundle inside to find the children. At the back of my mind is a spark, an idea that I'll sketch out and work on once Willow is asleep. How exciting it would be to get Marian involved in this charity event. How tempting to show Joe the powerful, romantic side of me that he's forgotten. And while I've only read a quarter of her book so far, how wonderful would it be to get a few moments with Marian, one-on-one, and thank her for her writing. Perhaps, if I'm bold enough, I'll tell her my story and be as authentic as she seems to be on the page, and perhaps, if she is all I believe her to be, she'll have the wisdom to tell me what to do next so that this will all work out alright.

Ginger

I don't know what I was thinking when I invited my girls to lunch today. It was bad enough hosting bookclub yesterday, and now I have to cook again. And of course my bookclub ladies left nothing – even though I mentioned about twenty times that Debbie and Lee-anne would be here today. The bookclub ladies were too busy squabbling over books and complaining that my house doesn't have enough off-street parking and asking me why I don't move into a complex instead of my house in Blairgowrie to remember to leave some food. It's not like Blairgowrie was my first choice. I wanted to live in Melville because the shops seemed more interesting and the neighbours too. But Roger said that Blairgowrie was good value for money and that the houses were sensible and that he didn't want to raise children surrounded by bohemian artists who might offer them drugs and pornography. So the house is not quite what I would have chosen, or the area, but it has become home and in the three years since Roger died, I've made it more my own and I do love the garden, which was always my domain. Anyhow, the bookclub ladies always suggest that I move into a 'nice, safe complex' or a 'good retirement village' and maybe they have a point. Still, they could have left some food while they bossed me around and told me how to live my life.

So here I am back in the kitchen, like a slave, making food for my adult daughters who are as unlikely to eat it now as they were when they were little. It's for different reasons now, of course. Lee is a vegan. She went from being a teenager who consumed animal protein like some sort of meat vacuum cleaner to not eating veal, and then chicken, and then all meat, and then dairy. God help us if she reads the article I saw the other day about plants having feelings ... I make a mental note not to mention that at lunch today. And then Debbie. Debbie's been on a diet since her teens, to my horror, and now that she's hit forty, it's got worse, not better, like I hoped. But she never quite commits to what sort of diet it is. You have to guess. And you're never right. If I cook a lean chicken breast, she's either not eating meat or she is on a high-fat diet. I mean, what sort of diet excludes a lean chicken breast?

Carbs are either totally not in favour or absolutely essential. All I know is that whatever I do, it's wrong. I can't help wondering if she does it on purpose and just makes up fake diets to annoy me. Well, today I'm on to her. I am cooking everything and she can choose. Like, literally anyone with any food fad will find something to eat. Whatever she doesn't eat I'll eat during the week. Take that, Debbie.

I sigh, straightening out my stiff back. Growing old has its downsides and as I close in on seventy, all my bones seem to be playing up. My daughters look at each other when I tell them this, like I'm admitting to wetting the bed or something. Loaded looks. Sometimes I wonder if I even *like* my daughters. I mean, I know I love them. Obviously I love them. And I loved it when they were small; I loved being a mom to small children. I loved their squishy little bodies, and their hugs, and their laughter. I even loved the tantrums, the whining and the sleepless nights. Other people complained about parenting small kids. Not me. But now, when every-one else's children have become easier, mine have become difficult, even though you'd think that they would be proper adults by now.

With Debbie, I guess I can blame the divorce. She's much grumpier and much thinner since that happened. And I miss her husband. I know I'm not supposed to say that. I'm supposed to call him a lying, cheating scumbag – and of course he is. But also, he was nice. Peaceful. And Debbie was nicer with him. But you can't say that. You have to nod and say 'there, there' and 'that lying, cheating scumbag'. You can't say 'I never liked him' though because then she'll be upset that you never said anything before. Lee-anne learnt *that* the hard way.

And Lee-anne. Except now we have to call her 'Lee'. Since she got to-gether with that Tex. Whoever heard of a woman called Tex? Honestly –

it's a chocolate bar, as far as I know. Lee-anne used to have the nicest girl-friend. Mary-Jane. That's a name you can take to the bank, as Roger used to say. And when Lee-anne and Mary-Jane were together, we could call Lee-anne 'Lee-anne' and we could call Mary-Jane 'Lee-anne's girlfriend' and we could call female people 'women'. But now it's 'Lee', and Tex is her 'life partner' and women are 'womxn' and when I said the word 'fe-male' the other day, I got lectured like I was some sort of bigot Republican. Which isn't fair at all. I kissed a girl at a party once; I'm not cabbage green.

But then, I remind myself as I start chopping carrots – because what diet on earth objects to raw carrot sticks? – it's not like I even loved my girls' names to start. That was all their father's doing. Roger. I'd wanted to call Debbie 'Clarissa'. We'd sensibly waited a bit before we had babies so I'd had plenty of time to think about names. I thought Clarissa was the most beautiful name in the world, which would guarantee her a wonderful life. 'Codswollop,' Roger had said. 'You need a name you can take to the bank.' And even though I had been with Roger for long enough to know that what I had thought was wisdom and calmness was more an inability to change and stubbornness, I didn't fight his view on names.

'But what about *my* name?' I'd ventured to him. 'I thought you loved it.'

I'm named after Ginger Rogers. When she named me my mom had wanted me to be a tap dancer.

'Your parents *are* a bit bohemian,' Roger had said, wrinkling his nose slightly. 'But it's worked out well enough with my name. Still, the baby will be Deborah.'

My parents weren't the least bohemian by any reasonable standards. They were God-fearing members of the local Presbyterian Church, and my father worked in the same bank as Roger. The only flight of romance that they'd ever had was that my mom wanted me to be a tap dancer so badly she sent me for lessons from when I could walk until the day in my teens when I just flat-out refused, and then she cried and cried. It's true that I *was* actually rather good at it, and now I wish I hadn't broken my mother's heart like that. What harm did it do, tapping to make my mother happy? I wonder if I can still dance … it's been years since I tried.

I put down the knife, and take a position in the middle of the kitchen floor. About a year after Roger died, I replaced the terrible seventies linoleum that Roger felt was 'perfectly serviceable' with lovely large white tiles. A pain to clean, but they still make me happy.

They'd make such a fine tapping noise too, if I had the right shoes. My sensible takkies aren't ideal for tap dancing and won't make a sound, but this is just a bit of fun. I put my hands on my hips and a smile on my face and I start.

It's like magic!

Like riding the proverbial bike, I can still do it. My muscles remember and they remember with joy. My back doesn't even hurt! In my head, I hear music and the tap as my toes and heels hit the ground. I spin around, arms outstretched.

Standing in the doorway to the kitchen, her mouth slightly open, is Debbie.

Bloody fucking hell, I hate the way they use their keys, appearing like ghosts when I least want to see them. I immediately stop dancing, and try to assume a look of utmost sensibility. Like she imagined the whole tap-dancing incident. I cannot stand another lecture about how people slip into dementia.

'Hello, darling,' I say, going over to hug her, even though she's like her father and stands like a dead man in my embrace, so far from the little girl she once was. 'How lovely to see you so early. What a delightful surprise.'

'Well …' Debbie looks like she's eaten curdled milk. 'It's certainly clear that you're surprised.'

Lunch starts badly. Debbie is all tight and angry because I was tap-dancing in the kitchen. I've set the table beautifully on the stoep, and for some reason this has also made her angry, although my garden is looking so lovely, and the weather is still warm even though we're at the tail end of summer, and the willow tree always makes it feel magical. When she was younger, she loved eating outside. When I bring out the food Debbie sighs and says, 'Oh, Mother, didn't I tell you?'

'Whatever it is you didn't tell me,' I hiss, 'I've catered for it. I can literally feed any food fad you care to throw at me.'

Debbie allows me a moment before she drops the bomb.

'Mother, I'm doing intermittent fasting,' she says. 'I'm sure I told you, but I guess you forgot. Only to be expected at your time of life, I suppose ...' She pauses and sighs, the weight of my age a burden on her shoulders. Then she brightens. 'Fasting is amazing. Sonja de Jongh lost seventeen kilos, and her skin is glowing.'

'What does that even mean?' asks Lee-anne, who arrived late, grumpy and sans the ubiquitous Tex. 'What *is* intermittent fasting?'

I'm so delighted she's asked this question that I beam at her. She scowls at me and Debbie flings down her fork (why was she holding a fork, I wonder, if she isn't eating) and says, 'I should have known you two would gang up against me.'

'Oh, darling, we're not,' I say quickly. 'But what *does* it mean?'

'It means that I can't eat now, okay?' she says. 'I'm on a fast.'

'How ...' I search for something supportive to say, but come up short. 'How interesting,' I was going to say, only it isn't really. It sounds deathly boring to me.

'Anorexic,' says Lee-anne. 'The word Mom is looking for is anorexic.'

'Don't be silly, Lee,' I say, just managing to stop myself from calling her Lee-anne. 'Debbie isn't *anorexic*.'

'Do you know, Lee ...' Debbie waves her fork again, over an empty plate. 'Mom was tap-dancing when I arrived. Alone. In the kitchen. With the front door wide open.'

I'm almost sure that isn't true, but not sure enough to object. I dish some poached chicken and home-made mayonnaise onto my plate. Lee-anne shares a loaded look with Debbie, before helping herself to three carrot batons, a lettuce leaf and an enormous pile of rice salad.

'It would be so much easier being a vegan,' she says, almost to herself, 'if I fucking liked vegetables.'

Now Debbie and I share a loaded look. Lee-anne has never complained about being a vegan before – but Tex is usually here.

'I had bookclub yesterday,' I say loudly, hoping to change the atmosphere. 'They didn't leave *any* food. They are the greediest people you ever met.'

'What book did you get, Mom?' Debbie is leaning forward – she likes to take the books when I'm done. Lee has looked up from her lettuce leaf. This is the thing we share; our love of reading. I decide to spin it.

'Well,' I say, 'I put in the new Marian Keyes.'

'Oh *yes*, Mommy!' Debbie is affectionate in her excitement. 'I *knew* you'd get that.'

'And then when we were choosing,' I continue, 'Sybil Portley-Smythe grabbed it from right under my hand.' I pause for effect. 'Literally, girls. As I reached for it, she put her hand under mine and just took it.'

I allow a moment for this to sink in. They're both looking at me like when I used to read to them.

'That woman's a menace,' Debbie says after a pause. 'Didn't she also take the new Douglas Kennedy last time?'

'No,' says Lee-anne. 'She took the new Celeste Ng.'

They look to me for confirmation just like they did when they were little. 'She took *both* those – and more,' I say triumphantly.

'Well, I'm devastated,' says Debbie. 'The new Marian is just what I needed. She's the only person in the world who can perk me up.'

Before I can take offence, Lee has pushed away her plate, put her head on the table and started crying. *Well, this is a one for the books*, Roger says in my head.

'What is it, darling?' I ask, tentatively patting her shoulder.

'All I want,' she sobs, 'is to be allowed to read a good, happy story. Or even if it's sad. I don't even care if bloody Sybil whatever-her-face reads it first – I just want to be able to read it without anyone telling me it's anti-feminist and imperialist and non-diverse. She's *Irish*, for God's sake – that's fucking diverse!' She looks at us, daring us to contradict her.

Look, even I know an Irish voice doesn't count as diverse, unless maybe you were tortured in the North while fighting for the IRA. Which I'm almost sure Marian Keyes was not. But I'm not going to tell Lee-anne that. Instead, I make an announcement.

'Girls, I'm going to buy you *both* a copy of the new book,' I say. 'And … ' I search for something to make it more special. '*And* … I will get them inscribed by Marian herself.'

Both girls look at me. Lee-anne's tears seem to halt halfway down her face. Debbie has a carrot in her hand that she forgets to pretend she isn't eating.

'Oh, Mommy,' says Debbie. 'You know you can't do that.' She sounds affectionate about this, not angry.

'Although a copy of the book would be lovely,' says Lee-anne. 'But, Mom, you do know that Marian Keyes lives in Ireland? She can't just sign our books for us.' The girls glance at each other – the same look they exchanged about my tap dancing.

Inside, I'm already panicking. What the fuck have I promised them?

But I tap the edge of my nose. 'I will get you signed copies,' I say. 'Just you wait and see.'

Debbie laughs – a nice change. 'Oh, Mommy,' she says. 'You're very funny.' Without any explanation, she starts to dish up a plate full of food. Full. She takes some of every single dish on offer. Even the mayonnaise.

'What?' she says when she notices Lee-anne and me staring at her.

She glances down at the food.

'*Intermittent* fasting,' she says, by way of explanation. 'It's intermittent.'

Matt

Picture this: the whole family is crying.

Why?

Because they're watching the 2019 Rugby World Cup Final. Again.

We've done this roughly once a month since the Springboks won. Yes, I've watched the game a shitload of times. I mean, by now I could practically play the game myself.

Don't get me wrong, I found the actual game as exciting as the next person. I leapt out of my chair and danced around the room waving my SA flag every time we scored. I shouted, 'Siya, you beauty!' and hugged everyone and cried at the end. And I enjoyed it the second time we watched it. Even the third – I picked up a few details I'd missed, appreciated the magnificence of Cheslin Kolbe's side-steps, realised Cheslin was only twenty-six and an international sporting hero (I am twenty-seven and not an international sporting hero), might've even said, 'Cheslin, you biscuit!'.

But now it's enough. I want to talk about other things, do other stuff. Maybe go to a book launch – they've been promoting quite a few on this Facebook group I'm on, mostly for women's fiction, which is cool. Personally, I love chicklit. Mom has shelves of it and I've devoured it since I was little. In secret, obvs – I went to an all-boys' school and I don't have a death wish. The stories are great, so funny, plus I feel like I'm in on the secret of what women really think about men. (Which is not a whole lot, as it turns out.)

And no, I'm not gay. It would be easier if I were, because then I'd fit into a neat little box: sensitive gay boy, likes women's fiction. Instead I'm a sensitive straight boy that likes women's fiction. Mom thought I was gay growing up because I used to call my sister to get rid of spiders for me (yes, like this is a very reliable indicator of someone's sexuality). I'd ask her to take them outside, but she'd just kill them. My big sister is pretty damn scary. If I was a spider, I'd run. Fast.

Most of the girls at our sister school were just as bad. Or good – depending what side of the feminism fence you're on. I'm definitely a feminist. Reading all those books and listening to Mom's stories has made me realise women have a seriously raw deal. So I consider myself an ally. A friend. If I'm honest, I'm really much more comfortable being in the friend zone. I really love having women as friends, because I just seem to have so much more in common with them.

Although they also think I'm gay. My best friend, Sadie (we've known each other since nursery school), loves to discuss my sexuality with Mom. It can go something like this:

Mom: I just want him to feel like it's okay to come out to me. I think I'd be a great mother for a gay son.

Sadie *nods*: The best.

Mom: Then what's the issue? Why doesn't he just tell us?

Sadie *rolls eyes*: I dunno.

Mom: He hasn't said anything to you?

Sadie: Not a word, Mrs M. I've spoken to him, more than once, but he hasn't confessed any liking for the great purple-veined throbber to me. (*Yes, Sadie actually says things like that to my mom.*) He says he likes women.

Mom: Yes, but does he like them, or does he *like* them?

Sadie: Not sure. But don't worry – I'll keep investigating.

I know all this because they'll have this kind of conversation in the kitchen while I'm bringing in the groceries or something – they're not exactly subtle. But Sadie will wink like they're both on some kind of secret mission, and I can see Mom already planning her gay son's wedding. She's probably also hoping my boyfriend will be black.

But there's no boyfriend. Or girlfriend. Not much sex either. To be honest, maybe I'm just one of those guys who likes sex to mean something. At varsity I did try the whole shagging-everything-that-moves thing, but it just wasn't me. I'd end up having feelings for the girl and she'd tell me to stop being so intense because all she wanted was a fuck-buddy … It got so confusing, I eventually gave up.

Sadie told me I was a pussy. That I had all these women throwing themselves at me (there were actually only one or two) and I wanted to have a relationship so I should stop being such a wimp. Then she remembered she was supposed to be a feminist so she told me she'd said 'wussy' not 'pussy' and then she hit me when I called her a liar.

'Argh!' I shout out without thinking. The family looks at me in annoyance.

'Could you shut the hell up?' my brother, Marcus, says irritably. 'Pollard's about to convert this try.'

'Um … You know he gets it, right?'

They look at me like I'd just ruined their favourite movie.

'It's okay, darling,' Mom says soothingly like she's speaking to a three year old. 'What's that you were shouting about?'

I'm dying to tell her – she'll be as excited as I am – but I won't get away with it in present company.

'Nothing. Sorry.' My hand is shaking as I go back to my Instagram feed.

Point is, Marian Keyes' latest novel has just been released. And that's not all – there are rumblings she might even be coming to South Africa. I know I'm probably a bit young to say this (maybe I just spend a bit too much time with Mom's friends), but I don't think most of us have ever gotten over the fact that in the bad old days of apartheid we were cut off from global culture; the only time an international star performed at Sun City was when their career was in need of mouth-to-mouth and ten firm pushes to the chest. So the prospect of a global icon like Marian Keyes coming to the country while her career is actually relevant … well, it's something.

And, I resolve, come hell or high water, I'm going to meet her. Fame-whore that I am, I'm already composing the tweet in my mind: 'Meet my new bestie, Marian Keyes.'

Mom doesn't know I'm on Twitter and I want to keep it that way. She's a total oversharer and insanely proud of all of us. God knows what for – it's not like we're exceptional in any way. Well, *I'm* not. But Mom still goes into raptures over everything I do, like she once read a book about boosting your child's self-esteem and hasn't stopped boosting mine ever since.

I might have mentioned that she reads a lot – there are books everywhere in our house. And Dad? No. Unless it's the news on his phone. (Maybe that's why there are no 'boy' books in our house.) No, Dad likes to watch sport and he likes to drink. A lot.

I kind of sensed he had a problem when we were younger. I wondered why he was so affectionate – too affectionate – in the evenings and then so grumpy in the mornings. As I got older, I realised why: it's because he's an alcoholic, or to use the correct term, he has alcohol use disorder. It's not so severe that he hides vodka bottles in the toilet cistern. It's more the functioning, acceptable kind. The kind that goes to the club for just one or two drinks and will be home by seven, and then, you know, just has to have a few drinks with old Jerry who's having such a hard time and ends up getting home at nine-thirty instead.

I seem to remember some whispered fights when we were younger, but Mom's mantra was always 'Don't frighten the children', so I think she eventually just accepted it. If Dad was at the club she'd serve dinner at 7pm as per usual and put Dad's in the warming drawer. She just got used to doing her own thing. I asked her once why she didn't leave. She said, 'I love him.'

My sister Micky doesn't get why I have a problem with Dad. She worships the ground he walks on. She's always been a daddy's girl and it irks me the way she treats Mom like she's her slave. The worse Micky treats her, the more Mom bends over backwards for her. I've told Mom to stand up for herself, but she just shakes her head and smiles at me and says, 'You'll understand when you have children one day, Matt.'

Yes, our names do all begin with 'M'. Really. Mom and Dad are Miranda and Malcolm, my sister is Michaela (or Micky), my brother is Marcus and I'm Matthew. Matt. I guess they enjoyed the idea of having a theme or something. Well, Mom did. Dad was probably too pissed to care.

He's already on his seventh beer – normal for a Sunday afternoon. Mom tries not to mind but I can sense her getting tense the more he drinks. The more he drinks, the less I want to drink, whereas Marcus tries to keep up with him, and Micky adds fuel to the fire by fetching him a beer every time he asks. Which is ridiculous, considering that her boyfriend once asked her to get him a drink when his foot was in plaster and Micky said, 'You're not a fucking quadriplegic.' That relationship did not last.

If Dad was a happy drunk it probably wouldn't be an issue. But he's cruel when he's drunk and he picks fights. Mom gets referred to as 'the handbrake', Marcus is a 'wuss' for not keeping up and I'm 'gay' because I don't drink at all when I'm around Dad. Micky is spared because she actively placates him.

Recently though he's started to get wary about picking fights with me, I think since I got taller than him and started studying psychology. Now instead of getting upset, I say things like:

'What's with the homophobia, Dad? Are you attracted to men – is that the issue?' I can see that he wants to hit me when I answer back, but he knows that if he pushes me far enough I'll probably knock him out. The only reason I haven't given him a running fuck-smack up to this point is because it would upset my mother; also there's not much honour involved in knocking out a drunk sixty-five-year-old.

The psychology is also an issue. Dad thinks it's quackery – right up there with healing crystals, not a subject for real men. (Mom had to fight hard to get him to pay for my studies.) He doesn't know that I'm specialising in addiction. I want to help people. Not the addicts themselves, but the people who enable them. People like Micky. And Mom.

I glance across at him. When he's drunk he gets this funny line over the bridge of his nose and his one eye droops.

I decide to go to my cottage before things go downhill – which they always do. I want to see where Marian will be appearing on her South

African book tour. If she's going to be at the Franschhoek Literary Festival, I'll book tickets for me and Mom. A Mother's Day present.

Maybe that's the real reason I love Marian. She's a recovered alcoholic who's been sober for almost thirty years.

If she can do it, why can't Dad?

Queenie

'You so lucky you can wear sleeveless,' Jennifer says with a sniff, the ever-present crumpled tissue at the ready in her hand. 'When I do, I feel like everyone in the office can see my arms wobbling like brown bladdy jelly on a plate.'

'What do you mean? No one cares about your arms – look at me, I could flap all the way to Pinelands Community Library and I bet no one would blink an eye!' I shake my arms so hard I nearly knock myself out. 'Though I guess anyone who signs up at the library for a bookclub called "Eager Beavers" wouldn't be the type to worry about flappy arms,' I add, taking a little twirl in my new blue-and-yellow floral sleeveless dress, my bare feet on the kitchen lino. 'It's the first bookclub of the year and today I'm in charge so it's Marian Keyes in the house, baby! *Grown Ups*. With a side order of batwings by me.' I give another shake and boob jiggle for effect. 'I tell you, they'll be begging for more.' Unlikely, but then I'm not one to let truth get in the way of a good story.

Jennifer finally cracks a smile. My heart lifts as it always does when I can make her smile, the habit of being the silly younger sister who cheers up the serious older sister so ingrained in me that I can't remember being any other way.

'Anyway, your arms are half the size of mine. You must get over yourself – you don't have to be so proper all the time. Shake up that office of yours,' I say, encouraged by the change in her mood. I give another shimmy so that my boobs threaten to escape from the top of the V-neck dress. Not difficult since those puppies don't easily stay down. I stick out my tongue so that it sits in the left corner of my mouth, curled up just so onto my lips.

For funzies, I pull the V-neck down and flash my purple lace bra at her. I mean, puppies need outings and mine haven't been anywhere in forever.

'You do that and there'll be a whole different kind of reader coming to check out books at the library,' Jennifer says, laughing as I get properly into the moves, pumping my legs and waving my long, curly brown hair from side to side, à la Tina Turner – if Tina Turner was a private dancer in the kitchen of our little house in Kensington. (Kensington, Cape Town, not Kensington, London. Like the complete opposite of *that* Kensington. Not posh, our home, but our home since forever.)

'You, Queenie Knight, are *simply the best*. A little cooked in the head, but still the best.' Jennifer wipes the laughter tears from her eyes as I keep going with my impersonation except now with my bra exposed. 'Oh my God, I am hot,' she confesses, moving her arms away from her body slightly. 'No, it's not seeing your boobs that did it,' she says, closing her eyes. 'Maybe it's not the best day for Ma's blouse after all …'

Her voice trails off and I seize the moment faster than if she'd said, 'Have a free Krispy Kreme.'

'Ja, it's going to be too hot for that shirt!' I eye her long sleeves. Ma's shirt. I see Jennifer's face shift. 'But my dress is only perfect because it's the same blue as the one on the cover of *Grown Ups*,' I add quickly, not wanting her to slip back into sad-face and undo the laughs. 'See?' I try to distract her by holding up the thick wodge of book that has accompanied me everywhere for the last week.

Her smile is back. Jennifer has always been a little bit of hard work but she's been even more tricky since Ma's death. I love my sister, but sometimes I wish I could run away and be free from worrying about how she is feeling all the time. Just worry about myself for a minute. I squash the feeling down. I love my sister. I'll save that other emotion for one of the characters in the little stories I'll scribble when I'm in bed later. In my head I hug the secret stash of notebooks in my bedside drawer. What would I do without a place to put all the thoughts and feelings that fill me? It's too horrible to contemplate.

'Let's see your whole outfit,' I say to Jennifer, hoping it isn't obvious that I have a whole other conversation going on in my head about her wearing Ma's shirt. She's changed the original gold buttons and replaced them with plain green ones, but it's still Ma's shirt. In itself it isn't too bad, if you ignore that it's Ma's shirt and Ma's been gone six years now. But the fabric is definitely not summer weight and it has a pussy-bow neck that's knotted too tightly, like it's strangling her. Thankfully the skirt isn't one of Ma's.

Dare I say more? Jennifer already complains that I nag her too much. I mean, seriously, how can she not understand that it freaks me the hell out seeing her in Ma's clothes all the time? They already look so much alike and seeing her sitting at the kitchen table in Ma's clothes does my head in. I know it's not what Ma would've wanted either. 'You girls must have all the fun, live your lives, don't just sit around the house,' she would've said. And I'll bet all my bras that her idea of fun would not have been for either of her daughters to live in her old clothes. Dammit. I miss Ma. I imagine our parallel lives, one where Ma was still alive and Jennifer wasn't always sad and I didn't feel like I was constantly trying – and failing – to make Jennifer feel better. In that life we would be happy. We'd be dancing in the kitchen together. I wouldn't just be writing about those kind of lives at night in bed.

'Wear your yellow shirt with that white skirt. Your gold necklaces. And those sandals with the heels. That'll definitely be cooler. And prettier,' I say finally, winking at Jennifer and going in for a side hug. Smelling my sister's flowery perfume makes me wonder what it would've been like to be part of a big family like the ones Marian writes about instead of just the four of us – and now only me and Jennifer left.

'Okay, fine, I'm going, I'm going.' She moves out of my hug and gets up from the table, shaking her head. 'I don't know why I ask; I know what you're going to say. You're so bossy. But I'm not changing my shoes.'

There's a reason Jennifer and I have always lived together even before Ma left the house to both of us. Jennifer keeps everything in the house in order. Because of her we will never run out of electricity, toilet rolls or bread. But because of me we sometimes laugh at breakfast and drink JC Le Roux on Sundays – Fridays too if I don't feel like Zumba class. She says she's glad we've never liked the same man as she was sure he would pick me. Honestly, if there were such a guy, I'd give all the chocolate in the world for him to pick her.

'And you can also get done already,' she says, looking disapprovingly at my bare feet, the nails painted electric blue. 'Ma was onto something when she nicknamed you Queenie, treating everyone like your loyal subjects who must be obeyed.'

'Well-l-l-l …' I pretend to think, drawing out the word. 'I think Ma just knew that I wasn't a Mavis after all.' I can't imagine myself as a Mavis even though *Mavis Anne Knight* is on my birth certificate and it's what people at school called me. Saying, 'My name is Mavis,' feels the same as when I tell people I'm an assistant librarian – they expect me to be old, grey, single, boring and wearing beige clothes. With spectacles and knitting in my bag. Mavis-the-assistant-librarian is a granny whose only joy in life is to date-stamp people's books. I realise that I'm probably being unfair to Mavises everywhere but Ma did me the best favour calling me Queenie – I feel like it fits me and it's how I always introduce myself now.

'Queenie suits me and anyway, all my subjects love me.' I grin, sticking out my foot so Jennifer can see the crown tattooed on my left ankle. 'Kevin also says so and you believe everything Kevin says.' I try not to think about when last he actually said he loves me. Or when I said it to him. Months ago definitely, maybe a year.

'Kevin? What does he know?' Jennifer teases. 'That guy will say anything after a few months on the rigs. Come, let's get out of here – we're both going to be late for work.'

'Haai, don't be so terrible about Kevin. I'm going to tell him when he calls me again.' I know she's joking. She loves Kevin and keeps trying to convince us to get married. I always tell her that we're only thirty-five, and we're happy as we are.

I never tell her the truth. That we *were* happy before Kevin left for the rigs but now it feels like it's not so much about being happy, it's more that we're so used to being a couple. In my stories, Kevin flies me to wherever he is working and we have holidays together. We go to exotic places and foreign beaches, we eat spicy food and drink cold beer. In that life we talk all the time, we can't get enough of each other. The distance makes no difference to us. I know it's not happening that way between us, but when I write it feels like maybe it could.

'Relax, it's only ten minutes to your office,' I say, pulling open the fridge to scrounge something quick for breakfast. 'And the library is just five minutes from there. Neither of us is going to be late.' I shut the fridge. I can eat at bookclub. I give Jennifer a sneaky smile so she knows what's coming next. 'But you know you can start up those driving lessons again if you don't like waiting for me to lift you? Lots of space in the driveway next to the Figo to park an extra car.'

'Shaddup, man.' She flicks a dishcloth my way, catching me on the arm. 'Always something to say. Why don't you think more about what you're going to say to those Eager Beavers? Can't just show them your bra and hope for the best.'

'Don't you worry – I've got plenty. I've read all Marian Keyes' books. I've been reading her newsletters. I follow her on Twitter and Instagram. I even follow some of her make-up videos – but we don't have all the brands she uses here, and it's too expensive anyhow. Or too "spendy" as she says – cute, hey? – but I still like to watch 'cause she gets so excited. I heard she's coming to this year's Franschhoek Literary Festival. Can you imagine? I mean, I could go to the festival – it's only an hour away. Maybe I can con-vince Esmeralda … but she'll say there's no budget. But imagine I *could* go, meet her, get signed copies for the library,' I dream on. 'Imagine if she actually *came* to the library how many people we'd get through the door … Think how exciting that'd be!' I'm getting as worked up as Marian does over Sephora.

Jennifer laughs. 'You sound like a flippin' stalker, man. It's a wonder you're not imagining yourself going to supper at her house.'

'Ahh!' I take a sharp breath in. Jennifer knows I can't help myself, there's no end to the lives I can picture myself in. 'Imagine I actually went all the way to Ireland to meet her!' I see Jennifer roll her eyes. 'Okay, okay. I'm ready. Let me get my bag and we can go.' I pad out of the kitchen, safe in the knowledge that I can return to that imaginary world, to any one of the stories I choose, at any time. 'But you better change your clothes fast or I'm leaving you at home!'

Three hours later, I'm standing in the Reading Room at the library observing my work: ten wood-backed chairs with padded seats placed at equal distances around the table so everyone has enough elbow room. Two extra cushions for Mrs Daniels because she always complains. I wonder what makes her the princess with a pea. A medical condition? She goes to the toilet at least three times in every club meeting. But she is also very particular about where she sits, always close enough to the water jug and glasses so that she doesn't have to stretch even a centimetre. Not too far from the door to get to the toilet and never close to Mrs Abrahams because she spits when she gets excited. She doesn't use a bookmark but folds over the corners of the page, which makes Mrs Daniels flick her handmade bookmark with its beaded tassel around like a magic wand. I'm convinced the inside of these two women's houses is like Opposite Land. But yet here they both are at the same bookclub. That's the magic about books and about our library – you will literally find all types.

I smooth the edges of the blue tablecloth I've brought from home and laid on the long trestle table on the side of the room. I check the hot-water urn, the tea and coffee things I've set up. A big plate of Lemon Creams, another of mixed muffins from Pick n Pay. At the head of the table is my copy of *Grown Ups*, my notes carefully tucked underneath – the ladies usually have a lot to say, but I like to have something ready in case Mrs Edwards starts on about her clever grandchildren. Most of the ladies don't mind her but it gets under the skin of Mrs Santo, whose grandchildren live in Dubai and don't like to talk to her on the phone. I check my notes again so that I'm ready for Esmeralda. Even though it's the assistant librarians who take turns running the Eager Beaver bookclub, as head librarian she attends every month. She doesn't ever ask questions, but she has a way of listening with her head tipped to the side that makes me stumble.

Fifteen minutes to go. A quick stop in the bathroom and then I'll go downstairs to wait at the desk for the first Eager Beaver. It's usually Mrs

Erasmus, my favourite. She always brings something for the table even though she doesn't have to. She says she knows the library doesn't have a budget for the bookclub and she knows I'm buying the snacks with my own money so she wants to help.

She reminds me of Ma. Always ready to turn anything into a party.

Last check in the mirror. I pat down my hair on top, push some of the curls back so they settle behind my shoulders and look less wild. I fix the wing-tips of my black eyeliner and sweep my eyebrows upwards with a little clear mascara (cheaper than a whole eyebrow kit). It's nearly time for me to pluck them, but at least the shape is still good. Essence lipstick in Pretty Polly on my lips and Have No Shame blush onto my cheeks. That's my face done. A last tug of my dress, puppies in place. A little Tina Turner shake and shimmy for luck.

Anyhow. I'm ready. Bring on the Eager Beavers – Marian Keyes and I are going to show them a good time.

Jess

With Willow safely tucked (or rather, wrestled with much anguish) into bed and Hannah furiously TikToking in the living room, I retreat to my bedroom. I love my girls feverishly and completely, but in their presence I can never quite find myself. Their needs, and Joe's, come first. I sink onto the printed linen that Joe called 'too bohemian' and light the Spiritual Guide incense that always gave him sinusitis.

Funny, I expected the room to feel lighter without him. His voice, clothes and non-fiction tomes filled our room so completely that sometimes I could barely breathe. I often felt there wasn't an atom of space left for me. Yet a heaviness has wafted in the room as distinct as the incense. Before Joe picked up his dreary read, I used to lie in his arms and tell him about my day. He'd remember to bring me some socks because my feet get cold. Practically speaking, I think, trying to get comfortable on the lumpy patterned mess beneath me, he was much better at putting on a duvet cover.

I consider reading more of my book, but pop open my laptop instead.

Facebook's soothing blue-and-white floods my screen. Here's a secret not even Joe knows: I'm addicted to Facebook Groups. I'm an active member of the Johannesburg Heritage Seed Society and Classical Music Lovers Club. I dip into Vintage Fashion Finds (although I cannot stand the acidic baby-powder scent of thrifted clothes). Sometimes, I even try out the Johannesburg Vegans depending on how ambitious I'm feeling. I love the highly specific heated conversations and the characters in each group – the more niche the better.

There's always an oversharer, a hyper-engaged best friend who seems to be online all hours of the day, a trouble-starter and a needy random who blasts everyone about some off-topic self-promotional service. I'm a people-watcher online and offline so sue me – I love that in these insignificant online spaces, people come together. It may be an echo chamber, but gosh it feels comfortable, the type of plush space you could lean back and settle into.

Ooh! My request to join a new group has been approved. As of this evening, I'm part of the South African Marian Keyes Fan Club. Online, I'm usually more eager-best-friend than oversharer, but tonight I need that little red ping of recognition that there are others out there who feel the same as I do.

'Hey, everyone! I'm Jess, a housewife from Johannesburg. I kinda feel like a fraud for being in this group because I'm – (I double-check the book next to me) – only a third of the way through my first Marian Keyes. But I've got to tell you, after reading it the whole afternoon, I was filled with the strangest feeling. My head grew all light and tears choked in the back of my throat. I've always struggled with this sense that I'm not enough, you know? Like I needed to meet this constantly growing checklist to be loved. I don't know, after reading her, I feel vindicated, like I can finally, maybe, let myself off the hook. Anyone else feel the same?'

I press 'Send', feel for my wine glass while simultaneously remembering I left it downstairs, and wait. That was probably a bit much. Maybe Marian Keyes fans have a specific code …

That new-comment chime. Thank God!

It's from someone named Queenie. 'Sistah, it's like you're living in my head. And welcome!'

Another one. Someone called Ginger.

'I'm just jealous you still get to discover all the books she's ever written. Hi and nice to meet you.'

I love this group already with its troop of highly responsive superfans with interesting names.

'You should have seen me after reading *Rachel's Holiday* ugly-crying into my pillow!'

A woman called Matt – of course.

I imagine all of us sitting on our various devices all across South Africa. What does 8.15pm look like in their households? What books are on their bedside tables and what have they had for dinner? Do they have children communicating in a language they don't understand on TikTok? Or young kids that both drain them of their sense of wellbeing and self while filling them with a joy they never knew possible? I think of Marian Keyes across the world in Ireland in what I imagine to be a cheerful, brightly coloured home, hopefully typing diligently in enviable silk loungewear. What makes her resonate so much with us South Africans? With me? Is it the shared violence in our national histories that has bred this dark yet emotionally vivid sense of humour?

Hey, I should make a note of that. It's the kind of faux-intellectual statement that'd make Beverly's ears prick up – an ordeal that'll be necessary if I want her on board for Marian's address at the charity event.

I turn my attention back to my new online friends.

'I just want to give her a hug and say thank you, you know?'

'Well, soon you can do just that,' replies Queenie. 'Rumour has it she'll be at the Franschhoek Literary Festival soon. No official announcement yet, but I read something about it on Twitter.'

'That was probably my mom blurting out whatever she's heard in bookish circles,' says Matt. 'The woman is a compulsive oversharer.' He smiles warmly, 'That's why I love her.'

'I don't know how Twitter and all that works but thank God she's coming. I've promised my bloody daughters signed copies of her latest book,' says Ginger.

A prickle of guilt gives me pause.

I should tell them about the charity function, shouldn't I? But isn't it a bit presumptuous, predatory even, to parade the poor woman at an event most probably in dry and downright deplorable company after only just discovering her work? I look at the chat bubbling before me – it's too pleasant to taint.

'It would be incredible to meet her,' I simply type.

'EVER WANTED TO LOSE 10KG'S FAST? ASK ME HOW. LOOSESTOOL SLIMMING TEA – AVAILABLE FOR THE FIRST

TIME EVER IN SOUTH AFRICA,' comments someone with a blurry profile picture. I laugh out loud. That sounds like the type of product my Gut Microbiome might deem worthy of her delicate constitution.

Then a chat window pops up. It's Matt. 'Hi everyone, I thought I'd take this into the DMs. Some funny types out there. You know how it gets when a famous person comes to South Africa. People line up around the block. It's going to be hard for us true fans to really connect with her.'

That shameful pang again, that feeling that I've been invited to an exclusive party by accident.

On the other end of the screen, Matt continues: 'I have to meet Marian, no matter what. We'll have to think of an idea ...'

Ginger

It started as such a positive idea.

Facebook. Debbie and Lee-anne told me I *had* to get on to it, that everyone stayed connected that way and I'd love getting in touch with friends who've moved away or who I haven't spoken to in years. It's certainly true that many of my friends have emigrated. With some I've been heartbroken, but others were a blessed relief.

'But maybe I lost touch with them for a reason,' I'd suggested, but Debbie and Lee-anne were having none of that. This was all when Roger was still alive and nobody was telling *him* to go onto Facebook and get in touch with people.

'What about Dad?' I asked the girls. 'Shouldn't he be on Facebook too?'

They'd looked at each other and had a silent conversation. They've been able to do that since they were small and sometimes I'm in on it and sometimes I'm not. This time I wasn't, but I could imagine what they were thinking. Eventually Debbie had said, 'Dad's not really the social media type,' and Lee-anne had said, 'I think Dad might be the person no one wants to get back in touch with.' And even though I felt terribly disloyal, I snorted with laughter and next thing the three of us were hooting, and Roger came through and said, 'What's going on? I can't hear myself think with all this carry-on.' And that obviously set us off again.

After that, we'd spent a lovely afternoon with them setting me up on Facebook, choosing my profile pics and entering important life events with pictures. They made me dig up a wedding photo with me looking so young and so awed by Roger, and Roger looking like the cat who got the

Chasing Marian

cream. All I could see was how stupid and naïve I was, but the girls oohed and aahed about how beautiful I was, which made me happier. And then we had great fun choosing baby photos of them to record their births as life events, and then Mary-Jane came and poured us all drinks, and we searched for people I might want to be online friends with and it looked like it was all going to be a happy shared hobby, like our reading.

And then I found my high-school friend Angela and they showed me how to send a friend request. And Angela accepted immediately and we scrolled through her photos and I could see exactly why everyone loves Facebook so much.

And then it happened. I was so thrilled to see Angela that I went onto her *wall* (I had the lingo down pat!) and started to write her a letter.

Dear Angela, I wrote. Then I left two lines. *How lovely to see you here on Facebook! How are things with you and your family? Did you hear about what happened to Louisa when she was in Paris, it was terrible …*

I was just getting into it when Debbie glanced over. And all hell broke loose.

'Jesus Christ,' she yelled. 'What are you doing?'

'Writing a letter to Angela on Facebook,' I said. 'Isn't that the whole point?'

Then Lee-anne turned on me. 'A *letter*,' she said, pulling the laptop so it faced her. 'Oh God. You boomers are all the same.' She started deleting my writing.

'What are you doing?' I asked.

But even Mary-Jane was with them on this. 'Ginger,' she said gently, 'you can't just write letters on Facebook. That's not how it works.'

'And you can't share gossip about other people, Mom. Everyone will *see* it,' said Lee-anne.

'And capital letters,' said Debbie. 'Do not type things in capital letters.'

'But I didn't,' I protested.

'You were *thinking* in capital letters,' she said. 'I know you were.'

Then suddenly there was this deluge of instructions about capital letters and not asking after people's ailments and not making irrelevant comments and not dramatising things and not sharing certain things but

33

definitely sharing other things and eventually I slammed shut the laptop and said, 'You know what? Forget it. I guess I'm too old for Facebook after all.'

But I did go back on when they weren't watching me. And I figured it out. I figured out how to send Angela a secret letter – it's called a DM for some unknown reason – and she then posted a whole long letter to my page and I sort of saw what the girls meant. It *was* a bit mortifying having her ask after my Auntie Myrtle's knees in front of the whole world.

So these days I don't 'post' anything on my 'feed' because of course I'm still 'friends' with my daughters, and even with poor Mary-Jane, so anything I post is open to their criticism. But I quietly follow what's going on in their lives and sometimes when I'm feeling brave, I even 'like' a post. I actually have Facebook on my new smart phone and I check it the whole time.

And then there's the 'Groups'. If I join any of those private groups, I can comment without my daughters seeing and I can say whatever I like without fearing their wrath. Since Roger's death, my Facebook groups have been a great comfort. I'm a whole other Ginger there. Chatty and involved. Maybe it's the only place I'm the real Ginger.

So when I saw a suggestion for a group for South African Marian Keyes fans, I immediately joined. I was one of the first few participants, which made me happy. If you join early and comment a lot, you get one of those badges or a steaming cup of coffee next to your name. It makes me feel important, which is obviously pathetic, but you take what you can get in this life, as my mom used to say.

So I joined in the first chat that someone called Jess started – lucky fish is new to Marian Keyes so she has all those delicious reads ahead of her. Then someone called Matt got into the mix and I found myself a bit confused. Is Matt a woman? Surely she must be because I've never met a man who likes Marian Keyes and admits to ugly-crying. And if Lee and Tex have taught me one thing, it's that your name can be anything you like. Then I look at the little picture next to the comment and it seems to be of a man. But that could be Matt's boyfriend or son or father – or really anything. Or maybe Matt is gender fluid. Lee has made it very clear to me that people don't have to be men or women, or even womxn, if they don't want to be. You can be whatever you want. Which is fine with me, no matter how much Lee likes to pretend that I'm some sort of arch conservative. I truly don't care who people sleep with or what gender they want to be while they do it. I think about mentioning this to Matt.

But before I can, his or possibly her or *their* face pops up on the side of my phone screen.

Well, this is new. I don't really know what to do with it and when I stab at it, it moves around. Eventually (I have no idea how) a little cross appears over it and it disappears.

I sigh.

I wish I was a bit better with my smart phone. Or had the sort of daughters I could ask. But I guess Matt's face popping up on my screen wasn't that important really. Maybe it was because I was thinking about him/her/them ... as unlikely as that sounds. At least I made it go away. It would have been mortifying to walk around with a stranger's little face on my screen for the rest of eternity.

Matt

Matt: So, I was thinking ... why don't we invite Marian to dinner when she's here? A proper South African meal? I have to admit this is not just for me – I also want to do it for my mom. She's like a Marian superfan.

Queenie: Ah ... that's really sweet of you.

Sweet *sigh*. Yep, that's me.

Matt: We won't invite the press so she'll be able to really let her hair down and we'll cook like bobotie or something and give her biltong.

Queenie: I don't know, Matt. I cook a mean bobotie, but I think she might be a veggie and she's probably got fancy PR people to keep her away from real people like us.

Jess: Mmm ... and who can blame her when you read some of the comments on social media? Do you ever look at the comments on Harry and Meghan?

Queenie: That makes me SO freaking mad. It's racist kak! The press just don't like her 'cause her mom's black ...

Jess: I think Princess Diana would've loved her.

Queenie: Oh, she totally would've! And she would've been so good with little Archie and Lilibet.

Jess: Do you think Di would've preferred Meghan to Kate?

Queenie: I think so. But she would've been too kind to let it show. That William's a chop anyway. I think he's so jealous of his brother ...

Okay, I can see we're just a hop and a skip away from discussing Charles and Camilla and him wanting to be one of her tampons. I need to nip this in the bud. Later.

Matt: Me too. Maybe it's 'cause Harry married a movie star. Have to say I was surprised. I mean, for a ginger with no formal qualifications to marry a woman who looks like that. Obvs he's a prince. But still. It gave us all hope.

Ginger: What's wrong with being a ginger?

Shiiiiiit. Ginger is back. There's nothing to do here but apologise.

Matt: Sorry, Ginger. That was really insensitive of me. I apologise.

Ginger: I'm messing with you, Matt.

Matt: Is this a trick?

The others are having a field day with laughing emojis – and a poo emoji from Queenie to represent the kak I'm in. Nice.

Ginger: No. I'm really just teasing. Sorry, couldn't resist. I'm not even ginger, you know.

Matt: As long as you're not hurt by what I said. I would hate that.

Ginger: What a kind boy you are.

A 'kind boy'? Jesus. I think my penis just shrank by three inches.

Ginger: You are a boy, aren't you?

Jess: I wanted to ask that myself. I wasn't sure if it was appropriate …

Queenie: Most men don't reads books written by women.

Matt: I guess I'm not most men.

Ginger: Is it men or is it mxm? You know, like women are now womxn?

Jess: Lol!! Mxm actually means something else, Ginger. It's when you suck your teeth or click your tongue. That kind of sound.

Ginger: Honestly, I can't keep up.

God, I hope Jess is not a know-it-all like my sister. I take a deep breath and remind myself that what we don't like in someone else is usually a reflection of something in ourselves and not about them at all. In shrink terms we call this projection.

Matt: Yes, Ginger, I am a boy-man-mxm.

Ginger: *poo emojis*

Matt: Um … Ginger. Why are you telling us we're speaking sh*t?

Ginger: What?

Queenie: You used the poo emoji.

Ginger: Oh! I always wondered what that was. How about :D? That is the laughing one isn't it?

Matt: Yes, that's the laughing one.

Ginger: Sorry! For the poo and for being late. As you can see I'm not that clued up with all of this. I couldn't work out how to look at my private messages on my phone. So I'm on my computer now. Did I miss anything?

Matt: I was just saying, @Ginger, that we should invite Marian for a meal when she's here. So we can meet her properly.

Ginger: I love that idea. And I'd be happy to have it at my house if everyone's keen?

Queenie: The only problem is I'm in Cape Town and it's not like I have the cash to fly up to Joburg for a dinner.

Jess: I'll pay for you to fly up.

Queenie: Are you mad??? You don't even know me.

Jess: I know that it wouldn't be the same without you.

Okay, maybe Jess isn't so bad, after all …

There's a faint 'knock knock' and Mom walks in. I live in the granny flat in my parents' garden. It's a very nice flat – double story with a big open-plan kitchen and living room downstairs and a bedroom with en suite bathroom and an amazing view of Joburg upstairs. In spring when the jacaranda trees are flowering, I look out on this purple haze that feels like something out of a story book. Now, in late summer, it's still lush and tropical and when you see all the trees you can believe that Joburg is the biggest man-made forest in the world – something that's actually been disproved but hey, if Cape Town's got the sea and the mountain, at least we've got our forest. There were big fights about who was going to get the cottage, but as I was the only one who was prepared to pay rent (Micky and Marcus thought they would get it for free), I got it.

'What're you doing? You working?' Mom asks, hovering. 'How are the scripts going?'

Besides doing a bit of lecturing at the university and some counselling,

I'm a consultant for a local TV company. They produce soapies and I give them feedback on whether the stories are believable or not. I was so earnest when I first started out until I realised that I was there kind of for my expertise, but really as a box-ticking exercise.

('The Head Writer: So, can she have a form of amnesia that also includes hallucinations and maybe, like, an imaginary friend because that seems to be where we're headed, and the actor really likes that idea?

Me: Well, that's not really believable—

HW *giving me the death stare*: We do not want to do rewrites, Matt.

When the head writer says that, I know I'd better come up with a relevant condition that fits what they've already written. Honestly, I should be adding all these amazing new conditions to the DSM, the official handbook of mental disorders.')

I'm about to pretend that I'm immersed in work even though I'm not, but then I look up and see a vulnerability I've never noticed before. My mom is lonely. I feel this fist-clenching-around-my-heart feeling that makes me want to go down to our local, The Blind Tiger, drag my father out and punch him in the face. He has no idea what he's squandering. He says Mom is the love of his life – he's always so over-sentimental when he's had a few (*Miranda is the first and last girl I ever loved*). But she's not. Booze is.

'No, no, it's fine. I'm just messing around on Facebook,' I say, and quickly type a message to the group: 'Wow, that's very generous of you, Jess. Guys, I have to go. I'll check in later.'

I close my laptop. Mom looks amused.

'You like Facebook? Marcus says it's only for boomers.'

'That's what he tells everyone, Mom. But he's forever stalking his old school mates on Facebook, checking how out of shape they are and if they're making more money than him.' Marcus does something in finance, earns a shit-ton of cash and is obsessed with his car and his abs. He could afford to buy his own place but it's cheaper for him to live at home and Marcus is so cheap he makes Scrooge look like an amateur.

She tries not to laugh.

'What?'

'You're awful.'

'You know it's true. Can I make you some tea?'

'Love a cup.'

We go through to my kitchen. In the cupboard I have coffee beans, coffee pods, coffee grounds, instant coffee … no tea.

She smiles. 'Let's go back to the house.'

Mom's kitchen is offbeat, kind of like her. All screed and colourful tiles with inspirational messages all over the bright-red retro fridge. I flick on the kettle and take two mugs from the cupboard. I choose 'Best Mom in the World' and 'Too old for this kak'. Mugs with messages are a big thing in our house.

'Orange and ginger, normal, rooibos or green?' I ask, looking through the selection.

'Orange and ginger is really for when you have a cold. Normal and green have too much caffeine. Is there any peppermint?'

I scrabble through all the boxes. 'Yep. Think I'll join you. I've had enough caffeine for one day.'

Mom grins, knowing this is not at all true. My love of caffeine is legendary – I can drink coffee right before bed and I'm fine. But I like to humour her by drinking the odd cup of herbal tea. I also do it to irritate Dad, who thinks that drinking herbal tea is one step away from auditioning for *RuPaul's Drag Race*.

Soon we're sitting across from each other at the kitchen table. The little red light indicates that the warmer oven is still on. I want to turn it off so badly – I hate the way she enables my dad – but I don't want to upset her. She should just throw his supper in the damn bin.

Mom is quiet as she squeezes the teabag in her mug, releasing the scent of mint. Too quiet.

'Mom?'

'What?'

'Is everything okay?'

'Everything's fine. Why wouldn't it be?'

I study her for a long moment.

'Stop doing the psychologist stare,' she says with a sad smile.

'But I *am* a psychologist – *almost* a psychologist. I can't help it.' I am supposedly in the home stretch of my studies, I've handed in my thesis, I've done my internship and I'm just about finished my community service so now I'm just waiting to write the board exam before I can officially call myself a clinical psychologist. It's taken me a bit longer than I imagined to get to this point, like two years longer – it was almost impossible getting accepted into the Master's programme – but the end is now in sight.

She's silent. But silence doesn't bother me – it's what makes me a good listener. 'I'm having this issue. With my breast,' she says baldly.

'Issue? What kind of issue?'

I'm shocked and I can't hide it. She sees my face and goes into mother mode, reassuring. 'It's like this redness, reminds me of when I had mastitis when I was breastfeeding you. Probably nothing, but it's just making me a bit anxious. I've got an appointment for tomorrow for a scan and they might have to do a biopsy.'

I try to act like a psychologist, to not react, to reflect her feelings back to her. I fail. 'Oh, Mom,' I say and I grab her hand and hold it. I'm scared for her but more than that, I'm scared for me. What would I do without her? I keep chanting, *This is not about you, this is not about you*, as I try and pull myself together. 'When did you find it?'

'Not long ago. Don't worry, it's not something I've been putting off.'

'Does Micky know?'

She shakes her head ruefully.

'I didn't want to worry her … you know, because breast cancer can be hereditary …'

'If it *is* breast cancer,' I add quickly. And as far as my sister goes, I know what she means, Micky can make anything about her, even someone else's illness. 'Do you want me to come with you? To the hospital, I mean?'

'Thank you, my boysie. But Dad says he'll take me.'

That explains the bender at The Blind Tiger. He's probably as shit scared as I am. 'Okay, well, if you need anything ...'

'I will. You're a good boy, Mattie.'

I keep holding on to her hand and decide I'm going with to the hospital anyway. Just in case.

A couple of days later, I'm sitting in front of my laptop looking at my Facebook feed and thinking about things. Is there even any point trying to plan this Marian Keyes surprise for Mom? I see there's a chat going on with my favourite fan group, but I don't feel like joining. Then I give myself a lecture on allowing myself to be vulnerable and think, *what the hell*.

Matt: Hey, guys. Sorry I've been awol, but I'm not sure this Marian surprise is going to happen in time for me ...

Ginger: Why not?

Matt: Sorry if this is a bit TMI, and it might be absolutely nothing, but my mom thinks she might have breast cancer. Doctor's appointment is tomorrow. She might even have to have a biopsy.

Queenie

Queenie: Fuck. That sucks.

I send the message before I realise what I've written. I really should think first. I know it's because when I write, the words come out exactly as I feel; there's no filter. Unlike when I'm speaking to people – then I am more considered, more careful. I watch their faces, see how they react to me, start to imagine what is happening inside their heads. I tailor what I say. I can feel how my words change from my heart to my head and then out my mouth. I think this is why I feel so close to Ginger, Matt and Jess even though we haven't known each other for very long. We've been group chatting on WhatsApp over the last few days. Sometimes I've found myself just popping off a message to them about whatever is happening. I say exactly how I feel in those messages and it's so much easier than having to speak the words. I don't have many people I can be like that with.

But now what do I say in my next message to Matt? He is no ordinary guy, or at least I don't know another man who would be comfortable in a Marian Keyes club, and I often forget he is a man when it's all online chat. I can feel myself start to overthink. Do men and women need you to say different things in a crisis? When Meagan at work had breast cancer she told me about the stupid things people said to her, how everyone knew someone who'd either recovered or died, and how they just *had* to tell her the story in every detail. How some people immediately took a cancer diagnosis as a death sentence and how messed up that was. Others started lecturing her on treatment options with unwanted advice on juicing organic vegetables and the oxygenated herbs that worked for their cousin's friend and that would definitely make every bit of cancer disappear.

Shit. I'm not good in a crisis – Jennifer is *that* sister. She has the sooth-ing voice and the calming disposition. I'm pretty sure she doesn't have the voices in her head either.

I can't have been the only one struggling with what to say because no other messages come through for a minute, and then Ginger's and Jess's messages both come at the same time.

Ginger: Matt, my boy, I'm so sorry. Try not to worry too much. Lots of women have biopsies. I'm sure it's going to be okay. One of the women in my bookclub, Sybil, had to have a biopsy last year. It turned out to be nothing but a lump of fat. But the stress she was under before the biopsy and the wait for the results were terrible! She didn't make it to bookclub that month and she never misses. It's normal for you and your mom to feel anxious.

Jess: It's going to be fine! Just think positive thoughts. Sending you both lots of love and strength for tomorrow.

Matt: Thanks. I'm so stressed about it. There's never anything wrong with Mom – she's such a rock. Always thinking about everyone else. It's the first time I've seen her look worried for herself, if that makes any sense. I don't know how to deal. I'm trying to keep calm but I'm freaking the hell out.

Queenie: Yes, what Ginger and Jess said! Matt, I'm sure she is going to be fine.

Matt: I'm going to go now. My dad's home and I want to check if he's still okay to take her to the hospital tomorrow. X

Before we have a chance to say anything more, he's gone. Jess and Ginger say their goodbyes and leave just as quickly. Mine wasn't my finest response, I know, but I was mortified that I was going to say the wrong thing and make it worse. I scroll through all the chats we've had. Tons of messages already. I realise that no one except me has said a single swear word – unless you count Ginger talking about her 'bloody' daughters – and I wonder if that's a thing for them. People can be funny about swear-ing. Some do it so much they don't even register, and others choke when they hear it like they're spitting up a furball. I'm careful at the library when the school kids are there wanting help in the afternoons, and I'm careful with the Eager Beavers (I once said, 'Oh my God' and Esmeralda went off about blasphemy like she'd just found twenty unchecked books in my car) but the rest of the time I swear more than Jennifer would like. I don't think about it except when she says that it's very un-ladylike and un-librarian-like to swear. Which I admit doesn't exactly discourage me – I just phone my friend Faheema and swear even louder so Jennifer can hear me wherever she is in the house. Faheema pisses herself laughing – she says I'm such a rebellious little sister. We take bets to see how long it will be before Jennifer comes to tell me off.

But I feel bad about Matt – I should've been kinder. I send him a DM.

Queenie: Hey, I'll be thinking of you tomorrow. If you want someone to chat to while you're waiting the time out, then message me, okay? It's not usually busy in the mornings at the library. You can even call if you want. I don't always know the right thing to say but I can talk rubbish to distract you :)

Matt: Okay, thanks! That's really kind of you. I might take you up on it. My dad says he's going to take Mom to the hospital but he's here falling over his own fucking feet. I don't know how he'll get her there for a 7am book-in. Now Mom's worried that I'm worried and she's trying to sober up my dad by force-feeding him supper while he's looking for the last beer in the fridge. It's a shitshow. Can't believe this is the same guy who puts on a suit and goes to work like a normal person every day. Sorry, talk about TMI, I've just had enough. Tomorrow I'll either be at the hospital waiting for her or somewhere pretending to listen to a lecture – it'll be cool to have someone to chat to. Will be in touch if I can. Got to go now.

Queenie: Don't worry about TMI. It's real. You all already know more about me than people who've worked next to me and seen me every day for years. I've told you things that I haven't even told my sister, my best friend or my so-called boyfriend. So please be in touch if you feel up to it. Whatever you need! I'll watch out for you on my phone tomorrow. Hope you get some sleep. xx

Thank God he swears too! I plug my phone into the charger next to my bed. It's the second time on the charger today – damn thing seems to be going flat too fast. Almost 10%.

I think of my new best friends on this Marian Keyes group. Our name sounds very boring. We should have a cool name, like Lady Gaga has Little Monsters – I'm definitely going to mention that to them next time.

I wonder what they're all like, as in their real lives? What's happening behind their closed doors? I can't help myself, I make up stories about them. I go through this with everyone I meet, even people I don't know who catch my eye. Jess seems like a yummy mummy with too much money and too much time. She absolutely only shops at Woolies, no Checkers for her. Offering to pay for me to fly to Jozi for dinner? That threw me. I don't want to feel like I'm taking advantage of someone like some kind of twisted literary catfisher, and I also don't want to be a rich lady's charity case.

Ginger is such a laugh. She pokes fun at herself about being technically challenged but she is up for anything. She is at least thirty years older than Jennifer but I so wish Jennifer could be like her, willing to trying something new, meet new people. If I get to go to the Franschhoek Literary Festival to see Marian Keyes, I'm going to drag Jennifer with me.

Matt is the kind of guy I would've liked to have as a little brother. I think a brother of mine, with a father like mine, would've read everything, including Marian Keyes. Pa was the only one I showed my stories to, he always took them seriously and would ask about the characters. How did I come to name them? What inspired me? Ma and Jennifer were more alike – practical and quickly tired of my imaginings. I didn't know that Pa was different from other men, but now I see it in Matt too. At the library it's mostly women who take out Marian's books – the men all seem to want to read crime or autobiographies written by other men. 'Where are the *real* books?' Mr Daniels once asked me when he came in to get Mrs Daniels. What a moron. I don't like to admit it but Kevin doesn't read at all unless it's something he's found on Facebook. I tell myself that when we do go on holiday together I'm going to pack some books by local authors that he won't be able to resist. I'm working on a list.

Anyway, Jess, Ginger, Matt – I'd never meet people like them in my everyday life here in Cape Town. Or maybe I would, somehow, at the library. But being friends with these white people? How would that happen here?

I pull my phone off the charger and go back into the Marian Keyes group on Facebook. Yes, we definitely need a better group name. I'll ask Matt tomorrow – maybe it'll take his mind off his mom. I stare at Jess, Ginger and Matt's profile pics again and send them all friend requests. I know no one puts their real life on Facebook, but you get a pretty good idea of people when you see what they decide to post. My page has all my check-ins and posts from Zumba and I follow some local authors' pages and there's some motivational quotes because nothing uplifts me like the right words on the page.

I know I post pictures of too many random things like yesterday's doughnuts we had for breakfast at the library. I do it because when I look back at my feed, it reminds me of the little things I enjoyed. Besides, if I waited for big, exciting things to post there'd be nothing there. There's also a million photos of our library events, anything to get people to see that our library is a fun place to be. I also do a word of the week. I know it's nerdy and random, but it gives me a laugh. This week's is 'Dewlap: Fold of loose skin hanging from throat, especially in cattle'. I sent it to Jennifer on WhatsApp and told her that if we grow dewlaps, we'll have something to match our batwings.

Wonder what the Marian Keyes group will think when they see all my stuff?

Doesn't matter. I love Fakebook. I share the best parts of my day there so if they don't like what they see, then it's too damn bad. And Facebook lets me see what other people get up to. So what if I'm curious – 'nosy', 'snoopy', call it what Jennifer likes – I'm interested in people. There's this idea that if you are a librarian you're only into books, but the best librarians I've met are the ones who love people. Books are nothing without people to read them, and it's my job to get people to read them. And sometimes seeing what other people are doing on Facebook encourages me to stop dreaming, to stop only imagining and writing about what I could do and to actually *do* it. Already the Marian Keyes Facebook group has made me think about how I'm going to get to Marian Keyes in Cape Town if I can't get to her in Joburg.

On my phone I switch into the draft section of my email box, where I've already started working on an email to Esmeralda. I read it quickly.

Dear Esmeralda

I'm sure you already know that the Franschhoek Literary Festival is coming up in May. I saw on Twitter that Marian Keyes will be at some of the events. I was thinking it would be good for the profile of the library if I went and got her to sign the library copies of her books as we have many of her fans in our area. I could write a newsletter (with photos) on what happened at the events, and this could be sent to all our members. I would also be happy to give a full report at any future Eager Beaver meetings. Once the full programme of the festival is available I will ...

That's all I have.

I want to say that I'd love to go for a day or two and attend as many of the events as I can. I want to beg her to sponsor me.

The screen of my phone blanks because I stare at the email for too long without typing. Dammit, I wish I could get a laptop but no one at work gets one, not even Esmeralda.

It's so frustrating – we're expected to come up with these amazing programmes to encourage the kids and adults to read, but we have no resources to do anything. Work from home? Forget about it. I can't get into any of the other systems we use – the only thing I can do is access my work emails from Webmail. No one can say you work at Public Library Services for the perks, that's for sure.

No use complaining though. Always the same response: No budget. No budget. No budget. You have to be a librarian because you love it, finish and klaar. Wish I could win the Lotto. A new phone and a laptop would definitely be on my list – hell, a bunch of laptops for the library would be on my list. And tickets to all the Franschhoek events, with an overnight stay for me and Jennifer. A spa outing also ...

'Anyway,' I say aloud to myself to stop the dreaming in my head. 'Rome wasn't built in a day.'

I'm going to sleep on it; maybe the right words to end my email will come to me in the night. As I plug my phone back into the charger, I see a new notification jump up.

Jess has accepted my friend request.

Jess

Woolies Hyde Park again. I pull up my trolley and begin unpacking my groceries onto the conveyor belt. *Paw Patrol* yoghurts for Willow, chicken nuggets for Hannah and a couple of bottles of Diemersfontein Pinotage for me. The transition from teetotaller to nightly drinker has been swift and red wine has enough heft to pull me down into slumber each night. And Diemersfontein is a good weekday wine – classy, but not too crazy, maybe even the healthy choice? I throw in a few slabs of Lindt, but not the demure 70% – tonight I want milk chocolate, with sea salt and caramel bits. Joe never liked it.

This is the only clue that he's gone: my grocery trolley. If Ubuhle, the cashier, takes any notice she doesn't say anything. What a strange life I lead that the only person I see more than my husband and children is the cashier at an upmarket grocery store. I hand over my card.

'Sorry, ma'am. Declined.'

My heart starts pounding. 'Oh goodness! I must have picked the wrong one. I forget what month it is, you know? It's probably expired. No time to pick up a new card, especially with the kids always in tow ...' I ramble.

Ubuhle remains expressionless as I hand over another one.

'Also declined.'

Shit. I scramble for my backup-of-backups card, the one Joe once gave me for emergencies, but which has moved to the front of my purse in recent weeks. I enter the pin code and breathe a sigh of relief as the little 'Approved' banner flashes across the screen. I almost expect a high five from Ubuhle, but there is none.

'Thanks, Ubuhle. Bye!' I smile, pretending we don't engage in this little dance every day.

'Have a lovely evening, ma'am.' Her eyes don't meet mine.

I take the long route to the car park so I can grab a coffee and swing past Exclusive Books. The air is rich with the scent of roasted beans. The tables at the entrance are groaning with hotly anticipated new releases. I run my fingers along their spines, an action that usually calms me. This is a path I trace often, but today feels different. Today, I feel as if I'm floating outside my body, observing the ridiculousness of my situation.

It all seems so pointless – strutting around in my overpriced bohemian garb and Gucci sliders, too wealthy to give a shit about wearing silk to buy chicken nuggets, pushing my overloaded trolley through the classist corridors of Hyde Park ... I act like I belong here, but I don't. Look a bit closer and you'll see the sag of my fading Botox, the black Gelish peeling off my nails like tendrils of soot. Here is the truth: I don't have money any more.

Worse, Joe and I are in deep financial trouble and I don't see a way out.

I float aimlessly through the bookstore, picking up books and putting them down as if merely holding them is enough to still my existential distress. This new Marian Keyes group has come at the perfect time. Since Hannah was born, hell, since I got married, I've been living a lie, an actress playing the part of what she thinks a wealthy Joburg woman should look like. It's refreshing to organise around something that isn't about the girls' school or Joe's dry circle of friends. I feel, I don't know, more myself ... not that I'm even sure what that is these days.

I use my *backup* card to pay for the parking, guilt twisting in my gut. Fear too. I've already offered to fly Queenie up to meet Marian, a promise I'm not sure I can keep. I'm inclined to offer my home as a location to host her too.

I checked out Queenie's page after she added me on Facebook – she's smart; really, really bookish and smart. Ginger is wry and wise and Matt, while he has a lot going on, seems to have a heart of gold. He presents as the usual South African boytjie, but there's something deeper running underneath.

What do I have?

Then it comes to me. Before I met Joe, I knew exactly who I was. I worked at a top public relations agency in Sandton. I could woo clients over drinks at The Westcliff and then stay up all night in media war rooms, preparing CEOs in times of crisis. In fact, that's how Joe and I met. I was the publicist for his investment firm. Of course, the moment we married and had Hannah, he made it clear that it was time for me to resign – good mothers couldn't possibly gallivant around the city every other night, clinking glasses with high flyers like him. My boss at the agency, Lindiwe, often bemoaned the fact that I'd left, calling it 'a loss to the PR industry'. I pushed down my complicated feelings and changed the subject whenever she said that. And then she left the agency herself, to start her own celebrity and literary publicity firm.

What are the chances she's in charge of Marian Keyes' schedule for her South African tour? Lindiwe and I managed the calendars of many celebs together in our time, from Candice Swanepoel to a particularly distasteful visit from Piers Morgan … I fumble for my phone and call her right there in the car park, the ill-begotten groceries at my feet. Part of me is intrigued about Marian, another part of me is reaching for a version of myself long past.

She answers immediately. 'Oh. My Gaaaaad. Jess?'

'Hah, it's been too long.'

'You're telling me! To what do I owe the pleasure?'

I pause. 'I'd like to ask a favour. But most of all, I want to see you again. Can I take you to breakfast?'

Her laughter tingles through the phone. I've forgotten how much I miss my work friends, miss dressing up in pencil skirts and blazers, brainstorming for pitches, bitching about clients and trading hot gossip over microwaved lunches.

'Sure, babe. But can we make it lunch at Marble instead? I'm hoping to win over David Higgs. May as well make it a bit of a thing and celebrate with some bubbles, you know?'

'Perfect, Lindi, my treat.' I gulp, my wallet burning in my hand. 'How's this Friday?'

'I'll look at my diary but consider it done. For you, my friend, I'll make the time. I gotta go – can't wait to see you!'

'You too.'

My heart is pounding as I hang up. Okay, this feels like something tangible, a way for me to help everyone else. Feeling victorious, I pop a message on the Facebook group.

'Hey, everyone – hope you're having a good day! I think I've made some headway in connecting with Marian Keyes. I'll explain in full later but I think we need a game plan. I'm thinking we maybe have a Zoom meeting soon, all together over a glass of wine?'

I eye the Pinotage meaningfully, then close Facebook before anybody has a chance to answer. Rejection isn't my strong point. An uncomfortable emotion beats through me. As if my enthusiasm for this group might strip off my designer layer of clothes and reveal what is underneath. Vulnerability, that's what Brené Brown would say it is. I get into the car, swerve out the parking spot and turn up the music so the image of Joe messily kissing Beverly doesn't inevitably flash through my mind.

Pull up to the parking boom. Shit. My ticket's already gone overtime.

This isn't my day, but it doesn't matter, does it? I have new friends, a new purpose and a new plan.

Ginger

What the fuck is Zoom?

My new friends from the book group want to have a Zoom meeting, with wine. At first I think maybe it's like Zumba, which Lavender Parker does every second Thursday at the gym. But I went with her once and I can't see how we could do Zumba and have a glass of wine. Or how it would help us plan anything. Or how Queenie from Cape Town could come without taking up Jess on her offer to pay. And that time I went to Zumba it was all middle-aged women and I can't see that Matt would feel comfortable, even if he is a bit unusual. No, if they're proposing Zumba, I'm not having anything to do with it.

I have two choices – ask the girls, or ask Google. I like an excuse to phone my daughters. Gives the conversation structure and direction, rather than me just listening to a list of reasons why they think I'm hopeless.

I try Debbie first.

'Debbie,' I say. 'Is Zoom the same as Zumba?'

See how clever I am? Setting up that I'm no fool, that I know my Zumba? It doesn't work.

'Jesus fucking Christ, Mom,' Debbie says. 'How can you think Zoom is the same as Zumba? Have you been living under a bloody rock?'

Honestly, I don't know where these girls get their foul mouths from.

But she doesn't actually tell me and after that I'm certainly not going to ask Lee-anne. I consider just telling my new Facebook friends that I don't know what Zoom is, but I don't want to be the demented old bat of the group.

So I google 'Zoom' and discover that it seems pretty straightforward. But I'm still not sure if I need to download something or register some-

54

where. And Debbie's always yelling at me not to click 'yes' on anything so what do I do about that? And in my Google search there was an article about how people can pirate all your data from a Zoom conference. I don't see how my data could be useful to them, but the idea of telling the girls that I've been duped makes me die a little inside.

I return to Facebook. At least there I know what I'm doing.

Except that it's doing that thing where it spies on you because now I suddenly have ads telling me to download Zoom.

I feel like crying. But then something catches my eye:

Don't know your Zoom from your Boom? IT support for the clueless. No judgement. No sarcasm. Just straightforward advice.

And there's a phone number, not an email address or an online form.

I phone before I can second-guess myself and a lovely girl says that James will be with me at 9am tomorrow and that I mustn't worry about anything – he'll sort me out. I'm so delighted I don't even ask what magical James will cost. Who cares – it serves the girls right if I spend their inheritance on the IT support they were too mean to give me.

I wake up in the morning convinced that I've made a terrible mistake.

James is probably a terrible young man who will come into my home and try to kill me, but will leave me barely alive after robbing me blind. The girls will be delighted and put me in an old-age place without another thought. Unless I actually do die. Then they'll simply bury me without another thought. But I'm too embarrassed to cancel so I put my panic button in my pocket and I wear lots of jerseys so that if he tries to rape me, it'll be really difficult to get in. I can hear the girls sighing with frustration even as I think this.

The bell rings just before nine. When I look at my security camera there's an older man standing at the gate. I sigh. It's going to be complicated trying to get rid of this man before James comes. I try to remember what it was I said to the last Jehovah's Witness that made her cry.

I open the gate a crack.

'Hello? Can I help you? I'm not in the market for God, I'll have you know.'

The man laughs. 'I'll keep that in mind,' he says.

He has bright-blue eyes and a good head of hair. You look for that at my age. It's rare.

'I'm James,' he says. 'I'm here to see Ginger.'

'I'm Ginger,' I say. The gate is still only open a crack. 'But you're not James.'

The man laughs again. He's got a nice laugh. Warm. Deep. Roger never laughed much. I like a man who laughs.

'I promise,' he says. 'James McKenzie, computer whiz, at your service.'

I open the gate, blushing.

'I thought you'd be younger,' I say. 'And more murdery.' Then I want to sink into the ground. He's going to think I'm crazy.

He laughs that treacle laugh again.

'I've had a few comments about my age,' he says. 'But so far you're the first to object to my non-murderiness.'

I smile. 'Silly man,' I say, showing him into the house.

James sits with me at the computer, which I have put on the dining-room table, and takes me through how Zoom works. He says he's impressed I got as far as I did, which I know is just good client relations, but it makes me feel warm. Then he takes his phone into the lounge and we do a practice Zoom call and it goes perfectly. And then he sets up a meeting for me to join so I'll know exactly how that works too. It's fun and I'm laughing and I can't help noticing how nice James smells.

In the course of all this, I find myself having to explain all sorts of things. The Marian Keyes group. My daughters. Zumba. (James has never heard of Zumba and is delighted by the story.) He shows me how to scroll back so that I can see the past posts of the people in my Marian Keyes chat on Facebook, not just the recent stuff, so that I can see more about them.

He says he likes the sound of Marian Keyes and asks which of her books I would recommend. Usually I'd have said they're not really the sort of books a man would enjoy, but I think of that lovely Matt and how much he likes them, so I recommend a few. And it seems silly for him to have to buy one when I have them all so I offer to lend him one. And then I make us tea while we decide which he should read first.

He admires the shelves that I had built around the fireplace after Roger died. Roger thought books should be kept out of sight but I love having them on display. I've organised them by colour after I saw someone on Facebook do it, and I think it looks lovely. Roger would be appalled. If he had to have bookshelves, then they had to be in perfect alphabetical order. But I remember books by their covers so the colour system actually works very well for me, thank you very much. James chooses *Anybody Out There?* because that's my favourite and he says that's good enough for him. Only afterwards I realise it might not be the best book for someone who's told me he's a recent widower.

Still, it's the best morning I've had in a long time.

After James leaves, I move the laptop from the dining-room table where James and I worked to sit on my red-velvet sofa, which I have placed where it catches the afternoon sun. I bought this after Roger died as soon as I had access to the money. He liked brown furniture. Said it didn't show the dirt. But then freaked out if there was any dirt.

I go back to look at my new friends' Facebook pages. Now I can see their lives through their pictures. I spend a happy hour doing just that and thinking about what a nice man James is.

It's quite a lot later, as I'm trawling through Jess's page, that something hits me. The Marian Keyes Jess is not just any old Jess. She's Jess Klein.

Which means her husband, who she's referred to as Joe, must be Joe Klein.

And I'm pretty sure that's the name Sybil Portley-Smythe gave us all at bookclub as the best investment advisor ever. She was full of how she had invested everything on his advice and was going to be rich. I'm happy with my investment portfolio so that was all academic for me. But a few of the girls took her advice and last bookclub they were all whining about how he wasn't taking their calls or answering their emails any more. People really have the most terrible manners. I hope lovely Jess isn't married to a man who's rude about answering emails.

She deserves a lovely man, I'm sure.

Someone who smells nice and has a warm, treacly laugh.

Matt

'It's not cancer!' I say and toast my computer screen with my glass of Creative Block 5. (If you're looking for a good Bordeaux blend, you need to try CB 5. You won't be disappointed.)

Why am I toasting my screen? Well, we – the MK Facebook Group (no, not uMkhonto weSizwe, ha ha) are having a Zoom bookclub. I fully expected Ginger not to know how to respond to my meeting invitation, but she's one switched-on old bird. Much more so than Mom, who honestly doesn't have a clue about Zoom and as for Dad, well, don't get me started.

'Matt, I'm so pleased for you. Jirre, I was so worried,' says Queenie.

I can tell she's genuinely pleased for me, not pretending. Queenie seems like a really good person, funny too. And sexy. From what I can see on the screen – and I'm getting a crick in my neck trying to look – she's got a voluptuous build that doesn't really go with the image I have of librarians (apart from the ones in pornos). Her very well-developed, er, chest kind of seems to have a life of its own. *Their* own.

I realise I'm actually ogling her boobs and I'm relieved when Jess interrupts my private perving session.

'I was sending you and your mom healing white light in my meditation this morning. Although a bottle of Prosecco might've been more useful. My meditation only lasted two minutes before I decided to read *The Break* instead. Reading counts as spiritual work, right?'

Jess comes across as this arty-farty, rich northern-suburbs lady who lunches. You know? Immaculate. Perfect figure. Perfect clothes. Perfect house. But there's something sad about her. I'm not sure if this is my shrink's intuition or if I'm just projecting.

'I think it's the most important spiritual work you can do, but I'm biased,' says Queenie.

Ginger is smiling. 'I *told* you it would be okay! So many of these biopsies turn out to be nothing. Look at Sybil—'

'Oh, she didn't end up having a biopsy. The doctor did another scan and he said it was an infection so there was no need to stick a needle in it, which I was really glad about because I think my dad would've puked. Plus, as a special bonus, I got to hear all about my mother's experiences with mastitis when she was breastfeeding me.'

Ginger nods, her smile fading.

'Well, that's great, Matt.' She hesitates. 'But ... just tell your ma to keep an eye on it. I don't want to be a Debbie Downer but Petunia Baloyi, a lovely lady from Zumba, was told that exact same thing – no need for a biopsy, just an infection. Next thing she knew, she had stage four cancer and it was untreatable. She was given six months to live.'

My heart falls. I want to be sick.

Queenie sees my face and quickly says, 'But I'm sure that's not the case with your mom.'

I don't ask if Petunia is still alive.

'Still,' Ginger carries on, 'it doesn't hurt to keep an eye on these things. Just in case.'

She can't bloody leave it alone. I feel unaccountably angry with her. Why is she pissing on my battery like this? I was in such a good mood and now I feel all anxious again. 'But you said Sybil was fine – it was just a cyst!' I can't hide my irritation.

'Sybil *is* fine. Petunia wasn't so lucky.' Ginger shrugs, but her connection is patchy so it happens in slo-mo.

Jess quietly pours oil on troubled waters. 'It's such a pain in the arse, isn't it? We used to think doctors were gods. We didn't have to wonder if the advice they gave us was sound – we just did whatever they told us.'

'That's why quite a few of my friends aren't around any more. They believed what their doctors told them ... and I suppose they were quite old,' says Ginger.

Jess starts laughing and then the rest of us join in – we can't help ourselves. 'Sorry, Ginger,' Jess says. 'I'm not laughing about your dead friends.'

Ginger looks sheepish. 'No, I'm sorry. I didn't mean to rain on your parade, Matt.'

'It's okay.' I realise she means well and I'm probably being oversensitive, something my dad accuses me of. Even after Mom had got the results, he'd made a comment: *See. Nothing to get all stressed out about. You didn't even need me here*, which was directed at me because I'd made him come to the doctor with a hangover. Because these days after his usual ten beers he doesn't even get a hangover, which is at least a bit of a warning sign that you have a problem with alcohol.

Mom could see I was getting ready to deliver a zinger so she quickly diffused the situation by taking his hand and saying, 'You didn't need to come with, Mal, but it made me feel so much better to have you here.' Mom is really good at defusing tension.

I force myself to focus on the call. I study Jess's face as she sips her glass of what I assume is Prosecco. Actually, she's also pretty hot, wouldn't mind running my fingers through that hair – and elsewhere. I feel the blood rush to my face. What the hell is wrong with me? This is supposed to be a safe space for women, dammit!

Come to think of it, I know exactly what's wrong with me.

I haven't had sex in … I count on my fingers … eight months! Are you judging me?

That's okay, because *I'm* judging me.

I take a gulp of wine and then start choking. On their screens, everyone's eyes are on me.

'Matt, are you okay?' asks Queenie. Her eyes really are the most amazing hazel …

'Put your arms up,' instructs Ginger.

Still coughing, I do as I'm told. 'Just going to get some water,' I say.

In the bathroom, I stick my head under the tap and gulp down some water. I glance in the mirror. My eyes are red and it looks like I've been crying so I quickly splash water on my face and head back to my laptop, where they've moved on and are talking about their plans to meet Marian.

From what I can gather, Jess knows the company that's doing Marian's PR. They seem to have a plan, but I'm too shy to ask them to repeat it, especially seeing my only excuse is perving and then choking because I was perving.

I'm none the wiser when they finish, but Jess says something about sending us all an email so hopefully I can work out what's going on.

'This has been so good. Thank you,' says Jess. You can tell it's heartfelt and I start wondering about Mr Jess – is she happy with him? What's the story there? And am I only interested because I want to jump her?

No, I think firmly. I'm interested because I'm a shrink.

Don't fool yourself, says a voice that sounds remarkably like Freud.

I say a hasty goodbye and leave the meeting. As I close my laptop and pick up my glass, which is now in dire need of a refill, there's a knock at the door. I go downstairs, wondering who it is – certainly not one of my family members.

When I open the door, my bestie, Sadie, is standing there. We have a code on our gate that we're supposed to keep to ourselves, but Mom has a nasty habit of dishing it out to everyone so there's never any chance to pretend you're not home.

'Hey …' I'm about to make some wisecrack when I see her face. 'Sadie? What's wrong?'

She shakes her head and bursts into tears.

I've seen Sadie cry, like, twice in my life: once when Nelson Mandela died and again when we won the Rugby World Cup.

'Come on, let's get you a drink.'

Queenie

'I can't believe you did a Zoom!' Faheema empties the full sachet of brown sugar into the foam of her cappuccino and watches the white puffiness sag.

Around us the tables in Mugg & Bean are emptying, the lunch-time crowd moving off to trawl the shopping centre. Canal Walk isn't my favourite – everyone seems to move so slowly, families spreading themselves and their trolleys-full of children across the width of every concourse – but it's the mall closest to home so I spend more time here than I want to.

Jennifer says I need to learn patience. Whatever. Canal Walk is easy for Faheema too so we usually meet up at Mugg & Bean because it's right across from entrance five (and because the muffins are as big as Faheema's head).

'Didn't you Zoom enough in Covid? If I never have another Zoom meeting for the rest of my life it won't be a minute too soon.'

'I don't mind it – Zoom, not Covid, obviously. Let's not even talk about that. I still want to gril when people get too close to me. But there are definitely things I like about Zoom that I wouldn't mind bringing into real life. You know, like the forty-minute time limit on free calls,' I say, sipping my tea. The rooibos is weak; I took the bag out of the pot too soon. 'There are some people you just want to shut up at forty minutes, but then you have to pretend you're still interested and keep talking. And you don't have to worry too much about how you look on a Zoom. When I was with the MK people, I was wearing pyjama pants with a vest, and no one was any the wiser.'

At least I *think* no one was any the wiser. Matt's face had been stuck in the same expression for so long I wasn't sure if his screen was frozen.

'Okay, you have a point,' Faheema says, laughing. 'I remember that – the rest of my house could be a tip but as long as the space behind me was tidy, I could pretend I was in control. So tell me more about this group.'

'Don't talk to me about control. You're looking at the baby in my family,' I say, pointing a thumb towards my chest. 'Control is something other people have. I'm barely in charge of my own brain,' I joke, but not really. 'So I met the MK group on Facebook,' I admit, knowing Faheema won't be impressed. (She thinks all social media is evil.) 'But it's totally legit – everyone's very nice. The bookclub Zoom was such fun, we talked about doing it every two weeks but already we're chatting almost every day. Shit, I wish I had a laptop – my phone's such a pain. Battery draining fast and cutting out. But anyway –' I shake my head, not wanting to get caught up in a moan '– the one thing I've learnt is that you don't have to meet people in the flesh to connect with them. It makes it easier when you can hang out like us, but you can still become good friends even if you're not in the same place.

I think of the group and all the things we've shared in the last few weeks. I've stopped thinking about a name for us Marian Keyes fans; I've decided we are Friends. Capital F. Who knows how long I would've had to know these people in real life before anybody properly opened up. *If* they opened up. People are so weird – you can see them every day for years and still know nothing about them. Then one FB chat and – boom! – all their secrets are out. I count myself in that group of 'weird' people, but I know it's because I find it easier to write a message than to speak about how I feel out loud. Thankfully Faheema has known me for such a long time that she understands me even when I am my least eloquent self.

'Hope they're not going to become better friends than we are 'cause I can't finish a Mugg & Bean muffin alone.' Faheema puts a vanilla-blueberry chunk in her mouth. 'And trust *you* to take it to the next level. You already have a virtual boyfriend; now you're in a virtual bookclub!'

I know what's coming. Faheema has never been Kevin's greatest fan, more so since she discovered that the last time he came to South Africa he only went to his parents in Durban. I haven't seen him in nine months.

'When is Kevin coming to Cape Town? Does he even bother to call any more?' Faheema raises her eyebrows at me. I should never have told her that since the Durban visit, he's only called every second week and our conversations have been ultra-short. Something is definitely up.

'I'm not sure. He only started a new round two weeks ago. He's making good money so he should enjoy it,' I say, defensive. 'His next break is coming up in May. He said he might come to Cape Town, but it's not confirmed.' My plan is to talk to him then and I'm not looking forward to it. How do you say, 'Where are we going? What's happening with us?' without sounding like a cliché?

'That guy is a real sweet-talker. I don't know how he gets you of all people to wait around for him. It's not like he can't phone you more often from the rig!' Faheema adjusts her scarf around her neck, flipping her straight, shoulder-length hair over the silk so that the ends curve upwards. I can see from the way she doesn't look at me that she's warming up for more Kevin-bashing. 'And he's making such pots of money, he could fly to Cape Town for a quick visit – easy. Or fly you to wherever he is. He's travelling all over the world; he could treat you to your first overseas holiday. Listen to me, girl – he is wasting your time.'

'Don't be like that, Faheema. I agreed to him working on the rigs and he's enjoying it. Kevin's a good guy. I don't want to be the one to put the brakes on – I don't want to be *that* girlfriend. I mean, *I'm* the one that told him to live his best life, and he says that's what he appreciates most about me. I'm not going to turn into a nag ...' I know I'm telling her all the things I tell myself about my relationship with Kevin. 'How's your life anyways? Work still so busy?'

'Work is always busy,' she says, rolling her eyes. She knows I'm just changing the subject – you don't get to be friends with someone from the age of six without learning each other's tricks. 'Performance is down on one of my funds and it's financial year-end so we've got auditors crawling all over the place. But before you distract me completely ... if I can't sort Kevin out maybe I can help with your other problem. But first you have to agree that none of those bookclub bitches will become your best friend? Doesn't matter how much you Zoom?' She sits up straight, pushes her chin towards me in mock seriousness.

'What are you on about?' I laugh.

'I have an old Dell laptop at home that I don't use. Didn't know you needed one otherwise I would've given it to you long ago. Zayn can make sure it's clean of all my old stuff. You want it?'

'What? Are you sure? I definitely want it!' I grab her hand so that our round wooden table wobbles, slopping some tea out of the teapot. 'How much is it? I can't afford much but I can make something work …' I start thinking of the money I'm saving up for Jennifer's birthday in May; a laptop isn't in my budget but when will I get a chance like this again? My heart sinks when I realise that at this point I can't actually afford *anything*.

'Don't be mad. It's just lying there. You'll be taking it off my hands and you'll make my husband feel better about making me change to a Mac. A deal's a deal though: if I give it to you, you can't make best friends with any of those bookclubbers.'

'We are best friends until I die,' I say in my best solemn voice. What I want to do is whoop around the mall and fist-pump the air. I wouldn't accept a gift like this from anyone except Faheema. 'Thank you, my friend, you always go beyond for me. Never mind best friend – if it wouldn't piss off Jennifer so much, I'd adopt you as my official sister.'

Faheema flaps her hand at me. I know she wants me to stop. If I had money, the first thing I'd do would be to pay her back for all the spoils she's given me. I'm tired of being the receiver; I'd like to be the giver for a change. I smile to myself, imagining the 'rich' me. I'd sit in coffee shops all day, drinking cappuccinos and making up stories – or maybe half the day. After lunch with Jennifer, I think I'd still want to hang out with the kids at the library.

'Jennifer would have me as a sister over you any day,' Faheema says, unknowingly interrupting my Lotto dreams. 'Speaking of which, I saw her in the downstairs coffee shop last week if that's interesting to you?'

Faheema and Jennifer work for the same financial company in Pinelands but Faheema is a portfolio manager in the investment business while Jennifer is a PA on the insurance side. They are two floors apart in the same building and regularly meet for coffee.

'Only mildly interesting. I suppose it's a step forward because it means she's left her desk for ten minutes.' I know Faheema doesn't want to talk about the laptop any more but my cheeks still burn from smiling. 'Thanks again.' I squeeze in the words before she starts talking again.

'Are you still saving for her birthday? Any ideas on what to get her?'

'Oh God, don't talk to me about that. I really want to go to the Franschhoek Literary Festival in May because Marian Keyes is going to be there. I even tried to get sponsorship from the library but Esmeralda said no, it's not in the budget. Then I thought about taking Jennifer for her birthday because she's also a Marian fan. Imagine – staying over for two nights, going to some events, maybe a spa, eating at some nice places … I reckon even if I can't make the whole dream come true, I can still get us tickets for the Marian Keyes event and just go to Franschhoek for the day.

'But now,' I pause as the waiter stops to check if we want anything else, 'these Facebook people, they're planning on inviting Marian – yes, I know we call her Marian like she knows we exist! – to this fancy charity function one of the ladies is organising. It'll be in Joburg and I *have* to get myself there. I literally cannot miss it. If I was a writer, I'd give my left kidney to be able to write the way she does. I mean, she can weave together a story so you feel you're right in it, that the characters are your friends. She can make you laugh out loud and cry real tears. To get into someone's brain and heart the way she does – that's a friggen gift.

'The one lady, Jess, shame, she even offered to pay for me to fly there, but I could never accept that. Sucks since I'm the only one without money in the group. Well, the ladies definitely have money. I'm not so sure about the guy.' I think of Matt confessing that he lived in the garden flat at his parents. 'He's still a student but his parents probably have money. I don't want to be a charity case.'

'There's a *guy* in the group?' Faheema asks, as if that's all I've said.

'Stoppit, man, he's nice but he must be ten years younger than me,' I say, sitting back in my chair. 'Anyway, I worked it out last night. Adding in my savings, if I want to take Jennifer to Franschhoek for her birthday and fly to the Joburg function, I need to make ten thousand rand by May.'

'Shit. How you going to do that? Are you allowed to take on other work?'

'I think I can. I don't know exactly how others are doing it, but I know many librarians have got side hustles. Some are into writing – poems, short stories, even novels. I could try that with my new laptop,' I say, shooting her another smile, 'but I've never heard any of them say they've made any money from writing. Some sell Avon and Tupperware. A few run baking and catering businesses but I'm useless in the kitchen so that's not an option. You're the money manager – any bright ideas how I can make some money fast?'

'Ten thousand in four months? Maybe you can get a Zoom gig as Queenie, the librarian Zumba dancer?' she cackles.

'Bitch,' I say as my phone rings and interrupts my laughing. 'Kevin,' I answer and I can hear my own voice full of surprise. I feel the smile forced onto my face and stretching into my cheeks. Kevin never calls during the day. Fine. Truth is that Kevin hardly ever calls at any time.

'Hello? Hello?' I say into the phone, trying to pretend that a call from Kevin is normal while Faheema watches me, her one eyebrow cocked into a question. He doesn't answer and I move the phone away from my ear to check the caller's name. Yes, definitely Kevin.

'Hello? Can you hear me?' I say again. This time I can hear men talking in the background, their voices indistinct. I hear Kevin: 'No, brother man, you are doing it all wrong. Watch me. See this is how it goes.' Obviously not talking to me. A bit of silence as I keep listening. He is laughing now. 'I told you guys, look and learn from the best. I got a lot to teach you.' A boast in his voice.

'Hello! Kevin!' I shout. 'Kevin! It's me! Queenie!' I'm so loud that the woman feeding her baby at the table next to us hesitates in putting the spoon into her child's mouth. Silence in my ear now. Then the sound of fumbling.

'Hey, Queenie?' Kevin says at last. 'What are you doing on the line?'

'You phoned me,' I say, trying to sound playful, aware that Faheema is listening to every word.

'Oh,' he says after a pause. 'I didn't mean to, I'm busy working. You know how it is … busy here, haven't got time to chat. My phone was in my pocket so it must have been a butt dial.' In the background, I hear someone say, 'Come, Kevin, let's get lunch.'

'Oh,' I say. The smile is still stuck on my face for Faheema. I look down, turn away from her eyes, and pretend I am listening to Kevin speak. 'I'm glad to hear from you,' I say eventually into the silence that stretches between us in the space where words should be. 'Maybe one day we can try to catch up in the day. Better than last thing at night when we're too tired to talk.'

'Ja, okay. We must try,' he says in that way that people say they are going to do something – coffee – but both sides know that it is never going to happen. 'I must go now, the guys are calling me.'

'Yes, okay. Talk later again.' I know that we won't talk again today. Likely not even the rest of the week. I wait for him to end the call before I turn back to the table.

'He just wanted to say hello.' I fake a smile to Faheema. 'Must be missing me.'

She knows I'm lying.

Jess

It's 3am when I put down *Grown Ups*, my wrists aching from the heft of it. A bereftness consumes me – I've turned the last page of the book that has been my bedside companion. Helpful, when the space next to me remains empty.

After finishing *Grown Ups*, it's a relief to know that Marian Keyes has so many other books out there. But how to know which one to choose? I've taken a slightly superstitious approach to this, combing the second-hand bookshops close to me for old copies. While vintage clothing shops fill me with existential sadness, second-hand bookshops fill me with hope and a sense of magic. To find the right book for your heart at the right moment on those muddled shelves, well, that doesn't happen by chance. I've left it up to fate to decide what Marian Keyes book I'll read next, at a time when I'm so unsure of my own path forward. I found *Grown Ups* at Bookdealers Melrose, a haven of eccentric spiritual texts and Jewish literature, and consumed the book in just two days. I wonder, as I place the finished novel on top of *The Break*, which Marian Keyes novel I will find next?

I walk zombie-like to the bathroom, drawing a reluctant boundary between the imaginary world and the real one. I hear the faraway hoot of an owl and a furious clattering on the roof. Genets, probably. Or maybe rats. Don't let anyone say South Africa isn't still wild. I splash some water on my face and reapply my ten-step Korean skincare routine. The demands of my Gut Microbiome have nothing on my fight against the signs of ageing. The regimented routine gives me a sense of control, although I live in fear of the day I miss a step and my face folds in on itself like a basset hound.

I drink a glass of water and get back into bed, making a big fuss of settling back under the covers. But I just can't do it – I can't recover from what I've just read.

I can't just sit like this, alone with myself.

I'm overcome with the need to tiptoe downstairs and pour myself a nightcap. If my father was still alive, he'd chastise me. My Uncle Ronnie was a notorious alcoholic and was often found with an empty bottle next to his bedside. This is different, however. I don't think I'm an addict, I'm just going through A Time. I mean, I've started enjoying a glass of wine each night, and I now believe that spaghetti bolognese shouldn't exist unless there's a glass of red alongside, but it's not like I have a *problem*. If anything, given my current circumstances, I should be drinking *more*.

Suddenly, my phone lights up. It's Joe. My pulse raises, my whole body buzzes with fear. My first instinct is to throw the phone across the room but he is my husband. Hurt as I am, I owe it to him to answer. I owe it to us. The thing is, the minute I open that conversation, I will have to face the truth. I can't deny it. I know that Joe has been lying, like in a really big way, over some really significant facets of his investment company and those lies are about to catch up with him.

'Jess?'

'Hey, Joe … how you doing?' I hear muffled sounds in the background. I imagine Beverly calmly stirring a boeuf bourguignon, or some other time- and skill-intensive dish I could never possibly make.

'Good, good … uh … How the girls?'

'Great, actually! Hannah is getting ready for exams and has finally ditched that catty friend we can't stand.'

'Candice?'

'Yes, ugh.' We chuckle together. 'Willow is amazing. She's got into Hannah's old wooden train set and is playing with that every chance she gets.'

'Whoa, Jess, remember when we first got that? We saved up for it and everything.'

'Different times …' I say, realising with a sinking feeling that those times of counting pennies are fast returning.

'We need to talk … ' he says quietly, caution and care humming across the line.

'I … I … can't right now.' I choke up. 'Willow's waking up. Nightmare I think.'

I end the call; the silence of the house consumes me. Time to go downstairs and get that bottle of wine. As I wrench out the cork, I imagine the shame of pulling Hannah out of Kingsmead and Willow out her posh preschool. I keep pouring as I imagine the sneers from my parental frenemies. Everybody knows there's something dodgy going on when a parent suddenly leaves the class WhatsApp group. Next thing they'll be sniffing out the source of shame like those untrained, unsocialised Rottweilers owned by the Sandersons down the street.

One glass is not going to be enough. Right, no other choice but to take the bottle with me up to bed. Looks like it's going to be an all-nighter. I don't care if alcoholism is in my blood, I'm willing to play with fire to keep these feelings at bay.

Upstairs, I set down my glass and turn on my laptop, poised to torture myself with a good Facebook-stalk of Beverly. I scroll impatiently through her sanitised content, trying to gather as much information as I can to feel in control. She's sharing a 'Save the Rhino' petition again and posting smug pictures of her latest literary event. Sorry, they are called 'salons'. I gaze at pictures of women with pashminas, sensible bobs and freshly Botoxed skin. How is it possible to look that put together? To appear as if you don't have a problem in the world? Must be nice, being Joe and coming home to a woman who's smart, in control and who always books her Brazilian wax on time. Must be nice to have a conversation over sparkling water and a gut-friendly meal about the latest literary sensation. Not the pulp I like to read.

'No,' I whisper to myself, so as not to wake the kids, 'we will *not* be doing any more of this tonight, Jess.'

Instead, I click off the offending profile and decide to get to know my new friends from the Marian Keyes group a bit better.

Ginger has the genteel, classy profile I'd expect from her, with a tasteful photo of roses selected as her cover image, even though there is something odd about it, like it's been uploaded upside down. Matt posts a lot of sporting memes I don't understand and talks about his favourite books, films and series. He's so passionate about it but I imagine he's holed up in his garden cottage a lot. He's actually quite hot, I think with another glug of wine, in a borderline-geek way. As for Queenie, I'm left wanting more. Although her feed bubbles with pictures of her laughing and partying with friends, there's a vulnerability to her infectious confidence. Maybe it's because she brings up memories of my younger self, getting five shots too many from the bar and going home with men that didn't have my best interests at heart.

I google her name and a few results come up. First, there's her official librarian profile with a picture that's far more reserved than her Facebook feed. There are one or two articles in the local newspaper reporting on bookclubs she's hosted. I smile as I recall Lassie, the librarian when I was growing up. Thanks to her, I read Enid Blyton's entire catalogue, and the blush-inducing Judy Blume. I'm so glad I'm tearing through all these Marian Keyes novels. Somewhere along the way, I've forgotten that books were always a solace for me. I've convinced myself that I enjoy cooking, golfing with Joe and hosting drawn-out dinner parties where a collection of well-heeled couples drone on about home renovations. I am torn between the love I always thought I felt for him, and a sense that this life was imposed on me without my consent the minute I quit my job.

Never again.

Suddenly, my eyes fall on a new search result. It's some sort of writing website where aspiring authors share their work. Queenie has her own profile and there's one piece of writing uploaded, time-stamped about two years ago.

'*I've never done this before,*' she says in the introduction, '*and this is probably really no good, but this story just came to me one night and I had to get it all down. Ugh, be kind, okay?*'

I click in and begin to read, first out of curiosity and then because I can't stop. I reread certain passages, my heart hammering and expanding. There's something really special about her writing – she's wry yet romantic, light but incredibly insightful. In fact, reading her reminds me of how I feel when I read Marian Keyes, but with a spicy South African spin.

I can't believe she hasn't told us she writes! It's far too late and I'm dangerously light-headed, but I don't care. I send a message to Matt and Ginger and include the link: 'Guys, I think Queenie's too embarrassed to mention this, but she's an amazing writer. Just look at this! Doesn't it feel a bit like Marian Keyes?!! Surely there's a way we can help her get out there?'

I'm plotting again, imagining introducing Queenie to Marian and sending Marian some of Queenie's stuff. That's not really done, is it? I'm sure she gets loads of hopeful people sending her work every day. But this is different. Queenie is talented – I just know it. Thinking about it, I've spent years around people who've cut corners to get rich, who've hidden the stench of their true personalities with expensive perfumes. Queenie spends her days helping others discover the love of reading. Imagine seeing her become successful, someone who really deserves it?

Buoyed, I scroll through the rest of the results, selfishly hoping for more beautiful writing. I go one, two … seven pages deep.

Until I spot something that sends chills up my spine.

The search result says, 'Hot breasty librarian getting screwed over her desk. Full frontal.' Underneath is her full name, as well as the name of the library she works for. The link is to Pornhub.

I slam shut the laptop, feeling light-headed and sick.

Queenie can't know about this, can she? Surely she would have found a way to take it down? This doesn't feel right at all – in fact, it feels like abuse.

Suddenly I feel drained. What is this about? Is money so tight that Queenie has resorted to … Do I tell Queenie and embarrass her, like a privileged, nosy, do-gooder? Or do I bide my time to see if she shares her secret on her own?

My paisley-printed sheets crumple and get soaked with sweat as I toss and turn into sleep.

Ginger

The Zoom meeting was fun. The others were all reminiscing about how much they zoomed during Covid, but I just did WhatsApp videos and I thought I was the bee's knees. My daughters were probably laughing at me the whole time. I make sure to drop it into conversation with Lee-anne the next time we speak; I obviously can't tell Debbie after the whole Zumba-Zoom debacle.

'I had such a lovely chat with my friends on Zoom,' I say, in what I hope is an offhand way.

'Christ,' says Lee-anne. 'Zoom is so last year. Literally.' She pauses. 'What friends?'

The child is like a bloodhound. I can't possibly tell her that I've met a group of strangers online and they suddenly feel like my very best friends.

'Bookclub,' I say.

'You know, Mom,' says Lee-anne. 'Tex's mom is in a lovely retirement village and they actually have a bookclub that meets right in the village. No need to drive around at night.'

'I just told you we met on Zoom,' I snap. 'So I wasn't driving. And we meet at lunch precisely so that nobody has to drive at night. Gill Henderson is virtually *blind* …' I start to giggle and after a moment Lee-anne does too.

Then I have to get off the phone because James is coming over to return my books. I'm not going to lie, knowing that he's coming over I get dressed up a bit. I put on my black slacks – Debbie says no one says 'slacks' any more so I make a mental note to call them 'trousers' should it come up in conversation – and my baby-blue jersey that matches my eyes. I even put on a bit of eyeshadow and I can almost hear Roger's disapproval from the beyond. Roger was of the view that nice women don't wear eyeshadow, though he seemingly didn't mind lipstick or anything else.

'Shut up,' I say to his voice in my head, only I say it aloud. 'You're dead, you old bore.' Then I laugh, thinking what the girls would say to that.

When James arrives, he has flowers. I'm immediately flustered but very glad I'm wearing the eyeshadow.

'You look lovely,' he says, handing me the bunch.

He's also a bit smarter than last time. He's wearing dark-blue jeans and a collared shirt. I hope that he's made this effort for me.

'You look nice too,' I say.

I make some tea and we sit on the red sofa and James tells me how much he loved *Anybody Out There?* and so I tell him all about my Facebook group and how we're going to try to meet Marian. Then I tell him how I wanted to ask Jess if her husband is Joe Klein who never answers Sybil's emails, but I felt I couldn't because I didn't want to make her feel awkward. And I tell him that I'm worried Matt's mom has had bad medical advice, but that I'd put my big foot in my mouth and then Matt'd looked so worried that I'd backtracked and then he'd stared at the screen in a mad way so I knew I'd worried him terribly. I tell James how Jess has discovered that Queenie is a writer, and very good, and we need to think how to take this forward for her.

James is an excellent audience. He nods and comments and seems really interested. I can't remember when last someone listened to me with such attention and I'm almost sure that no man ever has. Roger would have rolled his eyes by now and gone off to watch racing on TV, but James makes suggestions and seems very interested in the whole plan to meet Marian Keyes.

'What a brave idea,' he says. 'I'd never have the guts to try a plan like that.'

'What do you mean?' I say. 'You're an IT whiz. You're brave enough to do anything.'

'My son thinks I'm an old sad sack,' says James. 'He makes me think I can't do anything.'

'My daughters are exactly the same,' I say. I'm delighted that he understands. I thought I was the only person with disappointed children – I thought everyone else had wonderful children. Everyone at bookclub is always full of stories about their kind and caring offspring and their sweet grandchildren. I just have my angry girls, and since the divorce I only see Debbie's kids when she needs babysitting. She only bothers to see me on the weekends she doesn't have them. And it feels rude to tell her that I'd much rather see her with them.

I tell James all of this while refilling his tea and opening another box of biscuits.

He seems happy to sit. His son is divorced, just like Debbie, and is also trying to make him move into a home.

'I'm not entirely opposed to the idea of a nice retirement village,' says James, 'but every time Josh suggests it, I find myself just thinking how I changed his bloody nappies. And how dare he tell me to move. So then I say that I won't, even though I sort of want to.'

We both laugh. I know exactly what he means.

'We should introduce them to each other,' I joke, and then we look at each other.

'We should!' says James. 'That's brilliant. But before we do that, I was wondering …' He pauses, blushing slightly. 'There's a movie I really want to see, and I was wondering if you'd like to come with me?'

'Are you asking me on a date?' I say before I can stop myself.

'It seems that I am.' His smile makes his cheek dimple.

That night, as I fall asleep, I think about my life. I'm a woman with online friends, a plan to meet a famous writer and a date for Friday night.

Matt

I feel myself blushing.

'I slept with Sadie. It's the dumbest thing I've ever done. I don't know why. I mean, I do know why, but still …'

Ginger looks confused and when she's confused she kind of wrinkles up her forehead and brings her face right up to the camera on her computer.

'Who's Sadie?' she asks

'I guess she's like my best friend. I've known her forever. I mean, we went to Parkview Pre-Primary together.'

'That is such a good nursery school. I tried to get the girls in there but Roger, my late husband, thought it was a waste of money. All that money for the kids to do finger-painting, that's what he used to say.' Roger sounds like a dick and from the expression on Jess's face, she thinks so too.

'Women and men can never really be friends,' adds Ginger, in a confusing segue.

'*We're* friends with Matt!' insists Jess.

'That's because we're chatting on Zoom. If we were all together in a room it would just be a matter of time before things started to happen.'

'I disagree,' declares Jess. 'I don't think Matt would be trying to get into our pants …'

Actually, Jess … I want to say, but I don't.

'I *am* in the room, you know? You can talk *to* me. Not about me,' I say.

'But you're *not* in the room, are you?' Ginger says triumphantly. 'If you were, things would be different.'

I'm very pleased Queenie's not around. I don't want her to think I'm this slutty man-whore, which clearly I'm not. We're having a Zoom call without her because we're supposed to be discussing this short story she wrote. It feels kind of weird, doing stuff behind her back, but our intentions are good.

'Why don't you tell us what happened,' suggests Jess.

'Sadie came around. She was in tears and she, like, never cries. She was upset because her boyfriend was horrible to her – the guy's an asshole. Anyway, we had a couple of drinks together, one thing led to another and, ja …'

Ginger is serious. 'Have you ever got your leg over with her before?'

Jess changes her snort into a cough.

'Oh, we kissed when we were much younger. Like, twelve. But no, nothing since. We've just been friends. Really, really good friends until …' I tell them what happened.

I led Sadie into the kitchen and went into my therapist routine, reflecting what she'd just told me – you know the whole, 'So you seem upset with what's happening with Johnny …' And I thought I was doing pretty well until she said, 'Cut the bullshit and pour me some wine.'

I poured her a glass and slid it towards her, but she looked at it in disgust and said, 'Did I ask for half a fucking glass? I don't fucking think so!' I was about to give the self-medication speech (the 'You only drink to feel even better' one) but I saw the look on her face and decided she might hurt me. So I topped up the wine.

'More!' she shouted. Now, I have those really big glasses – it takes half a bottle to fill them – but she insisted I fill it right to the top. And then it was so full she couldn't even lift it. But she didn't let that bother her – she just put her face down and started lapping the wine like a cat with a bowl of milk. I shit you not. And while she was doing that, she explained what had happened with Johnny.

It's a depressingly familiar story. He came across his ex-girlfriend on Facebook, they started messaging each other and the messages turned flirty, then sexual, which progressed to them having virtual sex. It seemed like cut and dried infidelity to me.

'That's the problem! He doesn't think it's infidelity. He reckons because they've never played hide the sausage in real life, it doesn't count,' she wailed.

'I would have to disagree with Johnny on that score,' I interjected carefully, not wanting to say what I really thought, which was: *He's a complete tool; leave him already!*

'Of course he's fucking wrong – he's the most fucking wrong anyone can fucking be! That's what makes me most angry. That he won't just admit he messed up. Plus, she's really hot,' she added mournfully. 'She's got amazing tits. Perky. Even. Small nipples like rosebuds. Perfect.'

'Erm ... how do you know her breasts are so great?'

'Duh! Because she sent him pictures. *Lots* of pictures. I took screenshots because I want to use them as an example for the plastic surgeon when I eventually get my tits done.'

Sadie has always had a complex about her breasts. She thinks they're too big. She begged her mother to pay for a breast reduction, but her mother refused because she thinks Sadie will regret it if she's not able to breastfeed properly. Sadie's mom wants grandkids. She'd be thrilled if Sadie fell pregnant tomorrow.

'See!' Sadie waved her phone under my nose. On the screen was a photo of the side-chick's boobs.

I gently pushed the phone away. 'I don't feel comfortable looking at this woman's breasts without her consent.'

Sadie looked at me, her frown signalling that she was both pissed and pissed off. 'What is wrong with you, Matt? Do you even have a dick?' Then she tried to grab my penis.

I'll spare you the gory details, but I got angry and shouted at her and she got upset and started crying again and then I hugged her and we ended up kissing and ...

'What was the sex like?' Ginger shocks me, she really does.

'It was … amazing.' I feel myself going bright red. Again.

'For Sadie too, or just for you?' barks Ginger.

'She seemed to be having a pretty good time. I mean, I tried to make sure she … er … enjoyed it as much as I did.' I try not to sound defensive and I do not want to have to mention the word 'orgasm'.

I don't have to. Ginger does it for me.

'That's a good sign. Most women don't enjoy the first time they have sex with a new partner. Fake orgasms are the order of the day,' Ginger says reflectively.

'Mm. We've all been there, Ginger … the whole Meg Ryan in *When Harry Met Sally* slapping-the-table routine,' says Jess, nodding.

This conversation is starting to feel a bit too grown-up for me, but Jess thankfully moves it on from fake orgasms. 'What happened the next morning? Was it awkward?'

'No. I woke up because she brought me coffee. Which, I have to say, is a miracle – she never makes me coffee. She plonked it down next to the bed and said, "Sorry about last night," and I said it was fine and I hoped she was alright and she didn't feel I had taken advantage of her, and she kind of rolled her eyes and said, "You stupid fool, *I* took advantage of *you*," and I didn't really know what to say so I just drank my coffee even though it was really bad. I mean, just horrible. And then she picked up her bag and said, "So you really do have a dick. Quite a big one." And then she cackled, and left.'

'She's totally into you!' exclaims Jess.

'No, she isn't. She was teasing me,' I say.

'Jess's right!' says Ginger, firmly. 'All that stuff about your penis is not teasing. She's trying to tell you how much she likes you.'

I'm so worried that Ginger is going to start discussing my penis that I quickly change the subject. 'Enough about my huge penis –' this makes

Jess snort '– we're supposed to be talking about Queenie's writing.'

'Did either of you read the short story I sent you?' asks Jess.

'I did. I thought it was very, very good,' says Ginger.

'She's a really great writer,' I say. 'But I kind of want more. I want to read a whole novel like that.'

'That's *exactly* how I felt!' exclaims Jess. 'I want more.'

'So, what are we going to do?' I ask. 'Are we going to tell her we've read her writing?

Are we going to ask if she's got a novel stashed away somewhere?'

'I want to get her work out there. It's a crime she hasn't been published yet,' says Jess.

'Go for it,' says Ginger. 'Who knows? Maybe you can get her a big fat publishing deal!'

'Yes,' says Jess. 'With a blurb on the front cover by Marian herself!'

I'm about to suggest that we should consult Queenie *before* we start showing her work around and asking Marian for blurbs, but I don't want to be the wet blanket. I keep my mouth shut.

Queenie

'How was the late shift?' Jennifer looks at me as I slump onto the couch next to her in front of the TV.

The lounge is a mix of old and new, but not in a good way. Jennifer and I got the denim couch on sale from Coricraft and we bought the big wooden coffee table from a guy on the side of the road. On the other side of the room, Ma's worn-out imbuia ball-and-claw brocade sofa is pushed into a corner. Jennifer still keeps the doilies neatly on the backs the way Ma liked it. I don't mind the furniture, I don't need everything shiny and expensive, but I do wish our home was more a reflection of what we liked rather than a mishmash of impulse buys and Ma's things. Ma didn't even like that brocade sofa – she inherited it herself and never had the heart to give it away. Now here we are also hanging on to it for who-knows-why. I want to move on from doing things the way they've always been done to the way that I want to do them. In my dreams, I'd have a special private writing area with all my books and photos for inspiration. All the furniture chosen by me. Then I wouldn't always have to write in my bed.

'Wasn't too bad, except lots of extra organising because we've got our area head coming to visit tomorrow. Esmeralda was driving us crazy making sure everything is perfect.'

I kick off my sandals and stretch out my feet on the coffee table. I notice again that the crown tattoo on my ankle is fading.

'Is Esmeralda ever in a good mood? You complain about her all the time,' Jennifer says, her eyes back on the TV, the cutlery clattering on the empty plate on her lap as she tries to make more space for me on the couch. Her favourite show, *The Estate*, is on and she's completely in love with Dr van Wyk, the recovered morphine addict who euthanised his wife. Doesn't sound like much of a catch to me, but okay.

'Shame, sorry, I know. I don't mean to. Esmeralda can be nice when she forgets she's the boss, but mostly she's bladdy uptight. I know she's only doing her job, but I've been at the library since even before her so I know what I'm doing. She doesn't have to check on me all the time. I feel like a naughty schoolgirl she's caught scribbling in the library books. With overdue fines. Folding the corners of the pages.'

Jennifer knows I'm guilty of folding corners as a book mark. 'It's very unbecoming for a librarian,' she says.

'Did she say anything about you going to that festival you were talking about in Franschhoek?' Jennifer asks. 'I was thinking if you do go, maybe I can buy a ticket and take the day off. It could be a lekker outing. If you don't mind me coming along ...' I can hear the tiniest bit of hope in her voice.

Jennifer never asks me for anything, and she likes to think I have so many people other than her that I'd rather go places with. Hearing her ask about Franschhoek, I'm so excited that she is willing to try something new and I know more than ever that I want to take her to stay over for her birthday.

'Ja.' I shake my head with a sigh. 'She told me there's no money. Until last year there were still funds for conference fees but now it's a flat contribution that covers hardly anything.'

'If you find out what it costs, I can buy us tickets?'

Jennifer's trying to keep her voice neutral because she knows I hate it when she pays extra for me. Her salary is much bigger than mine and her annual bonus is more than just a thirteenth cheque, but she already covers the bulk of the household expenses. I wish I could contribute more.

'No, don't do that. But how about we both put in for leave on that weekend? And then closer to the time, I'll buy the tickets.' I know what she's thinking. 'And don't worry, I won't be imagining how to do it – I'm going to actually do it.'

'If I had a hundred rand for every time you've said that to me, we'd be rich enough to go see Marian Keyes in Ireland never mind in Franschhoek,'

Jennifer says. The truth in the joke stings. 'What's the plan this time? Are you getting another job you're not telling me about?' Jennifer looks at me quickly before turning her eyes back to the TV. 'What do people call it? A side hustle – oooh, lookit that Muzi there! He's mad! I dunno how he gets away with everything he does,' Jennifer interrupts herself. She loves to hate *The Estate*'s resident villain. I imagine what it would be like writing for a show like that. I know they've won awards but I wouldn't even need the awards; it would be enough of a dream just to write for a living.

'I'm thinking about it. But the side-hustle thing is a bit complicated. I asked Esmeralda and she said we're allowed to do extra work but I'll have to fill out a 'private work declaration form' that has to be pre-approved. That takes a couple of months because it needs lots of signatures and must go via a supply chain. I don't even know what a supply chain in a library is.' I think back to how I'd felt my eyes glaze as Esmeralda gave me all the details. 'Eventually a director has to sign it off too. Plus there's the usual stuff – you can't use work time or work equipment. Maybe I could get away with doing it secretly. It won't be forever, just a few months. Doesn't seem worth all the paperwork.' *Ten thousand rand is not nothing,* my conscience whispers at me.

'Asking forgiveness is easier than asking permission, hey?' Jennifer finally moves her empty plate from her lap to the coffee table. 'Be careful. You don't want to risk your job for something stupid.'

Later, I lie in my bed thinking about what Jennifer said. A little side hustle, short-term, once I've figured out what it's going to be couldn't get me into too much trouble, could it? It's not like I'd advertise on the library notice board or on my Facebook page. I won't do anything at work. Esmeralda need never even find out. If I follow the rules it'll be months before I get it approved and the Franschhoek festival would be over by then. Marian Keyes will be long gone …

I try to convince myself that this is a time when it would be okay to bend the rules. Like that time I sold the boys in high school tiny unmarked bottles of water and pretended like it was vodka. I only got away with it for one break time but I made enough money to buy me and Faheema a gatsby for lunch. It wasn't really against the rules to sell water and the boys were too full of themselves to admit that they'd been caught by a girl, so I didn't get into any real trouble. This time I just need enough for Franschhoek tickets!

My phone interrupts my snake-oil plans. Who calls any more? At eleven-thirty in the night. Not Kevin. We're down to texts every fourth or fifth night.

My screen is bright. Jess?

'Hello?' I say. The MK people have swapped numbers but I've never actually talked to any of them on the phone.

There's no answer. 'Hello?' I say again.

'Hellooooo, Queenie, it's me … Jeshhh,' Jess says softly, her voice breathy.

I sit up in bed, put on my bedside light. I don't know why I feel like I need to see in order to hear her.

'This is a surprise,' I say, hoping I sound friendly and not 'what-the-actual-fuck?'

'I *know*, right?' Jess says with a nervous giggle. 'But I was *jusht* shitting here at my kitchen table … thinking about who I could talk to … *who would understand the kind of day I had* … ' Her voice is little-girl sing-song. I want to laugh.

I hear her swallow. Then the sound of pouring liquid – I'm guessing wine into a glass. Shit. Maybe it's not so funny.

'*I could only think of you,*' she says.

'Are you okay?' I ask. On our Zoom calls, Jess is always kind and gentle. Composed. In control. She's never struck me as a woman who would drink by herself at eleven-thirty on a weeknight and then drunk-dial someone from her virtual bookclub.

'Have you ever done anything … reckless, Queenie? Something that made you feel powerful but then when it was out into the world it seemed maybe it wasn't such a good idea?' she asks. '*You know* ... something bad like that.' Jess giggles.

I feel like Jess is asking a question she already knows the answer to. And like there's something she knows about me.

'Sure I have,' I say. 'Everyone has done something wild that they regret.' I don't know what to say next and there's silence as I wait for Jess to speak.

'Well, today I did something wild that I regret and you are the only person I can tell. I think you will understand.' The giggles give way to a little sob.

I feel so sorry for her. This is definitely not the Jess of the Zoom calls.

'You can tell me. It's probably not that bad. Nothing worse than I would've done,' I joke and I want to kick myself as I hear her take another swallow and start crying softly.

After a short while she starts to talk.

'Today I went to Tashas for a late lunch by myself. Joe and I had a fight about money in the morning and I know I shouldn't have had an expensive lunch but I wanted ... I don't know, I wanted to feel a bit *normal*.' The little-girl sing-song has gone completely. Instead her voice is flat and hard on 'normal'. 'I had some time before the nanny left and I escaped ...' Jess's voice trails off.

Another sob.

'Tashas wasn't full and there was a guy there sitting at the table across from mine. Not a hot guy or anything, just a guy. An average guy in a suit with a nice face and good hair and who wasn't on his cellphone. He kept looking at me and smiling so eventually I smiled back and it was all very high school. When his wine came, he asked if he could come and join me and I let him. I shouldn't have. But that feeling of having someone *see* me, you know, in *that* way, it's something ...'

'Oh, Jess, that's okay. Having a little lunch-time flirt is not the worst thing you can do.' I feel heartsore for her. So much guilt over having lunch with someone.

'I had sex with him in the toilet.' Jess breaks into a gulp of a sob, a short, sharp laugh mixed in somewhere. 'Me and a *stranger*, Queenie. A quick fuck in the bathroom at Tashas at three-thirty in the afternoon. How ... *insane* is that? And it was my idea too.'

I'm not sure if it's pride or shame I hear in her voice.

'Their bathroom is unisex and it's got more than one stall so no one looked at us funny when we went in at the same time. I tell you, I didn't have to ask him twice. And if you were going to ask, I had condoms in my bag from six months ago when I found them in Joe's stuff. He said they were free with the *Men's Health* magazine ...' Jess goes quiet. And then I hear it. The full force of her regret. 'But, oh my God, Queenie, how could I have *done* that? What if someone finds out? It's like I was someone else. The only thing in my head was, "Fuck you, Joe. Fuck you. You're not the only one who can screw someone else, make our marriage trash." I felt like I was finally in control. What am I going to do?'

Jesus. I have no idea what to say to her.

'I don't know,' I say, deciding to be honest. 'Did you take each other's contact details? Are you going to keep in touch with him?'

'We know each other's names but that's it. I don't want to see him ever again. Can you believe it? Me of all people.' Jess is crying hard now.

I weigh my words. I don't want to say anything that will make it worse and I don't know how much she's had to drink. Will anything I say even make sense?

'Just let it go for tonight, Jess. It happened. Chalk it up to wild experience – everyone's got something. I've definitely done stuff like that.' I can still taste the regret from most of my teenage years. 'Maybe try and get some sleep and we can talk about it some more tomorrow. Everything always seems worse in the middle of the night.'

'Yes,' she says. 'I feel like the worst person in the world ... I knew you wouldn't judge me. Your video is out there with your name and everything and you're okay, you're getting on with life. You know what it feels like to make a massive mistake.'

My stomach falls.

'*Excuse* me?' I ask. I don't know what she's talking about.

The silence is long.

'The video!' she slurs. 'The sexy librarian one.'

'The *what*?' Suddenly, I want to vomit. This has to be a mistake.

'I'm sorry, Queenie. I thought you knew ...'

'No. I didn't. Send me whatever it is you've found.'

'I haven't watched it, don't worry. I just saw the link. I'll send it to you on WhatsApp.'

The WhatsApp is almost immediate. It's a Pornhub video link. With my name. Pinelands Library address. Kevin's name. His work address too.

My heart is pounding as I awkwardly sign up to the free trial period on Pornhub so I can view the video.

There's Kevin. Naked.

Grinning for the camera he must be holding in his hand. Having sex with a woman bent forward over a desk, her breasts big and bouncing as he grabs her from behind with his other hand. Her hair is wild like mine – it covers her face as she leans forward.

But a minute into the video she throws her head back. Smiles. Of course it's not me.

Jess

God, my head aches.

I apply a stage-level amount of make-up and drench myself in Chanel N° 5 with all the vigour of a fireman trying to extinguish a fire. If the fire was my flushed, pink, still-a-little-drunk skin, that is. I'm more of a Byredo Gypsy Water woman, but this fragrance – a gift from Joe – might just make me smell like the adult I'm supposed to be. The alcohol in the perfume only exacerbates the remnants of last night's wine still seeping from my pores.

Hangovers weren't always this bad, were they?

The problem with getting blackout drunk isn't the blacked-out bits per se – I quite enjoy disengaging from my current reality. No, the real issue is that at some point the lights have to be switched on again, and when they do, the flashbacks come with the force of a torch being shone directly into my eyes. The fact that these unwelcome memories all took place while my kids were having a sleepover at Granny's to 'give Mum a break' only adds to the shame.

Flashback number one. The toilet at Tashas Hyde Park. The stall was all tasteful rose-gold and cloud-like marble. I recall thrusting in a cramped stall to the muted sound of a Phil Collins track, bathed in the aroma of the bathroom's Charlotte Rhys's Oud diffuser (not my favourite, especially after this).

Was the sex even good? It was angry and … rapid. Does it matter how it felt? The feeling of commanding a man's complete attention for a few minutes – that was the drug.

Flashback number two. A long, rambling call to Queenie.

Shit. What did I say to her?

I told her about the sex, for sure. And I think I mentioned her porno, which she seemed to know very little about. That's rather worrying. A wave of shame crashes over me. I really like Queenie and I love her writing. I was hoping to become friends with her. But I'm pretty sure my intentions would have come out as garbled nonsense, although I think I remember that she exuded a quiet kindness that even now softens the full-body cringe I am feeling.

Flashback. Number. Three.

For this one I check the sent items of my phone.

No! No, no, no, no. I sent a message to Beverly. Not a message, a voice note starting with, 'Bev my girrrl!' I can't bear to play more than three seconds, which is enough to recognise me belting out the shrieking beginnings of Alanis Morrissette's 'You Oughta Know'. I just know the line I would have sung – that one about him thinking of me as she goes down on him in a theatre.

Good grief, there's a reply!

'I'm not sure if that message was meant for me. Quite an impressive free-association performance. Reminds me of *Milkman*, the 2018 Booker winner. You should give it a read.'

The cheek!

Another sent message. I was busy last night, wasn't I? It's a picture. Nothing too saucy, just me in my satin kimono, one shoulder slipped down to reveal a red-lace bra strap. It would have looked quite sensual if it wasn't for the thick smudges of mascara running down my face and the wild, serial-killer-type look in my eyes.

Bile rises in my throat.

I sent it to Matt from the MK group. I'm so confused. I've felt a fleeting attraction to him once or twice, but not enough to justify this.

I message Mum: 'How're the girls?'

'Right as rain and helping me bake banana bread. Don't rush – enjoy the time alone.'

I down a cup of coffee. Swallow more guilt. Throw a judgemental gaze at the dishes overflowing in the sink. Just when did Ntombi plan on loading the dishwasher?

Ah. Yes. We laid Ntombi off a few weeks ago to 'consolidate our costs'.

I look at my phone once again, shocked as I process what time it is. The dishes are later's problem; despite my best intentions, I've got to get to lunch at Marble with Lindiwe and I'm late.

Lindiwe is seated at an elegant table on the balcony that overlooks the Joburg cityscape. From afar, I notice her shaking chef David Higgs's hand with a brilliant smile. Looks like her deal with him is in the bag. And it's all his gain – with a few choice phone calls to her platinum network, Lindiwe can change your life. I wonder what would've happened if I'd let her change mine.

'Jess! Great timing,' she purrs. 'You're looking just gorgeous.'

I tentatively pull my sunglasses off my face. 'I wouldn't say gorgeous. I'm hungover as hell, have overcompensated in the make-up department and now resemble a caricature of myself.'

'Ah, Jess – you always did have a way with words.'

A waiter sidles up to me and fills my glass with cool sparkling water.

'Thank you so much –' I squint at the name tag '– Nosizwe.' Although on my clumsy tongue it comes out 'No-seez-way'.

'So, how have you been?' asks Lindiwe. Her skin gleams and her hair is poised in a perfect halo-like Afro.

'Okay, been better.'

'I'm sure. Joe's investment troubles must be keeping you up at night.'

A cold feeling rises in my body. My hands go clammy.

'But wait wha— I didn't think the news was public?'

Like a good media-trained professional she doesn't directly answer the question. 'Those accusations are pretty serious.' Several expensive-looking platters laden with hot, chargrilled bread, seared tuna and lamb skewers are placed discreetly at the table. 'I hope you don't mind,' says Lindiwe, 'I ordered champagne and something for us to snack on.'

Lindiwe tuts, her long gold earrings jingling as she shakes her head. 'I know the news before it becomes the news, my darling. I thought that's why you'd got in touch. Because you needed a fixer.'

'A what?'

'A fixer. Someone who controls the story and your image in the press.'

That all sounds too serious. And expensive. I don't like it one bit.

'No, no, I'm just fine, really. Using the time wisely, changing my life for the better. We had to let our domestic worker go, but I'm doing my own cleaning, which is quite humbling, you know? Like, why should someone else clean up after me ...? Good lesson for the girls.'

Lindiwe shoots a strange look in my direction.

'I hope you've paid her a good severance package,' she says coolly.

'Yes, yes, of course.' I try to anchor myself to another topic, at speed. 'I've also started reading again and—'

'How much?' asks Lindiwe.

'Pardon?'

'How much did you pay your domestic worker?'

'Four months in full?'

She nods. 'Okay, so you're reading ...'

'Yes! I'm part of this bookclub dedicated to Marian Keyes. That's actually why I—'

'Marian Keyes? You know, I like her, but I can never understand the South African obsession with overseas culture. We're so quick to fall for international films, authors, bloody chocolate bars.'

'I mean, have you tasted Peanut Butter M&Ms?' I venture.

'You're missing the point. When are we going to get excited about the talent we have *here*? When will we start forming –' she waves her hand in the air '– little clubs to celebrate our *own* Marian Keyeses?'

I smile. 'Funny you say that because I think I've just found her.'

'Really?'

'Yep. She's in my bookclub. A librarian based in Cape Town. Comes across a little shy but her writing! It's funny, raw, a little explosive. Anyway, that was one of the reasons I wanted to see you. We're desperate to meet Marian Keyes when she comes to South Africa, and I thought you, or someone in your team, might be handling her schedule?'

Lindi nods quietly, a grin playing on her lips. 'I like your style, Jess. This is the kind of hustle I like to see; the kind of drive you've lacked since you married Joe.'

I sigh. 'You know I'd still be working with you if I could, but he wanted me to quit.'

She wrinkles her nose. 'Are you sure about that? I recall you telling me it was your own decision.'

'It doesn't really matter now,' I say, getting agitated. 'My career has taken a backseat, and the thing that made me "me" is gone. I'm lost.'

Lindiwe shakes her head. 'I think a woman like you has more power than that. Maybe when you start raging, or whatever this is, you will realise you have some power in your own life after all.'

I shakily extend my champagne glass in a toast, even though I disagree. Already the alcohol is burning through the queasiness of my hangover.

Lindiwe continues. 'Anyway. *Of course* I have access to Marian's schedule, but I'm not going to release it that easily.'

'What can I do in exchange?'

'Let me be your fixer – you and Joe's – when the time comes. God knows you're going to need it.'

I feel sick, but hold out a hand anyway. 'Um ... deal.'

'Fabulous,' she says. 'I've got to rush. I'm running a listening session for Sho Madjozi's new album.'

'Of course you are.'

She calls over the waitress and taps her card. 'Lunch is on me.'

'Sure, thanks!' My body unclenches in relief. 'Enjoy the schmoozing!'

She shakes her head. 'Enjoy the house-cleaning.'

Ginger

My phone rings with a number I don't recognise. The girls are always saying I shouldn't answer those numbers because it's probably a telemarketer. But back in the day we *never* knew who was behind a ringing telephone and that was part of the fun. And also, those poor telemarketers. They're just trying to earn a living. It's not their fault that they're interrupting your day trying to sell you insurance for when you die. I try to be nice to them. And so what if I once ended up buying some timeshare that I didn't want. I don't see Debbie complaining about that.

But it's not a telemarketer. It's Queenie. Which just goes to show.

I know it's Queenie as soon as I hear the first tentative, 'Hello? Ginger?' She has that Cape Town burr to her words. It reminds me of Roger's PA, who was also from Cape Town originally. Poor Marli – she used to make Roger the most lovely food, like vetkoek and samosas and bredies, and he'd bring them home from the office. 'Foreign muck,' he used to say, which made no sense but there was no persuading him to try it. But the girls and I loved it. I got her to cater for after the funeral, actually. Told her it's what he would have wanted. She was so delighted. It's important to make people feel special, I think.

Queenie's never called me before so this is a big deal. 'Is everything okay?' I ask.

'Yes, of course,' she says. Then she pauses. 'Actually, no. It's not. I don't know what to do about Jess.'

'Jess?' I must sound like an idiot, like I don't know who Jess is. But Jess doesn't seem like someone to be worrying about. Personally, I think we should be worrying about that poor Matt, having sex with that girl.

But then I remember that Jess is married to that dreadful man who's not responding to Sybil's emails so maybe we *should* be worrying about her. 'What's happened?' I say to Queenie as I settle into my armchair. I have a feeling this will be a proper story. And we all know that Queenie's a proper storyteller.

First Queenie tells me that she's called because she's worried about Jess. Queenie lives in Cape Town and the rest of us live in Johannesburg so she can't just hop in a car, you see. She's thinking maybe *I* can help, being physically closer. She says that she thinks maybe Jess needs someone wise to lean on. Someone wise like me. Huh! I wish my daughters saw it like that.

Then Queenie swears me to secrecy and tells me that Jess has 'committed an indiscretion with a stranger'. And you don't have to tell *me* the mortification one feels after committing an indiscretion with a stranger. The less said about New Year's Eve 1979 the better. Although in fairness, Edmund wasn't exactly a stranger and his wife, Marlene, is still in my bookclub. Roger might be dead but Marlene isn't, even if it was forty years ago and they weren't exactly married yet. But still, I know about regrettable indiscretions.

Of course I just say, 'Well, haven't we all made mistakes?' and Queenie says she's sure I haven't made such terrible mistakes and I just say, 'You'd be surprised,' and then she says nothing surprises her any more, and she tells me another story – this one about her and her boyfriend and a video and another woman and Queenie's name being dragged through the mud on the Internet.

I really hope that if I've taught my girls one thing, it's never to have sex on camera, or at the very least not to show their faces. It was totally different in my day when digital cameras first came out and you could just delete it straight away. Good times. But these days, you'd have to be an idiot to let a man film you. Or a woman, or even a womxn. I say this to Queenie, and *she* says you'd have to be an idiot to have sex with her Kevin, and that makes us both laugh. The biggest problem Queenie has is how to get her name taken off this video.

Well, I have no idea how to help her with that, but I know someone who can: James. I tell her about James and she agrees that I can ask him to phone her. I'm delighted. A legitimate excuse to call him!

After I speak to Queenie, I call Jess and suggest that seeing as how we both live in Johannesburg and not even that far from each other with her in Sandhurst and me in Blairgowrie, why don't we go out for lunch. I'm worried she might suggest that Matt joins us because I don't know if she'll want him to know about her indiscretion, even though we all know a great deal about *his* indiscretion, but she just agrees to lunch without suggesting Matt. I propose we meet at Tashas at Hyde Park because it's close for both of us and because my girls seem to like it there, but I must have got it wrong because Jess yells, 'No!' and suggests we meet at Olives & Plates in the bookshop. I make a little note to myself not to make the mistake of suggesting Tashas to my daughters because it is obviously no longer acceptable. It's awfully hard to keep up with these things.

We agree to have lunch tomorrow and I'm quite surprised that a woman like Jess has time in her diary for me. I guess nobody's surprised I have time in my diary for her.

That done, I turn to the pleasing task of calling James. We first have a lovely chat about the movie we saw together, and how we've both been thinking about it. And then we talk about the last Marian Keyes I lent him and what we best liked about it. I suggest he might enjoy Jojo Moyes and he's never heard of her so I say that next time he comes over, I'll lend him one and then I blush at my presumption but he doesn't seem to even notice and enthusiastically suggests that we go for lunch tomorrow. Which obviously I can't because of Jess so I explain that to him without mentioning her indiscretion, or New Year's Eve 1979, and he's very understanding. Roger would have been most put out but James just says, 'Well, what about dinner?' and I accept.

Finally I tell him about Queenie's Internet problems and we both agree that things have got much more complicated than when we were young. He says that he'll give her a call and see if he can help, although it's not something he's had to try before. 'I'll do some research first,' he says with a confidence I like.

Well pleased with my day, I put down the phone only to have it ring again. Debbie. 'Mom,' she says, 'I'm busy tomorrow so I'm going to drop the kids at you at lunchish and pick them up after supper.'

'I'm afraid that doesn't suit me, darling,' I say.

'What on earth do you mean?' says Debbie.

'I'm having lunch with a friend tomorrow. Not at Tashas obviously. And I have a date tomorrow night. So I'm afraid you'll have to make another plan.' I feel slightly bad, so I add, 'I'd be delighted to have them the next day, of course.'

I know it's nasty, but I have a small smile on my face as I listen to Debbie stumble over her words trying to persuade me that I don't actually have any plans I can't cancel.

Eventually, I interrupt her. 'I'm sorry, darling,' I say. 'The landline's ringing. I'd better go. I'll see the kids the day after tomorrow. Love you.' And I hang up.

Landline. Hah! Do I really seem like the sort of fossil who would get a call on the landline?

Matt

I'm sitting at the Service Station Café, waiting for Sadie, who doesn't seem to get that I have work to do and can only afford to take an hour off for lunch, but I've given up trying to make her be on time. Like everyone around me, I'm staring at my phone. But I'm not on Insta; I'm trying to make notes on the latest batch of scenes I've been sent, which are the craziest to date. The executive producer of the series loves a bit of incest and we keep having the same scenario where people end up falling in love and then finding out they're brother and sister (as one does). But this time they want to do a mother-son scenario, which they say is a riff on the whole Oedipus vibe.

Frankly, I'm starting to wonder if the producer did have a thing for his mom. He says things to me like, 'Growing up, did you ever think your mom was really sexy? Mine was so hot. So. Damn. Hot. You know what I mean, Matt?'

Actually, I don't, and I'm trying to find a tactful way to say this but I keep getting distracted by a picture. One that Jess sent me. It's disturbing because although she looks sexy as hell (God, I do love a red bra), she also looks a bit out of it and there's no message or anything. At first I thought she'd sent it to me by mistake but then I wondered if it wasn't a cry for help.

'Brrrrrrsh!' I feel a big, wet zerbit on my neck.

'Hey, big dick,' is how Sadie greets me, grinning widely as she slides into the chair opposite me.

'Could you maybe keep your voice down? There's a bunch of mom's friends over there.' I flick my eyes to a group of well-groomed women all with identical blonde bobs and dressed in top-end gym gear.

'Ah ... the Karens of Facebook. Hiiiii, Karen!' Sadie shouts, waving.

They look around, puzzled. I try to kick her under the table and end up kicking the wrought-iron table leg and nearly breaking a toe.

'Fuck, fuck, fuck!'

'That'll teach you,' Sadie says. 'Who do I need to fuck around here to get a cortado?'

The waiters at the Service Station know her and are not at all put out by her brashness. Lungi makes a sign that I think means her coffee is on the way, but could also mean she has to fuck him to get the coffee. Whatever.

'Anyway,' she says, 'why am I here?'

'I just thought we should clear the air after ...'

'After we had sex?' She doesn't lower her voice. 'You're pretty good in the sack, Mattie. I think you should add that to your LinkedIn profile.'

'Nobody goes on LinkedIn any more.'

Sadie just laughs. 'Look, we had a good time; I'm not feeling used. I made up with Johnny –' (*Fuck*, no.) '– so it's all good, Mattie. You don't have to marry me because you took my virginity.' She tries to bat her eyelashes and simper. It looks kinda scary.

'Your virginity left the building a looooong time ago, girl.'

'You know it. You were there after all.'

I was indeed. And no, she didn't lose it to me. It was in our matric year (Sadie attended our sister school) and she was determined to screw like it was a badge she'd be able to pin on her blazer. She'd decided who she wanted to lose her virginity to, and once she'd made up her mind the poor guy didn't stand a chance. He was the captain of the rugby team – very good-looking but extremely conservative and he didn't believe in sex before marriage. Which frankly was like a red rag to a bull. Sadie was determined but she was also nervous – 'Those religious dudes can be really rapey and twisted, Mattie' – so she'd made me hide in the cupboard while they did it.

Most excruciating five minutes of my life.

He came in about two minutes. Sadie'd said, 'Is that it?' and he'd started crying. She, of course, had zero sympathy but I'd almost got out of my cupboard to counsel the guy. Almost, but not quite.

Sadie appears to be thinking fondly of the incident; her eyes have a faraway look in them. 'How is ... what's his name again? You're still in touch, right?'

'Nick.'

'How is he?'

'Recently left his wife and went off and became a priest.'

She starts to laugh. 'That explains so much. Probably a paedo.'

'Or has a calling and wants to serve God.'

'Nah, definitely a paedo. Otherwise why was he so shit in the sack?'

'He was seventeen. And you, Sadie, were scary as hell.'

'I was hot.'

'And scary.'

'Shuddup. What're we eating?' She kind of bats my head out the way so she can see the menu on the blackboard.

'One macadamia nut cortado!' Lungi presents it with a flourish.

'Thanks, Lungi.' She flashes him a megawatt smile that has him melting on the spot. She *is* very beautiful, I acknowledge, and I feel ... I dunno.

'Why are you looking at me like that?'

'Like what?'

'Like a weirdo.'

'I *am* a weirdo.'

'True story.'

As usual, Sadie can't make up her mind when we order our food and makes me order her second choice so she can have some of mine. I'm used to it by now.

'So, Sadie, what do you think? Do you think the woman in this picture is ... okay?' I show her the picture of Jess on my phone.

Sadie peers at it frowning. 'She looks fuck-drunk and like she's just had a one-night stand.'

'Do you think it's a cry for help?'

'Help as in, "Bring me two Myprodols, an Energade and the day-after pill"? Why do you think it's a cry for help or is that just part of your need to rescue people?'

It's on the tip of my tongue to point out that she didn't seem to object to being rescued the other day.

'She's a newish friend and she sent it to me the other day with no message or anything.'

'She's coming on to you.'

'Nah.'

'She wants some of that.' She gestures crudely to a sausage on another diner's plate. 'Just ask her why she sent it.'

'I don't want to embarrass her.'

'Oh, for fuck's sake, Matthew!' She rolls her eyes. 'I know you have balls – I've *felt* them. So start acting like it!' And before I can do anything, she grabs my phone and starts typing.

'Sadie, no! I mean it, don't—'

But it's too late. She's already sent Jess a message.

You know that feeling you get when you're dreaming you're in a lift and the cord thingie has broken and it's plummeting to the ground? (No? Only me?) Well, that's the feeling I get now.

She returns my phone with a huge grin on her face.

I check the message: 'Hey, did you send this to me by mistake? Just checking you're okay. Matt'

'See, I'm not a complete bitch,' she says. I don't say anything, just raise an eyebrow. 'I'm *not*,' she insists.

I shrug.

So she thumps me.

Lunch – what I get to eat of it – is delicious as usual. Carmen's food is always amazing. I try to pay the bill, but Sadie slaps my hand away and with what can only be described as a leer says, 'I owe you for services rendered.'

Her jokes are starting to get on my nerves. It would be worse if we were so embarrassed we didn't want to see each other again, except ... I don't know ... her casual attitude freaks me out.

Basically, I found it amusing until I was the one being laughed about.

After Sadie's left, I head to the bookshop next door. Buying books and drinking coffee are my two forms of self-medication. I buy yet another copy of *Rachel's Holiday* because it has a different cover that now matches my other Marian Keyeses. I balance that out by buying four local books: the latest Sue Nyathi, a short-story collection from Mohale Mashigo, the new chicklit from Fiona Snyckers and some griplit from Jo Macgregor. (Aside: it really gets on my nerves that some people still don't realise that South African fiction is not just *Cry, The Beloved Country* and JM Coetzee.)

Before I go to my cottage I swing by my parents' house to give Mom the Fiona Snyckers. (Mom lurrrrrrves Fiona.) Micky is in the pantry eating Nutella out of the jar. With her fingers. No, Micky doesn't live here but she spends so much time at my parents' house she may as well.

'Okay, that's disgusting, and Marcus will kill you if you finish the Nutella.'

'Let him try.' (Good point.) She eyes me speculatively. The way our cat, Blackie, looks when she's toying with a mouse. 'So, Mattie ... heard you had a drunken shag with Sadie.'

No, no, no, please God no.

'Don't be ridiculous,' I say, drawing on every bit of acting ability I possess which, granted, is not a lot.

'Don't bother. I heard it from Sadie.'

I feel a flash of anger and something else I can't identify.

Mom wanders in. 'What's this about Sadie?'

I'm shaking my head so hard at Micky, I'm afraid it might actually fall off.

'Matt shagged her.'

My mother swings around to me. 'You and Sadie are in a relationship? Oh, I'm *so* pleased, Mattie. I always thought you might be—'

'Gay,' Micky finishes for her. 'Don't worry, Mom, we *all* thought he was batting for the other team.'

'Not that it would've been a problem if you were. I just wanted you to feel that you could tell me if you were sexually attracted to boys because you know Mrs Harris's son from my yoga class is gay and between relationships.'

Someone kill me now. Rupert Harris is, how can I put this in a charitable way? Rupert is plain and although I'm not planning on dating him anytime soon, I am insulted that my mother thinks Rupe is the kind of guy I would be interested in.

'Oh, I'm so happy for you.' Mom comes and gives me a big hug.

'It's not a relationship, Mom,' protests Micky. 'It was a shag-and-release situation. Turns out your favourite son is a bit of a man-whore.'

'Nonsense,' says Mom. 'Mattie's not that kind of guy.' She claps her hands. 'Oh, I've *always* hoped you and Sadie would get together. It's been worrying me for so long that you've never had anyone, Mattie. Life is better when you have someone to share it with.'

There are tears in her eyes. Actual fucking tears.

'I'm so glad you've finally found love in each other.'

Jesus.

If I had the energy, I'd attempt to fit the entire Nutella jar in Micky's mouth and be done with it. Instead I say, 'You know in Ireland "Micky" is a slang word for penis,' before I turn and walk out the door, forgetting to give Mom the book. Never mind. My *relationship* with Sadie seems to be gift enough for now.

I stomp out of the kitchen door and turn left up to the steep path to my cottage, slapping the white blooms of the irises out the way as I go and avoiding the sharp thorns of the rambler roses. The path to the cottage has definite Hansel and Gretel fairy-tale vibes (without the Wicked Witch) and a better view than the house. I can see across to Melville Koppies on the one side and to the Magaliesberg on the other. Usually, the beauty of the flowers and the view cheer me up, but this time I am swearing as I trudge up the path. I get a startled look from William, the gardener who comes in a couple of times a week to sort out the garden and who also likes to stand at the gate asking people if they know Jesus. 'Not fuck you, William – fuck Micky. She's a complete pain in the arse.'

William gazes sorrowfully at me muttering. 'Watch the way you talk. Let nothing foul or dirty come out of your mouth,' which sounds like something from the Bible and I'm scared he's going to ask to lay hands on me to rid me of my obvious possession by a demon.

'Never mind. Sorry. I'm just angry.'

I get inside and flop down on the couch. I lean back and close my eyes for a second.

I'm not just angry with Sadie for telling Micky about us – I'm hurt. And now Mom thinks we're an item and I *hate* disappointing her. I know, I know, sounds like me and Oedipus are besties and that I have an enormous amount in common with the producer who's got a thing about incest, but it's not that. It's that Mom is always giving and she asks for so little in return and now I'm going to have to disappoint her with the fact that I *did* have a one-night stand with Sadie. Fuck, fuck, fuck.

My phone pings. It's a message from Jess. A facepalm emoji followed by: 'Need to explain that pic in person. Having lunch with Ginger tomorrow. Want to join us?'

I really should be studying for my board exam and finishing the notes on these scenes and I do mean to say no, but it's as if my fingers have a life of their own: 'Yes, please. I've got myself in a bit of a mess and I need some advice.'

Queenie

The library is busy this afternoon; small groups of kids spread out, chatter in the air. People like to think of libraries as silent places and maybe it used to be like that, but it's not the case any more. Our library is more of a social centre than anything else, especially today when it seems that every teacher from every grade at the local school has assigned a project.

I love it here.

To look around there is nothing obviously special to see. There's the fadedness of the old government-style building, beige-painted walls covering concrete stipple from the seventies, rows of slightly battered dark-wood shelving. Rough short-haired carpet tiles, green to hide the wear of foot traffic. There's nothing modern about it; you might even say there is a tiredness in the bones of the library. We librarians do our best. We put up posters, keep our newsboards pinned with quotes from the latest books, but the library could use more colour, fresh paint, new tables and chairs in the research area, couches where the magazines and newspapers are. Computers that don't take up half the desks with their big box screens. But without fail, when I stand still and feel, not just look, there is always a steady hum that grows into a buzz as the day wears on and more adults and children arrive. It feels like the air is sparking with energy as they find the books they need. Then it doesn't matter what the shelves look like, or the carpeting or the couches. The magic is all in them discovering the possibilities of what is on those shelves.

The books, the books, the books – each one of them ready to transport you to a place where it doesn't matter what it looks like where you sit or stand. I had books, of course, to keep me escaped during Covid, but it's this feeling of communal magic in the library that I missed most.

I watch the kids. As usual some strut around purposefully, others hang about. Not all the librarians agree with me but I like to let the kids wander and find what they need for themselves. I've chanced upon some of the most unexpected reads just by trailing my fingers along the spines of a row of books. Stopping simply because a title, or author, or colour, or crackle of a spine folded over too many times caught my eye. Finding what I didn't know I wanted; if it were up to me, every child would know that delicious joy. The world is not only for those who strut around purposefully. Not all who wander are lost. I know Esmeralda wants them to go directly to the counter to ask for help, but my style, when I'm not on counter duty, is to hover in the aisles with my trolley as cover while I shelve books. I keep an eye out for the kids who can't find what they're looking for or who are too shy to go up to the counter – the ones helplessly staring at the shelves as if the right book will suddenly jump out. Sometimes I leave them for a little while and hope they start touching the books like I do and that the right book will reveal itself. Other times I start chatting to them about non-bookish things as I fiddle with my trolley, then I hand them a book – any book, all casual like – and ask them what they think of it. It's a starting point. I know where to go with them from how they respond.

Esmeralda thinks I'm hiding in the aisles so I can slack off, but I re-member what it's like to be that child. People think it's simply about being shy because you're either shy or not, right? Sometimes the kids *are* shy but I wasn't a shy child myself. I was middling, in between, ordinary. But completely overwhelmed by choice. So many books.

How would I choose? What if I got the wrong one? It took a while before I learnt that there is no such thing as the 'wrong' book – I always found something in any book, even if it was realising what I didn't like – and once I knew that it made it easier to choose and to go forward. I wish that ability extended to the rest of my life. I can imagine all these possi-bilities, all these choices and I get overwhelmed. And I do nothing. Never follow through, as Jennifer reminds me.

But I am going to follow through on Marian Keyes, I tell myself. I feel sure about it. With Ginger, Matt and Jess, I have a chance to start fresh.

They don't have the baggage of others who know me; I don't have to be the friend that doesn't follow through and do as she imagines.

This morning, Ginger messaged to say that she and Jess would be having lunch today and I made her promise to send me a pic. So when my phone pings with a notification from Messenger, even though I should resist during work hours, I click it.

And there they are – with Matt as a surprise addition. I zoom in to see them sitting around the table, half-eaten desserts and coffees close at hand, smiles on their faces.

Who are these people? I want to ask myself. I mean, obviously it's Jess, Ginger and Matt, but I don't know anyone else who can just go out for a long lunch on a weekday afternoon. Everyone else I know works full time – they'd have to take leave to be able to do that. It reminds me of that advert for a private bank that was on TV years ago – it went something like, 'Who are these people, living like this on an ordinary Tuesday?' and it showed this couple sliding along in their convertible, seemingly without a care in the world. 'Those people' were obviously the clients of the private bank so not me or anyone *I* knew. And Jess, Ginger and Matt look like *those* people.

But that, I remind myself as I hurry to shelve the dog-eared copy of *Our World of Water* that all the Grade 4s wanted, is the power of books. Sharing the same taste in books can connect you, help you overcome nearly everything. It transcends all the things that would make you hesitate. Doesn't matter your age, gender, social standing, occupation or where you live. Ordinarily I would have been intimidated by how beautiful Jess is, or how sharp Ginger can be, or how young Matt is. I would have been conscious of not living close to them. But when we chat about Marian's *Grown Ups* or share our excitement about a sequel to *Rachel's Holiday* none of anything else matters. It's our sweet spot. If it wasn't for the MK bookclub, I'd likely never have met – or honestly, wanted to meet – Matt, Jess or Ginger. They just look too different, live too differently, and stay too far away for me to imagine that we would have anything in common. But because of bookclub I know them as more than 'those people'.

Don't judge a book by its cover, as the saying goes.

'Wish I was there!' I type. 'Chat later xxx'

Of course the one time I'm on my phone, Esmeralda sees me.

'There are kids at the desk needing photocopies,' she snipes, giving me such a fright that I drop my phone and have to get on my knees to reach where it's fallen under the trolley.

'Coming!' I say, still scrabbling for the phone. I really meant it – I really do wish I was there.

I wonder whether Jess has told Matt and Ginger about the guy in the Tashas toilet. Or was she too embarrassed? Ginger and Jess both know about the Pornhub video though Jess still thinks it's me. Have they told Matt? I wish I was at the lunch to make sure everything came out right. And I really think Jess could do with having a friend close by.

As for me, the Pornhub thing is embarrassing and overwhelming and I want to die when I think about it, but at the same time I'd give anything to be able to talk about it with other people. In fact, I want to be angry about it, to swear out loud, have a tantrum. Cry.

I really, really want to cry. I stay on my knees with my arm stretched out under the trolley for longer than I need to. My face endures the scratching of carpet and my hand is on the phone but I'm not ready to get up. I need the threatening tide of tears in my chest to subside. Esmeralda cannot see me with a wet face. She might feel sorry for me and that would make it worse. I will not be able to tell her the truth and she will feel like she has more control over me than she already does. I don't need that.

I haven't told anyone besides Ginger. Not even Jennifer. She loves Kevin; loves the neat little box Kevin and I fit into. Love. Marriage. Kids. That's where Kevin and I are supposed to go, according to the world of Jennifer. She hasn't yet managed it for herself but she wants it for me. As if she's decided that she can't be happy so she needs to make sure it's going to happen for me. 'Ma and Pa would've wanted it for you too,' she says, as if I need more pressure. Their deaths nearly killed her, both of us, and I'm not sure I could handle her falling apart about me and Kevin too. I don't want to disappoint her.

I haven't told Faheema for the exact opposite reason. She doesn't miss an opportunity to tell me all the ways that Kevin isn't a good boyfriend, and this would confirm that she was right. I don't want to have to deal with her rage on top of my own. It's not my face or my body in that video but it *is* my name and this library. What if people here find out? Oh my God, imagine someone sent Esmeralda that link! Not exactly the kind of adult outreach programme she'd want for the library. I want to shut down my brain at all the possibilities.

While I am doing the photocopies, I think of how easy it had been to talk to Ginger. When she'd first suggested James, I really wasn't that keen – I felt a little like she was trying to save me (Faheema would say I have a chip on my shoulder about accepting help). But the truth is, I wasn't exactly sure what more he could do. I've already found the online content-removal request on Pornhub and submitted all the information. But since then I've started panicking. The Pornhub form doesn't say how long it will be before they respond. What if they don't remove it? What if other videos pop up with my name? I don't want this thing following me around forever. What am I saying – I don't want it following me around for another day! By the time James messaged to say he was researching it and would ring me tomorrow, I was so glad Ginger had suggested him. I don't want to deal with this thing alone.

But the other great thing about Ginger is that she didn't pry. Faheema would've demanded to know how many ways I was going to make him pay, while Jennifer would've been making excuses for him, insisting it was all a misunderstanding. Ginger didn't do any of that.

I still can't believe what Kevin has done and I've watched the clip more times than I should have. Stupid, but I've tried to convince myself that it isn't him. That it's some weird twisted joke where someone has put our names to another couple's video. But it is burnt into my brain. All three minutes twenty-one seconds of it. Quick one, Kev. Bastard. It's his face. His smile. The curve of his cheek. His eyes squeezed squinting closed as he stares straight into the camera. The tiniest bit of tongue sticking out between his teeth. His hair long, the curls falling onto his forehead. I can't bear to look at the rest of his body, but I don't have to.

It's him.

No mistake.

I sent him the link the same night Jess sent it to me – but after I'd watched it the first ten times, or was it fifteen? I'd say he was a dog about it, but that would be unfair to dogs.

'I can't really talk about it now, I'm on shift,' he'd messaged. 'You know my phone was stolen a few months ago – whoever had it must have uploaded the video. I'll try to call you later.'

No apology. No explanation for why he'd had sex with another woman. Why he'd filmed it. No outrage that it was on Pornhub. He must have known about it even before I sent it.

'Why is my fucking name on it? And the name of the bloody library?' I'd messaged back. I knew we weren't the most loved-up couple on earth, but I still burned with questions: *How could you do this to me? Why? Who is she? Why didn't you tell me?* But through my tears I understood that it didn't matter. I hadn't wanted to admit it to Faheema or to Jennifer, but a part of me had always guessed that Kevin wasn't faithful to me when he was away. He was living his best life, wasn't he? And hadn't I encouraged him to do exactly that? Nothing like a video of him fucking another woman to make the blinkers fall from my eyes.

'I don't know. Maybe they saw your details saved as Girlfriend in my contacts,' he'd messaged.

My heart broke a little more. Kevin had made a big deal when he'd saved my name under 'Girlfriend'. He'd done it on all his social media too. At the time it had meant something to me.

'You'll have to change my details to Ex-Girlfriend,' I'd lobbed the message at him with the most certainty I'd felt in a long time.

This was it. All the silences between us, the awkward phone calls, the pretence that we were making the long-distance work, it all came down to this. No more denying it. I couldn't imagine my way out of this disaster. The video was real.

'I'm sorry,' he'd said at last. 'It was just a girl I met in Durban. There must be a way to get the video taken down … It doesn't have to be the end of us, Queenie.'

The words sat there. Flat. Meaningless. He wasn't trying very hard to hold on to me.

I thought about it for as long as it took him on that desk with that girl. Honestly, I didn't even need that long.

'Oh, but it does, Kevin. It is the end.' Then I switched off my phone.

Turned on my new laptop from Faheema. Opened up a blank page. And wrote and wrote and wrote. All my feelings out. It was, as always, the only way.

Jess

The Le Creuset kettle shrieks on the stove. Hannah bounds around the kitchen with worrying enthusiasm, telling me the talking points for to-day's inter-school debate meet in ALL CAPS. Willow scampers beneath my feet, emitting a high-pitched whine that might only be completely audible to a humpback whale.

I wish I had such saintly patience that I could continue making break-fast unflustered. But the noise, that bloody noise! I sometimes wish my children had been born with a mute button.

The headache doesn't help. Next to the growing pile of Marian Keyes novels next to my bed there is another empty bottle of Diemersfontein Pinotage.

The more I crave quiet, the louder the girls seem to become. I ache for Joe's grounding presence on mornings like this one when his calmness could absorb it all.

'Hannah. Hannah! Take the bloody kettle off the stove and pour me some tea, will you? Five Roses, milk and two rusks.'

'But I thought you were only drinking almond—'

'I said dairy, Hannah. I don't ask you questions, do I?'

She shrugs, her bright face gleaming with innocence. Darling Hannah, there never is anything to ask her questions about. She glides through life with the principled confidence of a child who has always got what she wanted and never had cause to believe otherwise. She doesn't know how privileged she is.

I pull Willow onto my lap, busy her with a YouTube clip of a child somewhere across the globe unboxing a Barbie doll, promising myself that

113

I will unpack the various layers of why this is problematic later. I stare at the flotsam of my disintegrated rusk with such focus it's like I'm doing a tea-leaf reading. Except the only thing these soggy pieces of sugary gluten are telling me is that my Gut Microbiome is going to be furious with me later.

My eyes land on my copy of *Rachel's Holiday* – my latest Marian Keyes read. I didn't even need to hunt this one down because Ginger gave it to me as a gift at our lunch. I'm sure she said something meaningful about it, but I was too busy having shame flashbacks about my time in the Tashas bathroom. It's good timing though, because Matt said he'd bought another copy from Love Books the other day.

'We can buddy-read,' he said, holding my eyes until my face got hot.

That's another reason I felt off at lunch! I didn't have a drink. I was hyperaware of what my behaviour must look like to my new friends and I hadn't wanted to come across as *that woman*. Then I'd been too busy plotting our next move to meet up with Marian Keyes. I'd had a glass with dinner and the comfort bottle next to my bed – I mean, I'm not *crazy* – but I was able to go the whole lunch without drinking. That must count for something, right?

I slurp my tea feeling goddamn awful.

'Okay, you lot,' I sigh. 'Time to get you to school.'

'Mom!' Hannah looks appalled. 'Dad is taking us, remember?'

I feel a pang of sympathy for my resilient girls, who are soldiering on, no questions asked.

The bell rings. Shit. No time to run upstairs and make myself look more … I don't know what exactly. More of what he wanted me to be? More *Beverly*? I cringe, wondering if she shared my unfortunate voice note with him. Pleasing him used to feel so important, but somehow it doesn't matter as much any more. A realisation has been dawning on me lately that maybe, just maybe, I need to focus more on pleasing myself.

Our heavy steel gate shudders open. I feel light with the strange, out-of-body sensation of greeting my own husband as if he were a guest.

He's got thinner. But thanks to Beverly, no doubt, his shirt has never looked so crisp. I fight back the shame of knowing more about wine vintages than bleach or fabric softener.

'The gate needs oiling,' he says.

'I know.'

'I should have come by sooner, taken a look. This always happens after the first summer storms.'

'It does.'

A house is a funny thing. It holds the life of a marriage long after it's over, like bricks retaining warmth after a hot summer's day. I don't want to remember all the times Joe fought with the damn gate, or painted the walls, or mowed the lawn, or hauled his thick frame up our wonky ladder to replace the bulbs in the downlights. When his investment company took off, we were going to remodel the kitchen. We had dreams too.

This toxic cocktail of feelings is overwhelming. I long for the cushion of a glass of something, anything. Mimosas at this hour, perhaps, to keep things civilised.

He looks at me searchingly, about the gate perhaps, or something else. *How would I know?* I think bitterly. *He was probably schtupping Beverly for months before I figured it out.* There it is again, that unwelcome image of Beverly's lips in a papery 'O'.

'The girls are going to be late.'

I smile widely at their waves and 'I love you's and blow them a few dramatic kisses. I need to pull myself together, dammit! My beautiful girls deserve so much more than the confused, muted version of myself that I am right now.

Since I'm already on the gluten spiral, I toast myself an English muffin. Then pour a glass of orange juice with only the slightest glug of champagne … to temper the bitterness. Open the fresh copy of *Rachel's Holiday*. There's a new bookmark inside the front cover. A note from Ginger:

> *Dear Jess*
> *Books speak for us when we can't find the words, and answer questions to which we don't have the answers. Books find us when we need them most. I hope this one gives you what you need.*
> *Best, Ginger*

Bless her, but Ginger couldn't be subtle if she tried. I'm not sure if I'm insulted or amused. Good grief, the lead character is even called Jessica!

I'm about to start tucking into the book when my phone pings. It's a message from Lindiwe: 'You and your fan club are going to be disappointed, but Marian's trip to SA has been cancelled. L xx'

No reason. Just 'Marian' and 'cancelled' in the same sentence.

I feel like I've been punched in the stomach. What's Ginger going to do about getting her signed books? What's Matt going to do about treating his mom? How are we going to get Marian to look at Queenie's writing?

I know I'm going to have to tell everyone, but I really, really don't want to. Because somehow it just adds to the guilt swirling in my stomach. What I want is to blast away this discomfort and escape into my book. And what I really want is a large glass of chilled Chardonnay.

Ginger

I have a sleepless night after the lunch with Jess and Matt, and the dinner with James.

First, I'm worried about the note I slipped into Jess's copy of *Rachel's Holiday*. I was about as subtle as a bat over her head with that gift. And she didn't drink at lunch, so maybe our instincts weren't even right.

Although the story she told does sound like she's in trouble. Turns out she *is* married to that awful man who doesn't answer emails, only he's been having it off with someone else and has left. And reading between the lines, I hope to hell that Sybil didn't invest all her money with him because I don't think she's going to see a cent of it. I can criticise Roger all I want, but the man was very sensible with his money and no fly-by-night sweet-talking scamster is going to get his claws into *my* money, that's for sure.

Anyway, we reassured Jess that if her husband is having an affair and has moved out, it's perfectly acceptable to have sex with strangers in toilets; necessary even. I assured her that if *I* saw a decent-looking chap at another table, I'd whip him off to the loos tout de suite. Shame, it took Matt a long time to stop choking on his Appletiser.

And poor Matt. In this situation with this Sadie girl. She sounds like quite a handful, always on about his performance in the sack. But the heart wants what it wants, as Craig Lyons whispered to me in the corner at a dinner party in the nineties. So poor Matt wants this Sadie, but he can't admit it, so she's gone off with someone else probably just to hide her embarrassment. What I'd like to do is just sit them down and tell them to have an honest conversation – but I settled for just telling Matt.

Jess and Matt both seem to see me as some wise old woman. Totally unlike my girls – but I suppose my girls have the advantage of knowing that I'm an old fool who was once a young fool who married the wrong man for the wrong reasons and wasted the best years of my life being a Good Wife. And now I have one unhappily divorced daughter and one un-happily paired-up daughter, and really, who do I think I am giving people advice?

So that's why I don't sleep.

We didn't talk about how to go about meeting Marian, which worried me a bit. I mean, I know it was a crazy idea anyway, but I keep thinking about how I bragged to the girls that I'd get them a signed copy and I kind of want to deliver.

When I told James about this at dinner he said not to worry, the answer would come to me because that's the sort of woman I am. I rather liked that version of myself and I nearly asked him in for a drink afterwards when he dropped me off because maybe *that's* the sort of woman I am. But actually, I was aching all over after my day out, which hardly makes sense at all because I mostly sat, but I explained this to James, and said, 'Next time?' and he raised his eyebrow like Jack Nicholson and I rather regretted not inviting him in.

Debbie phones me early in the morning while I'm still drinking my tea and worrying that Jess won't speak to me after she realises that I've basically called her an alcoholic. I'm wondering if she knows that Marian herself is an alcoholic so really it's quite alright to be one. I'm trying to think how I can casually slip this into conversation when my cellphone rings.

'I'm surprised you answered, Mom,' Debbie says in greeting.

'It's 7am,' I say. 'What else would I be doing? Sleeping?'

'No,' says Debbie. 'We all know you're an early riser. No, I thought maybe you'd be off jolling with your friends. You seem to be awfully busy these days.'

'Also,' I say, instead of arguing that 7am is a bit early for socialising. Or for phoning. 'Also, I could have had company. *Overnight* company, if you get my drift.'

Oh, I know it was mean of me. Small-minded. But she does ask for it.

'What do you mean, Mommy?' Her voice is small, like a little girl.

'Like … if Sybil was too drunk to drive,' I backtrack.

'Sybil's always too drunk to drive. That's never stopped her before.'

We both laugh; it's true.

'Oh Christ, Mommy, you're not having it off with Sybil are you? One lezzer in the family is enough.'

'I did not bring you up to use language like that, Deborah Jane,' I say. 'And why on earth would you think I'm having it off with Sybil? She's the *last* woman I'd choose. If I was going to choose a woman, I'd choose one with enormous boobs.'

'Mommy! You said you had a date and now you're talking about Sybil staying overnight. And boobs. I don't—'

'Oh. Oh, I just said that because I didn't want to say that James might have stayed over last night. I thought Sybil would upset you less.'

There's absolute silence on the other end of the phone. So long that I think maybe we've been cut off.

'I'll drop the kids at you at two,' Debbie says eventually. 'Perhaps you could refrain from having either James or a big-boobed woman over while they are with you?'

'I'll think about it,' I say. 'But it's going to be hard to explain to them.'

'Ha ha, Mommy,' Debbie says with no hint of a laugh. 'You think you are so hilarious.'

Of course, Lee-anne is on the phone twenty minutes later.

'Debbie says you're an out-of-control sex maniac having an affair with a womxn?'

'Honestly,' I say, 'where does Debbie come up with these things?'

'I thought it sounded too good to be true,' says Lee-anne.

'You would actually hate me to have an affair with a woman,' I say.

'I can hear that you're saying it without the "x",' says Lee-anne. How the hell can she tell? Although she's right. The 'x' was far from my mind.

'The woman I'm having an affair with doesn't like the "x",' I say.

'Wait, what?' says Lee-anne.

'Ha! Got you,' I laugh. And then because I don't really know what else to do, I just hang up.

Bloody Debbie. Deliberately causing trouble.

When Debbie drops off the kids, she brings me a whole pile of new magazines. I know it's a peace offering of sorts and I'm pleased. I never buy magazines for myself – Roger didn't approve and I can't seem to break the habit. But there's nothing like a cup of tea and a pile of glossies, is there?

Of course, it's only much later that the grandchildren actually give me a break to look at my magazines. But the front cover of the second one I pick up is worth the wait: *Win a trip to meet Marian Keyes*, it says.

I can't believe my eyes and hastily page to the relevant section: *Write a winning short story and win an all-expenses-paid trip for you and three friends to meet the one and only Marian Keyes!*

The deadline is six weeks from now and the story has to be written with humour, à la Keyes. The winners get flown to Ireland to meet Marian and eat a meal in her home. This is exactly what we need!

Now if it were just me, this would be a problem. I can tell a fine tale, but ask me to put my words on paper and I become incoherent, and end up saying the opposite of what I mean. Which, actually, is how I ended up marrying Roger, but that's a story for another day.

The fact is, I can't write.

But that doesn't matter. Because … Queenie.

Matt

It's the day after the lunch and I'm busy organising a Zoom call for the MK bookclub – first Jess said she had something she needed to tell us and then Ginger chimed in that she also had BIG NEWS. Ginger tried to organise the call but got the time wrong so instead of it happening at 6pm, she scheduled it for 6am. I said I'd sort it out, so that's what I'm doing. I send everyone the link and think back to the advice Ginger gave me over lunch yesterday.

1. Do not have a relationship just to please your mother.
2. You are in love with Sadie so stop fannying about (yes, she really said that) and tell the girl, otherwise I will. (I believe she would.)

Trouble is, I like pleasing Mom, and I know the thought of Sadie and me being an actual couple makes her very happy. And as for me being in love with Sadie … yes, fine, I do have feelings for her. But it's a bit like being in love with a black widow spider or a praying mantis that will kill you after you've done the deed. My therapist (yes, even shrinks need a shrink) says that I want to get close to women but I have a fear of being smothered, and I'm afraid of crossing them in case they retaliate. No shit, Sherlock! I'm not just *afraid* of Sadie hurting me, I know it's an actual prospect. It's like she can't help herself. Those stories about women being more sensitive than men are such bollocks. Practically every womxn in my life is waaaaaaay tougher than me. (Ginger says people can tell if you're not spelling it with an 'x'.)

Anyway, it's time for our Zoom call.

I let Jess into the meeting. Except it's not Jess, it's a miniature version of Jess.

'Hi.' Miniature Jess waves.

'Er … hello?' Awkward silence. 'Um … my name's Matt. And what's your name?'

'Willow.'

'That's a very beautiful name.' God. I sound like a creepy paedophile.

'Willow! You're not supposed to play on Mom's laptop!' Another mini version of Jess appears – this one older and frowning suspiciously at me. 'Who are you and why are you talking to my sister? I've got Childline on speed-dial.'

Shiiiit, I immediately feel guilty – I'm not sure of what.

'I'm a friend of your mom's – Jess's. I thought it was her.'

Mini-Jess is still eyeing me suspiciously.

'Mommy's having a wee-wee,' Willow says helpfully.

'Thank you for that, Willow.' Jess walks into view and I heave a sigh of relief.

'Hi, Jess.' My voice high-pitched and panicky.

'Go and play, you two.'

Willow looks unimpressed. 'I want to say bye.'

'Okay. Quickly.'

'Bye, Matt.'

'Bye, Willow. Bye, Willow's big sister. Well done for looking after your sister so well.' Was that the right thing to say or will Mini-Jess think I'm a patronising asshole?

'Thank you, Matt,' Willow's sister says gravely, so perhaps it's alright.

'God.' Jess looks concerned. 'What did she do?'

'Threatened to call Childline when she saw me talking to Willow.'

Jess smiles. 'They've been doing stranger danger in class. Every person who comes to the door is treated like a prospective pervert.'

'A good thing. Although I do feel like a grubby paedophile right now.'

'Sorry.' Jess is still smiling.

I let Ginger into the Zoom call. We can see her face but we can't hear her. 'Ginger, you're on mute.'

'Unmute yourself, Ginger.'

Jess and I are both over-enunciating and gesturing wildly at the screen, as one does.

'Hello? Hello? Can you hear me?' Ginger has reacquainted herself with the mute button. Now she's shouting.

'Yes, Ginger, how are you?'

'Good for someone who's knocking at death's door.'

'Why are you knocking at death's door?' Jess asks, concerned.

'Oh, I'm not. I mean, obviously we're *all* knocking at death's door but no, there's no immediate issue, it's just what my daughter Debbie always says. It's her little joke with me.'

I really don't like the sound of Ginger's daughters.

'Matt, I can only see you and Jess – hello, Jess. Where's Queenie?'

'I sent her the link – she could just be late,' I say. 'So, what's all this we have to discuss so urgently?'

'Can I go first?' Suddenly, Jess isn't smiling any more.

'Sure, Jess.'

'I hate to be the bearer of bad news, but Marian's book tour to SA has been cancelled.'

She explains what's happened – apparently it's not just Marian's trip, the whole festival has been cancelled and no one knows why. There are all sorts of rumours flying around. Some people are saying it's because the main sponsor has pulled out, others are saying that the organisers spent all the money doing a world tour of lit fests for 'research' purposes, and the latest rumour is that the festival is just too filled with old white people and is no longer relevant. Whatever. Either way it's still cancelled and I feel completely pissed off with Lindiwe and the people who were supposed to be organising the whole thing. But Marian said, 'Sure, it's fine. I'll come another time.' (She didn't actually say that; I can just imagine her voice in my head.) That means that we're not going to see her and I can't take Mom to the festival, and maybe our Marian fan club will fall apart because we'll have nothing to focus on. And I really like these people; I don't want to lose them as friends, but I'm not sure what we can do. Then I realise I am catastrophising, which is a classic sign of generalised anxiety disorder. I count my breaths to calm myself.

'All is not lost!' declares Ginger. 'I have a plan, but as it concerns Queenie, I feel we should wait.'

This only makes us more curious and after we try to call Queenie and she doesn't answer and another fifteen minutes go by and there's still no sign of her, Ginger eventually tells us about the competition from the magazine.

So maybe we'll get to see Marian after all!

After lots of 'Fuck yeahs' (me) and punching the air (Jess) and laughing and talking over each other, we calm down enough to discuss what this means.

'But do you think Queenie will think we're just using her to win the competition?' asks Jess.

'Well, we are,' Ginger says bluntly. 'But it's not as if we wouldn't write the story ourselves if we could. It's just that *presumably* none of us can write like she can.'

'What if she wants to take three other friends, not us?'

'The pair of you really are Debbie Downers,' exclaims Ginger. 'But I'll tell you what. We'll tell her about the competition and give her the option of taking three other friends. How's that?'

'She's far too nice to ditch us,' says Jess.

'Exactly,' Ginger says with a cackle.

We still haven't been able to get hold of Queenie. Jess volunteers to track her down because I have a deadline for tomorrow.

The scene from the show where the son and mother start getting fresh with each other is beyond vomitous and I soon find myself in full procrastination mode, googling the mating habits of praying mantises. What I find is not good: the bigger female will bite off the smaller male's head – or any other body part – if she's hungry or if he's pissing her off. I imagine Sadie taking a large chunk out of my thigh …

I know I won't be able to concentrate until I've spoken to her. I decide to message her: 'Drink?'

'Can't. Dinner with J.'

Fuck. Fuck. Fuck. 'Another time then.'

'Nah. I can fit you in. Just promise not to jump me.'

She follows that with six laughing emojis, which gives a the-thought-of-having-sex-with-you-again-is-hilarious vibe. It's irritating, actually, but I still make a time for her to pop round. I know I should settle down to an evening's work, but I decide to make some snacks. In my fridge there's half a shrivelled lemon, some tonic water and a slightly tired cucumber that will be okay for tzatziki. I head out to raid my parents' fridge for some Greek yoghurt.

As I climb the steps up to their kitchen door, I hear someone crying.

It's my father. He and Mom are sitting opposite each other at the old wooden kitchen table and she's patting his hand.

He's saying, 'I can't lose you, Miranda. I just can't.'

I know I should give them their space, but I'm too freaked out. My mouth is suddenly dry and my heart is thumping in my chest.

'What's going on, guys?'

My father's eyes are weepy and puffy. Mom is pale, serious.

'Come sit down, Mattie,' Mom says patting the chair next to her and I sit. 'You know the infection I had in my breast …'

She doesn't have to carry on – I already know what she's going to say. Turns out the doctor was wrong and Ginger was right. Mom has inflammatory breast cancer. The worst kind with the worst outcome. I can tell she's trying not to upset me, but it's too late for that.

'What made you go for a second opinion?' I ask.

'I don't know … I just had this feeling that things weren't right. And Dr Burns is getting on a bit – he's not as switched on as he used to be.' Mom is big on listening to her gut and for once I'm really glad she believes in angels and spirit guides and dead people speaking to her and all that stuff.

'What are your options regarding treatment?'

She hesitates.

'Mom?'

'I'm not sure I want treatment.'

'What?'

'If it's spread, I don't want treatment, Mattie. I saw how my own mother suffered. And I don't want to go through that; I want a good death.'

I want to scream at her, tell her I don't care how far gone it is, she *has* to fight, we can't lose her, we're not ready to lose her, *I'm* not ready, I *need* her. But instead of expressing my feelings, which is what I tell my clients to do, I shut my mouth, push the anger and the shock waaaaaaay down, and ask her how she's feeling and tell her I will support her no matter what.

I can see she's relieved at how well I'm taking it. But inside ...

I hug both her and Dad, tell them we'll talk more when we've processed the news and that I'll help them tell the others, then I go back up to the cottage, the snacks for Sadie forgotten. I open the door and sit down on the couch. I am so angry, I want to punch something – like Dr Burns' face – hard.

'I brought you this.' Sadie walks in without knocking, 'It was all I had. Maybe you can have it on toast or something ...' She puts a jar of chocolate body paint on the table. Then she sees my face. 'Mattie? What's going on?'

I tell her. She puts her arms around me and she starts to cry. I am too numb to cry.

'I think my snot's on your shirt,' she says eventually.

'God, I need a drink.' I pour her a gin and tonic, slicing the dried-out bit off the half a lemon.

'Okay, Mattie, let's think this through clearly. She hasn't said she won't have treatment.'

'No. Only that if it's spread, she won't – she said there's no point.'

'You gotta admire that. Your mom's got balls.'

'I could admire it if it was someone else. But because it's Mom, I want her to fight. I don't want to lose her.'

'I don't want to lose her either. Okay, we have to stop this otherwise I'm going to cry again.'

'You have to do something for me. Well, for her.'

'Anything.'

'You have to pretend we're dating.'

Sadie's jaw literally drops open. 'Me and *you*? You're shitting me.'

I explain what Micky had said and how happy Mom was about us being an item. Sadie thinks for a while. 'Well, if it'll make her happy, let's do it. Your mom's the mother I never had.' Sadie has a mother who is perfectly sweet, she just gets on Sadie's nerves. 'Should I cancel tonight with Johnny?'

Yes! He's an A-grade asshole! I think on the inside, but outside I'm fantastically mature.

'No. If she asks, this is your break-up dinner and the two of you have decided to stay friends ... I mean, I don't want to ruin your relationship,' I lie. 'Will Johnny be okay with this?'

'Duh – I just won't tell him!'

I'm not sure if that's such a good idea, but I'm too exhausted to argue.

As soon as she's gone, I pick up the phone and call Ginger. I need to talk to a grown-up. But before I can say a word, Ginger says, 'Mattie, I'm so pleased you called. Something terrible has happened. Queenie's gone missing!'

Queenie

I wasn't sure what he was expecting when we arrived last night at the little lodge in Colesberg. There was only one room booked – obviously, because he'd booked it *before* – but I was still relieved when he asked the receptionist to make up two single beds.

Decent. But she needn't have bothered.

Charl. If you'd told me two days ago that right now I'd be on my way to a luxury five-star lodge in the Pilanesberg National Park, making the trek north in a dusty bakkie with a handsome stranger but without any luggage, I'd have told you I'd been kidnapped. There would simply be no other explanation. Two days ago, I didn't even know where the Pilanesberg was (a couple of hours from Joburg, Charl says). I haven't been to Joburg since cousin Chriselda got married and that was ten years ago when Pa was alive. Our car broke down three times and Ma had to try keep Jennifer calm when she had a panic attack each time. Also, I've never been on a game drive in my life. I don't even watch wildlife shows on TV. The closest I've come to anything vaguely related is reading James Hendry's *A Year in the Wild*.

Charl had laughed when I said that to him. 'Typical Capetonian! Can't imagine life away from the mountain and the sea. I'm telling you, being in the bush is a good life.'

I'd had to remind him that *he* was the one on the Sea Point Promenade having a last lingering look at the ocean when we'd met.

Though perhaps 'met' is not the right word. Collided, maybe. I think it was luck; he says it was fate.

I steal a look at his profile while he focuses on the road. Not sleek and groomed, Charl is heavy-set with slightly too-long brown hair that covers half his ears. Lines crease his forehead and fan from the corners of his eyes and the short, stubby beard that scratched me last night fades into his neck. The bare forearm resting lightly on the gearstick is brown and weathered, his hand scarred.

Is this what a rebound guy looks like? I wonder. Does it even matter?

Don't you also need to have been in a relationship to be on the rebound? The truth that I haven't wanted to admit is that Kevin and I haven't been in a real relationship for years. I know it's sudden and seems unlike me to be with someone like Charl, but I like this calm man with his kind face. He's comforting and sexy and exciting all at the same time. And no ways am I giving *this* up to mourn my already dead relationship with Kevin. It's not often I get to experience something that is better than what I can imagine.

I shake my head. I can't believe what's happened in the past twenty-four hours. I mean, whoever heard of anyone being rescued by a game ranger on the Prom on a Thursday morning, and then driving fourteen hours across the country to go on a game drive with him.

Although 'rescued' is maybe too strong a word …

Yesterday started slower than usual. I don't like to let things get me down, but the whole thing with Kevin was starting to sink in. And then, soon after the library opened, Esmeralda had called me aside and she didn't mince her words.

'Queenie, there's a problem. I've been getting strange emails for a week now – men asking for you or looking for librarians to "have fun with".' Her mouth pulled into a tight line. '*Sexy* fun,' she added, her eyes bulging as she made a tiny (and I hoped involuntary) thrust with her hips.

I would've laughed if I wasn't so mortified about what was coming.

'I didn't know what was going on until one of them sent me a link.

Now it's your beeswax if you and your boyfriend make a porno, and I wouldn't normally want to know about it –' like hell she wouldn't '– but you had to go and put it on the Internet with this library's contact details. I haven't watched, *sies*, but obviously I had to send it on to the director.' She folded her arms across her chest. 'I don't know the procedure for something like this. He might suspend you pending investigation, I don't know. Nizam is a nice guy, but I don't think he can let this go. And you're lucky no one has tagged our Facebook page. Bringing Library Services and the City of Cape Town into disrepute is a serious thing, my girl. It can get you fired.'

I had an urge to laugh – I'd spent so much energy writing out my feelings about Kevin that the only thing left was black humour. Like that guy who made a whole podcast series about the bad porno his dad wrote. Maybe I could write a series titled 'So My Boyfriend Made a Porno And It Wasn't Fucking Me'. Pun intended.

'But it's not me,' I said. I meant my voice to come out strong and sure; instead it was thin and whiny. I cleared my throat, suppressed the inappropriate giggle and started again. 'Okay, so it *is* Kevin and it *is* my name and it *is* this library's contact details, but it's not actually *me* in the video, and *I* didn't put it on Pornhub. I'm trying to get it taken down but …'

It's been a week already. Ginger's James says I've done all the right things to get it taken down, but I've heard nothing back from them yet. He says that if they drag their heels, I should get a lawyer involved, but I don't have money for a lawyer. I'll give it another week. Two max.

'Not you?' Esmeralda said, suspiciously. 'But it *is* Kevin. And Kevin *is* your boyfriend? You mean … he did it with someone else and recorded it?' As she started to understand that I'd been cheated on and that the evidence was out there for literally thousands – if not millions – of sweaty wankers to see, her face changed. Now here was a juicy story she could pass on to her husband tonight. 'Holly-ha, that is very bad,' she said thoughtfully. 'You could still get fired, you know? The whole disrepute thing is serious. Remember that *other* intimate video …'

'We've broken up now,' I said, as my bubbles of misplaced laughter completely disappeared. In the back of my mind, I remembered the story of a library assistant who'd accidentally loaded a private video onto her library's Facebook page. I never saw it and I don't know that Esmeralda saw it either, but she'd said at the time that it was 'intimate'. The Pornhub video is much worse than 'intimate' and *that* incident had got the library assistant a disciplinary hearing. I can't quite remember if she quit or if she was fired, but it was certainly more than a slap on the wrist. And of course everyone knew about it.

Fuck you, Kevin.

But cursing in my head didn't stop the nausea that had replaced my urge to laugh. I wanted to offload the morning's muffin straight onto Esmeralda's annoyingly tiny feet. She isn't one to keep something like this to herself so I knew it wouldn't be long before Carol and June started giving me looks.

'Do you think I could take the rest of the day off?' I asked. 'I don't feel very well.'

Esmeralda hummed and hawed, but eventually agreed that I did look a bit green and could take a sick day. I fled before she could change her mind and drove straight to the Prom. I know it's so Cape Town to seek out a bit of sea air when you're feeling naar, but I had to do it. It was like the suburbs were closing in on me and I needed to be reminded that life was bigger than this overwhelming moment.

At first I simply stood and stared over the concrete sea walls and watched the water move and splash hard into the underside of the walls. The sea sprayed a salty mist onto my face. As I calmed, I leant forward into the breeze and pushed my hands against the cold concrete so that my head hung close to the edge, my body as close as I could get to the sea. My hair would be wilder and curlier after the sea air, I knew. Like me, it was usually freer here than it was at home. I repeated a new mantra to myself as each wave rolled and crashed: 'I'm not going to lose my job.'

When I'd calmed down enough, I moved away from the sea wall and sat down on the closest bench. I put my bag on the bench next to me and messaged Jennifer: 'Bit of trouble at library, too long to type – will tell you when I see you. I've taken the day off, might be late for supper. Don't wait for me okay? Xxx'

It was as I put my phone back into my bag and stretched my legs out in front of me that I noticed Charl.

Short – well, still taller than me – with strong, muscled legs in khaki baggies, he was leaning forward over the concrete barrier where I'd just been standing, looking at the sea, pressing his arms into the wall like he was doing some kind of weird sideways push-up. I realised that was probably what I'd looked like less than five minutes earlier. He was breathing so deeply I could see his chest rise. Something about that made me smile – maybe it was just seeing what I must have looked like, or knowing that another human was also taking a moment to gather themselves when everyone else seemed to be hurrying along getting their steps in. He must have felt me looking at him because he turned and smiled a squinty grin.

And then the asshole stole my bag.

Not Charl. An asshole on a bicycle swooped right past me and scooped up my bag from the bench. And Charl sprung away from the wall and gave chase, getting so far as to tug at my bag, which was slung over the thief-on-wheels's arm. My wallet tumbled out.

But just my wallet. Not my car keys. Or my phone.

So how did we get from me open-mouthed screaming at a sea-sprayed thief on a Thursday morning, to a sun-drenched luxury lodge nestled in thorn trees somewhere in the North West Province two days later?

I don't know.

I do know that it felt good to scream until my lungs hurt, to cry in frustration as the bike sped away.

It felt good to have a kind stranger steer me to a nearby coffee truck and then pour two sugars into my cappuccino – 'For the shock, you know' – while we sat on the grass. It was as if he knew that I needed to tell my story and to tell it immediately, in a place where the sun and sea and wind could spirit the drama away. With the soft earth grounding me, it certainly helped that the stranger had beautiful brown eyes and that he really listened and that he smiled only when it was the right time to smile.

It felt good to let the drama go and to sit in the sun and talk and laugh and then order ice cream from the ice-cream guys cruising slowly past on their bicycles. It was as if I was one of those people in the private-banking ads who didn't have to worry about losing their jobs. It felt good to have him treat me as I was interesting to him and to find out that – yes! – he was interesting to me too. We shared about ourselves and he told me how he lived a life so different from mine, but still loved the sound and smell of the sea, just as I do, and came once a year for a medicinal dose of it. Three ice creams and another coffee later, I don't know how long in time except that the sun no longer burnt me and the breeze had become cooler, the kind stranger became Charl. I only knew I wanted to know more than an afternoon with this man.

'Take a long weekend with me?' Charl said. He looked surprised at himself. 'I've got to be back at work on Saturday, but I can get you a place to stay at the lodge. I don't have a private jet to get you there, only my bakkie with GP plates,' he said with a smile, because I'd just joked that if we were in a Mills & Boon, he'd own the game reserve and would fly me there in his plane. 'We'll stay over halfway at a B&B in Colesberg, but in the Pilanesberg I'll take you on the world's best game drive. You won't be imagining it – being in the bush is beyond imagining.'

I think that's what got me. I'd just told him how I was always imagining the places I'd go and the things I'd do, but that I never ended up doing. Imagining how I'd be brave. Imagining how I'd get me and Jennifer to stay over in Franschhoek in a fancy hotel. Imagining seeing Marian Keyes. Imagining meeting the MK bookclub in Joburg.

I know I should've been at the Sea Point Police Station reporting my stolen bag.

I should've been trying to cancel my phone.

I should've been making a plan to get my spare car keys from home.

I should *at least* have tried to reach Jennifer to tell her what had happened.

Instead, I clutched my wallet and did the quickest maths. I had enough savings for a one-way flight home from Joburg. A little bit extra to buy myself what I might need for the next few days. I could call in and ask Esmeralda for leave. Usually she wouldn't give it on such short notice, but after today I think she would be happy for me to be out of the library for a few days. I've not done many crazy things in my life. But I didn't only want

to imagine what could happen next. I wanted to know this man.
'Okay,' I said, like he'd asked if I wanted another ice cream.

Jess

A notification pings on my Facebook: 'Do you want to accept this call from Queenie?'

I didn't even know you could make phone calls on Facebook.

The voice comes through with a slight echo and delay. 'Hello? Jess?'

'Oh my God, Queenie!'

I check the kids. Willow is drawing like the angel she is while Hannah and her friends are practising another bloody TikTok with all the precision and fervour of a North Korean military parade.

'Uh, it's Queenie.'

'Oh! Hello!' My enthusiasm is possibly overstated. It's the first time we've spoken one on one since my unfortunate drunken incident.

'Queenie? Are you okay?'

'Yes, sure. I've just got myself in a bit of a situation ...'

I can hear a man's voice bellowing for her in the background. I'm crap at a lot of things, but when it comes to getting out of 'a situation', I'm your girl. I make sure the door is shut tight.

'Carry on ...'

'Okay, don't judge. It's a long story but ... I've ended up in this fancy game lodge in the Pilanesberg. With a guy who works here. A conservationist. Charl ...'

'Queenie!' I whisper. 'Have you been kidnapped? Just say yes or no. Or a safe world, like "Marian", really loudly.'

'No! No, no, no. I like him. He's gorgeous. It's just ... the trip was a spur-of-the-moment thing, it happened so fast and—'

I realise that the tone I initially read as anxiety is actually excitement.

'And?' I'm rather jealous. I wish I could be swept off my feet by a rugged conservationist hunk instead of being hustled into the Tashas toilets by a K-Way-wearing Joburg drone.

'Anyway, it's just that … I'm stuck up here and I don't have enough … you know … protection.'

'Like condoms? Or pepper spray … I mean, you don't know this man very well.'

'We bought condoms but I didn't really have a chance to pack so … I left my birth control at home.'

'You know, my homeopath says birth control is like an atomic bomb to a woman's hormones. The rhythm method, on the other hand—'

'Jess! Now is not the time,' Queenie says through gritted teeth.

'Okay, my doctor will write me up a script for anything. Want some Valium while we're at it?'

'Uh … no?'

'Good plan. That stuff is like a fire extinguisher to the libido.' Suddenly I realise what is really going on.

'Queenie, this isn't about the toiletries, is it?'

A gulp on the other end of the line. 'I really like this guy, but I'm scared. What if my judgement is wrong? You, Matt and Ginger are literally the only people I know in Joburg.'

I don't have the heart to tell her the Pilanesberg is actually a few hours away from Joburg. Still, it gives me an idea.

'Queenie, I'm sure all of the MK clan would love an excuse to come and see you.'

'It's not very out of your way?'

'Not *at all*.'

Queenie's spontaneous trip couldn't have come at a better time. It's Joe's turn to take the girls this weekend, and he messaged earlier to say he plans on packing up some more of his stuff. What better antidote to my jilted-wife status than to be away on a mysterious holiday of my own?

I send a message to Matt and Ginger: 'Queenie's in the Pilanesberg, a last-minute thing. What do you say to a spontaneous long weekend for the MK bookclub? Could be the perfect time to tell Queenie about Marian and convince her to enter that competition?'

'Is there room at the lodge?' asks Ginger.

'Yes,' I say, logging onto lastminutesafari.com, which I frequently used when I spent money like water. 'We can even get a 40 per cent off special.'

'Hell, yes! I need a break from my drama – speaking of drama, I wonder if I should bring Sadie?' writes Matt.

Ginger video calls the group by mistake and I spend a few seconds staring at the underside of her chin. I take that as a yes from her side.

I throw a few leopard-print kaftans and a wide-brimmed hat into my Country Road tote. I hustle Hannah's friends out the door and they herd into a waiting line of their parents' four almost-identical SUVs. I quickly select some clothes to fill the girls' bags for their visit to their father.

'Will you be okay, Mom?' says Hannah, her forehead creased. I worry about how much she worries.

'Of course, my darling. I'm going away with my bookclub friends for the weekend!'

'But, like, will we be okay, as a family?'

I hug her tight. 'Daddy and I will do our best to make sure we are.'

Joe arrives on cue and I say my goodbyes. As they drive away, my heart pounds. This feels good, closer to the Jess I used to be. Spontaneous, but within reason. Making choices for myself.

Ginger

Well, of course I'm going to join the others on this madcap trip to the Pilanesberg. I'd prefer to make a plan to drive together because I don't like driving such long distances myself, but when I try to call and ask them, something goes wrong with my phone and I somehow end up taking a photo of my chin instead.

But then I have an inspired idea. I could ask James to join me, and then *he* can drive. We were supposed to have a date tonight and he's often told me how much he loves escaping to the bush. But I'm not sure what the protocol is – will the others be upset if I bring him along? I can't ask them because of course they'll all say, 'Yes, fine,' even if they don't mean it. So I phone Debbie.

'Debbie,' I say. 'Say a person was hypothetically going away on a girls' weekend, could they bring someone with them?'

'Is this about that woman with big boobs again?' says Debbie. 'Are you going away together now?'

'Debbie, I've told you, I'm not having an affair with a woman. I just want to know what the norm is here.'

Debbie sniffs. 'Well, are there any other men going?' She pauses. 'I mean *partners*. Don't tell Lee I presumed all the partners would be men – she'll kill me. She's already cross because I said "folks" in a WhatsApp group we're on together. I spent ages thinking of that, Mom. After the great Christmas debacle when I called them "guys", I thought "folks" was perfect.'

'It seems very neutral,' I say. 'Why was she upset?'

'Apparently I should have spelt it "f-o-l-x".'

There's a pause, and then we both start giggling.

'We shouldn't laugh,' I say. 'I actually worry about her. I'm sure this isn't her speaking. It's that bloody Tex.'

'So, Mom,' says Debbie, after we finish reassuring each other that Lee-anne will be fine. 'Instead of telling me about these hypothetical people going on a trip, why don't you tell me what's really going on?'

And so I do. I tell her about my Marian friends and how we are going to go and rescue Queenie, who probably doesn't need rescuing, and how I want to invite James to drive me there, and then stay. I keep waiting for Debbie to say something about how stupid I've been, making friends with strangers and even thinking about having a dirty weekend with my boyfriend. But instead she asks all sorts of relevant questions, like what ages the others are and whether they have partners, and whether I expect to share a room with James or not and if that might not be awkward. It's weird, but while we're talking, it's like I could be talking to Jess or Quee-nie, and not Debbie at all.

Debbie thinks I could phone one of the others for a lift and that would be fine, but that maybe this is a nice opportunity to take it to the next level with James. I can't believe my daughter has just said, 'take it to the next level,' and it wasn't a discussion about a diet or exercise. Then after she realises that we are in fact gatecrashing Queenie's own dirty weekend, she's adamant that I can take James – 'If you're sure you're ready, Mommy.'

I don't want to admit it to Debbie, but the fact is I'm not sure. But in for a penny, in for a pound.

After I talk to Debbie, I phone James and explain that I can't make our date. I decide to be honest: I tell him that I'd like to invite him along, but I'm not sure I'm ready 'to take it to the next level'. I'm rather grateful to Debbie for the wording.

James is quiet for a moment. 'I *would* love a weekend in the bush,' he says. 'And without our date, my weekend is looking rather boring. How about I get my own room – would that be better for you?'

'But what if we don't need it after all,' I say before I can think and then I blush.

James laughs. 'Then that will be money I'd be delighted to waste. I'll call them and book it for both of us.'

Sometimes I can't believe all of this.

Two hours later, James picks me up, planting a kiss firmly on my mouth and no awkward discussions about bedrooms. I feel giddy with excitement. This is the best thing to happen to me in years!

I've always loved driving out of Johannesburg. Roger didn't like going to game reserves – couldn't see the point – but he did like going to Sun City. Not to gamble – Roger was certainly not the sort – but something about the ubiquitous hotel-ness of it appealed to him. He liked that he knew what to expect, and when they opened The Lost City he even splashed out on a more expensive room one weekend.

But now I am watching the city give way to bush, knowing that soon we will be in an actual private game lodge. Not even a SANparks one – a private one. I give a shiver of pleasure and James turns to smile at me.

'Excited?' he asks.

'Very,' I say, and then get worried that he thinks that I'm excited about sex. So I explain about Roger and Sun City and James laughs in all the right places. I like that he talks while he drives. Roger wouldn't. Said it distracted him from the road. The girls and I would have to sit in silence because music distracted him too. But James has the radio playing *and* he talks.

We're about halfway there when my phone starts pinging. It's the Marian WhatsApp group.

Matt: Ladies, on my way and just saw something on Twitter that a famous writer is in the Pilanesberg. What do you think the chances are?

Jess: Could be anyone, Mattie. Hang on.

Queenie: Having a massage. Can't talk.

Jess: Checked Marian's Twitter feed. Says they got to South Africa before the festival was cancelled! Says that Himself is taking her away for a weekend to a surprise destination instead.

Matt: OMG. She's there. It's fate.

Jess: WhatsApped Lindiwe, my PR connection – she can't technically say anything, but it sounds like we may be onto something …

Me: I hope you kids aren't texting and driving.

There's a long silence and I regret saying anything. Why do I always have to be the worrywart? James tells me I have a very good point – texting and driving is terribly dangerous, especially the way people race on these highways.

I can't help noticing that James himself is driving exactly the right amount of too fast – Roger stuck doggedly to the speed limit and drove me mad. Worst was, if he couldn't see a sign, he'd presume the limit was sixty, even if we were on a major road. But James is going fast enough that I am not pulling my hair out with annoyance, but slow enough that I feel completely safe. I look at him, his blue eyes on the road, the music playing in the background, a smile on his face.

Maybe I am ready for the next level after all.

Then the conversation on my WhatsApp starts up again.

Jess: No worries about driving. Stopped for coffee. Been looking at her social media. I swear, I think it could be her at the Pilanesberg.

Matt: Ginger, I would never text and drive. Mom would kill me. Xxx.

Matt again: The gossip sites are saying it is a female author of world renown …

Queenie: Having a Cosmopolitan. Can't talk.

Me: If she's there, we'll find her!

'What are the chances really?' James says when I fill him in.

'You know,' I say, 'usually I'd think it was impossible. But I'd also have said it was impossible for me to be speeding down the highway for a weekend away with a group of people I met on the Internet, a man that I rather fancy and not a care in the world. Marian Keyes being there doesn't seem so impossible after all.'

'Rather fancy, eh?' James says with a smile.

'Rather.' And we both laugh.

My phone pings again.

Queenie: About to have sex. Can't talk.
Jess: *big-eyed emoji*
Matt: *laughing emoji*
Me: *thumbs-up emoji*
Jess: There in 20 mins, so hurry up.
I laugh again. Nothing's going to go wrong this weekend.

Matt

'Fuck me!' exclaims Sadie craning her neck to get a better view as we drive up to the reception area of the game lodge. 'Your friends have good taste.'

It's the ubiquitous thatched-rondavel game lodge décor surrounded by lush indigenous plants, but not in a two-tone khaki-shirt kind of way; it's upmarket and screams money. I was surprised at how reasonable the rates were, but I think we might've got a further discount courtesy of Queenie's shag.

I hadn't actually meant to bring Sadie, but she'd decided it'd look weird if we were supposed to be dating and she hadn't come along on the dirty weekend. Also, Sadie's nosey as hell and wanted to meet the other members of the MK bookclub. I'd had a momentary twinge of misgiving in case, after a gin or three, Ginger decided to tell Sadie how I really felt about her. But I've been feeling so overwhelmed by Mom's diagnosis that I couldn't wait to get away and try and process everything.

Mom was so thrilled when I told her Sadie and I were going away together this weekend.

Mom: I knew the two of you would be so perfect together!

Me *cringing*: It's early days …

Mom: Still, a weekend away.

I gave Micky the death stare to make sure she didn't ruin Mom's fantasy about Sadie and I being love's young dream, but she was too upset after the trip to the oncologist to say anything.

The oncologist had been blunt and told Mom if she was going to have treatment, she needed to do it now, otherwise there would be no point. 'You'll be dead within six months,' he told her. As a shock tactic,

143

it worked superbly well on my dad and Marcus, who immediately start-ed blubbing while I tried to hold it together and take notes. I'd started researching breast cancer the minute Mom told me, and one of the first things I'd read was that you should always have someone with you at your doctor's appointments to take notes. I'd decided that person had better be me. Also, Micky had said, 'Matt, take notes.'

As it happened, though, the whole family had come to the appoint-ment. Unfortunately, Micky hadn't taken well to the oncologist's manner and had told him to fuck off, which is par for the course. What she actu-ally said was, 'Who the fucking hell do you think you are, you fuckwit? If you think we're impressed by your fucking degrees, we're fucking well not.' There were more fucks – I've cut out a few of them but you get the gist. I expected him to tell all of us to get the hell out of his office, but he gazed at Micky with this sort of reverential awe and then apologised if he sounded abrupt and explained that he felt it was important not to sugar-coat the situation.

Did Micky melt at that? Of course not. She bastardised Maya Ange-lou: 'Just because I am in pain, doesn't mean I have to be a pain.' Which is so rich coming from her that my jaw practically hit the floor – when Micky's in pain, we don't just have to know about it, we have to feel it too. Anyway, the guy just nodded meekly and then almost begged my mother to start treatment. If he doesn't ask Micky out on a date, I shall be very surprised. I almost wanted to warn him (for his own sake) but I wasn't crazy about his manner either.

I stop the car outside the lodge's reception area and we get out. We're immediately swarmed by a bevy of men wearing Madiba shirts, playing drums, singing in perfect harmony and inquiring after our journey while simultaneously offering us hot towels to wipe our sweaty brows.

'Wow, tourists must really lap this shit up,' exclaims Sadie.

But I am lapping it up myself. The Pilanesberg air always feels so lush and tropical and I love the smell of the thatch. As we go inside, yet another man in a Madiba shirt welcomes us with a tray of what I think are mimosas, but which turn out to be passion fruit bellinis.

'Niiiiiice.' Sadie takes a large gulp.

I exhale and immediately feel the tension draining out of me as I take a sip. Delicious. Sadie elbows me in the ribs.

'Ow! What?'

'Someone's waving at you. Is that one of your bookclub buddies?'

Over at the reception desk, Jess is dressed in white and as I move towards her I smell something fresh and citrusy.

'Hey –' I blush slightly as she kisses me on the cheek '– how cool is this place?' I try, and fail, to act cool.

'Wait till you taste the food.'

'You've been here before?'

'With the ex. He was playing in some company-golf thing. It's much better being here on my own.' She forces a smile and I wonder if she really means it. 'I can't wait to hit the spa.'

'God, yes,' I say. 'I'd kill for a hot stone massage.'

'You are such a girl, Mattie,' Sadie says. I see that she's managed to get another bellini out of the concierge.

'You must be Sadie,' Jess says, smiling and holding out her hand.

'Have you been talking about me to your new friends?' demands Sadie.

I panic, but decide to brazen it out. 'Yes,' I say – more bravely than I feel.

'Good,' is all Sadie says as she drains her drink. 'The only thing worse than being talked about is not being talked about.'

My laughter is tinged with relief. Jess gives me a quick thumbs-up when Sadie isn't looking.

'Have you managed to find out if Marian is actually here?' I ask Jess. 'Did your PR connection say anything?'

'Haven't been able to get hold of her, sadly. And the people here are too damn discreet. But maybe we'll see her at dinner.'

I feel excitement bubble up in me at the thought of meeting Marian in real life.

'See you on the viewing deck for sundowners,' Jess says with a wave as she sashays off to her chalet.

We check in and then head back to the car to drive the short distance to my chalet. Ours, I mean. Me and Sadie's.

I've just realised I'm going to be spending a weekend with Sadie and I quickly do a check of my feelings. I am feeling … nervous. Nervous, LOL. I'm shit-scared and hoping it won't be completely awkward and filled with her making jokes about my penis.

'She's very beautiful,' Sadie says as I get into the car.

'Who? Jess?'

'No. The woman at the reception desk.' Sadie rolls her eyes. 'Of course I mean Jess.'

'Yes, she is very attractive.'

'She's not just attractive, she's beautiful,' Sadie insists.

'If you say so.'

'I do say so.'

'I haven't slept with her. If that's what you're getting at.'

'You totally should. Older woman. I'm sure she could teach you a thing or two.'

Now, the rational psychologist part of my mind knows that Sadie's only saying this because for some reason she's feeling threatened by Jess. I'd love to flatter myself and say it's because she's jealous, but I've seen this behaviour from Sadie before and it's more like she doesn't want to be outshone (like with the picture of the woman with the perfect boobs on Johnny's phone).

The less rational part of my brain immediately thinks back to the male praying mantis being killed by the female … And I assume she's having a go at me because my sexual technique is lacking, ergo I could do with some lessons from an older woman.

But I don't feel like starting off the weekend with an argument.

'I'll keep that in mind,' I say as I open the boot, retrieve our luggage and start lugging it up the path – although the name on the brass plaque outside the rondavel stops me in my tracks. Guess what it's called?

The Praying Mantis. I shit you not.

It gets worse when we go inside because although I asked for two single beds, there is just one king-sized bed romantically draped with a mosquito net. It's all very *Out of Africa*, but it makes me cringe. Sadie is bound to think I've planned it like this.

'Sorry. I did ask for twin beds,' I say as I drag in our luggage. 'I'm sure that's a sleeper couch.' I gesture to the leather couch that sadly has no mosquito net, which of course means I won't sleep a wink.

'Don't be such a martyr, Mattie. You know you'll never sleep with all those goggas parachuting down from the thatch and landing on your head while you're sleeping –' it's not like she's read my mind or anything '– we'll just share the bed. I'm sure I can control myself. You're not that hot.'

'Oh, I was going to put *you* on the sleeper couch,' I say airily and nearly fall over when she whacks me with a pillow.

'Right,' she says, picking up her vanity case. 'I'm going to go shower and tart up. We can't have your bookclub buddies thinking you've got an ugly fake girlfriend.'

'Stop fishing for compliments. You know you're gorgeous.'

She stops and looks at me. 'You really think so?'

'Yes. Why do you sound so surprised?'

She suddenly looks a bit bleak.

'Johnny always says I'm sexy. Not gorgeous.'

Johnny's an asshole who deserves a running fuck smack. No, I don't say that. 'Johnny needs to go to the optician and have his eyes checked,' I say instead. 'Believe me, you're beautiful.'

Our eyes lock. We look at each other for what feels like an eternity.

'That deserves a fake kiss,' she murmurs and leans in and kisses me.

'I don't think that's a good idea, do you?' I say and pull away.

No. I don't do anything of the sort. Although in my defence, I really do try and tell myself that she's someone else's girlfriend and I should put on the brakes. But then the blood rushes from my brain to other parts of my anatomy and for the next thirty minutes I am rendered incapable of rational thought.

Who am I kidding? It was more like ten minutes.

And I'm so shattered by the end of it, I do feel kind of like the male praying mantis. Sadie must also be tired because we fall asleep and only wake up when some monkeys start making a helluva racket outside our rondavel.

I reach for my phone and see it's fifteen minutes till we have to meet the others for drinks. I make some coffee for both of us – they even have a Nespresso machine in our room and one of those fancy jars filled with what looks like home-made shortbread, which is my favourite. I eat about five pieces for strength before I wake Sadie up – not a pleasant experience at the best of times.

She doesn't want to get up.

'Sadie, if you don't wake up, you won't have time to shower or put on any make-up …'

She staggers off to the bathroom cursing me under her breath.

One thing I'll say for my fake girlfriend, she can get ready in record time. We're only five minutes late as we stroll through the restaurant area and out to the viewing deck. I've also made a bit of an effort with my appearance (I'm wearing a button-down shirt instead of a T-shirt), seeing that this is the first time I'm going to meet Queenie IRL. I say as much to Sadie and she says, 'Why? You want to shag her too?'

'No, Sadie. It's just a sign of respect to look decent when you meet someone.'

She sighs theatrically. 'It was a joke, Mattie, lighten up.'

I do my 'there are no jokes' shrink spiel, while wondering if maybe I *do* actually want to shag Queenie. But as I'm pontificating, Sadie kisses me to shut me up and then grabs my hand, which pushes all thoughts of Queenie out of my head.

I think, fuck, yeah! And feel a rush of pure joy, but I don't have time to enjoy the moment because Ginger rushes over and grabs my other arm.

'*Don't. Look. Now,*' she exclaims, whispering loudly out the corner of her mouth. 'But I think that's Marian's table at the end of the restaurant – and she's sitting there as we speak!'

Queenie

'I hope Ginger gets a better view. From here all I can see are the backs of their heads,' Jess says, leaning in towards me as we wait at our table. She takes a big sip of wine. 'I can't *believe* this is actually happening.'

'Me too,' I say. I can't believe *any* of this is happening. This place! I'm here! The main lodge, with the dining room, is all sophisticated dark wood with plush cream soft furnishings, contemporary African art on the walls and soft lighting set into the thatched rafters overhead. Uniformed lodge staff hover discreetly on the edges of the room. It's dark out, but through the floor-to-ceiling windows I can see lights dotted on the deck overlooking the watering hole – I think I want to spend the whole day out there tomorrow.

And I'm here with these people! I'm trying not to stare at Jess – she is so much more beautiful in real life than in any of the Zoom calls we've done. Her skin is perfect and even though her clothes are all floaty and casual, everything about her looks expensive. I don't feel uncomfortable around her though; when she speaks she is still the same Jess from our Zoom calls. Faheema says I focus too much on whether I'm the poorest in any group; she says no one thinks about it except me. Maybe she is right, but I *do* notice. I don't want anyone feeling sorry for me. Pa always told us how poor he was growing up, but he was also very proud and told us how his family never accepted handouts from anyone, so maybe I picked up on that from him. I try not to worry about that now. I just want to enjoy being here.

'Charl says he doesn't know for sure – and he'd be fired if it came out he spilt the beans – but he knows there *is* a famous overseas writer here this weekend, and he thought he remembered that her name has an M in it. It *has* to be her, Jess.'

I don't want to say it in case I sound too Cape Town, but I feel like this whole weekend was simply meant to be. Meeting Charl, driving to the Pilanesberg, having the MK club drive out to stay here ... as if it was some mad twist of fate that conspired to bring us all together this weekend. And now, after the disappointment of finding out that Marian wasn't coming to Franschhoek, we're going to meet her after all! It can't all be coincidence that got us all here. And it's funny – they feel like old friends, just in sharper focus now that we've actually met in person. Take Ginger – so much funnier and wittier in the flesh. I hadn't considered that the medium of Zoom and chat would inhibit her. Not a lot mind you, but speaking to her in person has made me realise exactly how hilarious she really is. I haven't even met Matt yet, but I suspect he's even more interesting in real life. Seemingly such a regular oke on the surface, but with so much going on underneath.

'Clever Charl,' Jess says. 'I like him. He seems so down to earth and he has such good taste,' she teases. 'He really seems to like you, Queenie. Pity he can't stay for dinner.'

I feel the smile spread over my face.

'Yeah, he has work, but he said he'd swing by our table later if he gets the chance. I definitely got lucky with him, Jess. Can you imagine if he was a dick? It could so easily have been a disaster!'

He could've been a 'murderous psychopath' – that's what Jennifer had said when I used Charl's phone to call her from the road. The minute I told her I was driving with him to the Pilanesberg she made me share our location on WhatsApp, and she wanted all the lodge details so that she could phone to check that he actually worked here (something I probably should've done myself before getting into Charl's bakkie). I don't regret it for a minute though.

For once, I actually did something, I didn't just fantasise about it. And if I hadn't taken that chance, I would've spent the next how many months wondering about what would've happened ...

'Listen, thanks again for organising that everyone came for the weekend. I didn't realise how far this actually was from you. Maybe I had a small panic attack about being in the middle of nowhere with someone I don't actually know. I needed to hear a friendly voice.'

Jess had been so kind when I called her – nothing was too much trouble. And she'd also offered to come to my room and do my make-up before dinner – I had nothing with me and there was no way I wanted to meet Marian with a naked face. I'd thought Jess was beautiful on the screen, but the more we talk I think it's her kindness that makes her more beautiful in real life. It's not just the skin, it's what's under the skin. That husband of hers is an idiot. And that guy in Tashas must still be pinching himself.

'Honestly, you did me a favour,' Jess says. 'I would've spent the weekend without my children, feeling sorry for myself. And this way, thanks to you, it looks like Matt and Ginger are also getting their own dirty weekends on. Everyone is happy. Well –' Jess pauses, staring at the scowling girl who's just walked into the restaurant holding hands with the man I instantly recognise is Matt '– maybe *she's* not happy.'

'So that's Matt. And Sadie.' I take in the way Matt is looking from Sadie to Ginger, as if he's desperately trying to include Sadie in the conversation. In contrast to Sadie, the guy with Ginger – who I guess to be James – is relaxed and smiling. 'From the way Matt described her, I'm not surprised. She sounds like hard work to me.'

As if they've heard us talking about them, Ginger looks up and gives a little wave like she's suddenly remembered who we are. It seems she's mid-sentence when she drags Matt towards us, sulky Sadie on his other hand and a laughing James following them all.

'Did you see Marian?' Jess asks, slight panic in her voice, as they arrive at the table. 'Is it her? Do you think now's a good time to go and talk to her? I've got my copy of *The Woman Who Stole My Life* here with me – that could be an icebreaker? We could ask her to sign it.'

'Hang on just a minute, can I please say hello to Queenie?' Matt says, reaching over to hug me before I can even get up from my chair. 'It's a special moment this; we've only ever seen each other online.' His hug is gentle and warm. 'And another hug for you, just because,' he says to Jess, leaning in.

I'm surprised – and thrilled – that Matt has it in him, what with Sadie staring us all down. *You go, boy*, I think. I don't know how Sadie has managed to keep Matt dangling the way she has – just looking at him, you'd think she would have snapped him up. Tall, dark-haired, olive-skinned with strong features and soft eyes. Muscley. Not too much. Enough for it all to be Gorgeous. Definitely a man and not a boy. It is an absolute no-brainer that Matt is a catch. I must remember to tell him because it doesn't seem that he knows it. Also, I must tell him that his Zoom lighting is very, very bad.

'I couldn't see her face – the women had their backs to me,' Ginger says when they all sit down, 'but there's only one dark-haired woman and I swear it's her. I heard her accent, definitely sounded Irish, didn't it, James?' James doesn't have a chance to answer, but he doesn't look upset by this. I wonder if Ginger realises that he hangs on her every word. 'Shall we go over now? Or let her have dinner first?'

'I would get it over with before she realises there's nothing decent on the buffet,' pipes up Sadie, as if Ginger was talking to her alone. 'South African-themed dinner tonight so I bet it's trays of bobotie, curries in mini-potjies and piles of koeksisters and milk tarts. God, nothing original at these places. If you've been to one, you've been to them all.'

Matt looks embarrassed. I would be too – everything here at the lodge has been exceptional so far, the very definition of luxury and attention to detail. My room was free because Charl organised it, and it isn't the top of range, but there was a complimentary bottle of champagne on ice, all-natural biodegradable toiletries next to the outdoor bath and electric blankets turned on by housekeeping at night. Gowns so thick and white and fluffy I didn't need to use a towel. A mini Nespresso machine and a fully stocked bar fridge that included munchies to satisfy all cravings. That's just the tip of the iceberg, there's more that I messaged Faheema about, but one thing's for sure – dinner is not going to be ordinary.

'I quite like a bit of bobotie,' Ginger says, not making eye contact while she folds the white-linen napkin beside her plate. I can tell that Sadie irritates her by how carefully she places the heavy cutlery on top of the napkin. 'Maybe Marian will too.' Ginger seems to gather some patience;

I guess it comes from dealing with her daughters. 'But maybe you're right and we should try to catch her before dinner. With a buffet, who's to say how long dinner will take and no one likes to have someone come up to them when their mouths are full of food.'

'So we're going *now?*' I'm already halfway up. *This is it – we're going to meet Marian!* 'Jess, you go first – you've got the book. And you're the one with the PR experience so you're used to talking to famous people. I think when I come face-to-face with her, I'll forget my own name—'

'I'll stay here, thanks very much, keep James company,' Sadie says as if someone was asking her. What's with this girl? 'I'm sure we can entertain ourselves …' She gives James a coquettish smile that makes my jaw drop. How does Matt not see this?

Ginger's hand is wrapped tightly around the fork in front of her.

'Err, yes.' James puts his hand over Ginger's and gives it a squeeze. 'Sadie and I can check out the buffet while you chat to Marian. I'm sure it's a moment the four of you want to yourselves anyhow. We'll report back when you're done over there.'

'That's a great idea, James.' Matt looks relieved as he gets up from his seat. 'I say we just do it. I'm so nervous, I don't think I can eat a single thing anyhow.'

Sadie lets out a little snigger, but we all pretend not to hear it.

Our chairs scrape on the floor as Ginger, Jess and I form a little huddle with Matt. 'Okay, let's do it,' Jess says, book under one arm.

She hooks the other arm into Matt's and off we troop – Jess and Matt leading the way, Ginger and I behind them. Our table is close to the window and Marian's table is all the way across the room, but Jess suddenly stops halfway causing me and Ginger to crash into her back while Matt tugs ahead. Luckily the tables are spread quite far apart from each other so the other diners don't immediately notice us.

'Oh God, I'm too nervous. What if she chases us away?' Jess says, worry in her eyes. 'I know I used to meet famous people, but now I'm just a washed-up housewife. A soon-to-be-divorced, washed-up housewife.'

'She's not going to chase us away,' Matt says calmly. 'According to her social media, she's always very nice to fans. And if that's the worst that can happen, it's still not very bad. No one's going to die if Marian turns out to be mean.'

I feel bad, thinking of what's happening with his mother, but I'm also impressed at how he has pulled us all back from spiralling. All I want is a bit of an adventure and to meet Marian, but Matt has so much more on his plate.

'Also,' he continues, talking to Jess, 'you are not a washed-up, soon-to-be-divorced housewife – you're a gorgeous woman moving on to the next chapter of her life.'

Jess nods, not entirely convinced.

'I definitely don't think she'll be mean,' I say. 'You've got her book, your make-up is Marian-worthy and your shoes are spectacular – all things she loves. Plus, we're all here together – we're all about to make potential asses of ourselves. You're not alone, Jess – it's just that your book is the starting point.'

'Are *my* shoes good enough?' Ginger asks worriedly, looking down at her Green Cross slip-ons. 'When I put them on, I wasn't so much thinking of meeting Marian as much as kicking them off later.' She blushes slightly. 'I guess I'll let you in on it – I told James he didn't have to book his own room.'

We all whoop loudly, then promptly shush ourselves as the other diners look at us curiously. We're not exactly inconspicuous – three women and a man huddled in the middle of the room, whispering together for no apparent reason.

'Never mind the shoes. Let's keep going,' Matt says, rallying us into action.

In one last push we arrive at Marian's table and station ourselves behind her chair.

'Hi, Marian,' we chant together, holding hands like preschool kids, smiles plastered on our faces.

The other people at the table stare at us. Marian turns.

It's not Marian.

It's not Marian.

It's not Marian.

Jess, Ginger, Matt and I all turn to each other: 'It's not Marian.'

I scan the table. No Marian. There's a blondish woman who looks vaguely familiar, but I can't place her.

Ginger recovers first.

'Oh, so sorry about that,' she addresses the dark-haired woman sweetly. 'See, we thought that Marian Keyes was at this table. We heard there was a famous author here that staff were calling "Mrs M" and we couldn't think who else it could be. We are *such* Marian Keyes fans we just happen to have a copy of *The Woman Who Stole My Life* here with us, and we thought she could sign it for us. So, so disappointing. We're really very sorry for interrupting your dinner.'

'There *is* a famous writer at the table,' someone pipes up. 'She's one better than Marian. More than a missus, she's a dame.'

'Oh, now you're having us on,' Ginger says, chuckling. 'I'm sure we'd recognise someone famous. And when it comes to famous writers, it's Marian Keyes or bust for us!'

'You don't want to meet Dame Hilary Mantel?' asks the blondish woman I've been trying to place.

Shit. Shit. Shit. I *do* recognise her. Esmeralda would literally die if I told her I hadn't recognised the first woman writer to have received the Booker Prize twice.

'Dame *who*?' Matt asks, leaning forward and peering at her. The dame bristles with annoyance.

Before we have a chance to dig ourselves out, we hear a retch echo around the room and the sound of a loud vomit coming from the direction of the buffet.

And there is poor James, shock on his face, as Sadie leans over a round wooden bowl on one of the tables, and throws up in it.

'Mopane Worms' reads the chalked sign beside it.

Looks like sulky Sadie ate a sour worm.

Jess

I know all about a morning after these days, but this one's different. It's 5.30am, with only the slightest blush of sunrise. There's a riot of birdsong and an ominous rustle and bellow as I make my way to the others who are gathered at the designated meeting point for the first game drive of the day: James and Ginger, who are holding hands and looking decidedly sheepish, and Queenie, with ruffled hair and a perfectly styled oversized khaki shirt bearing the lodge's logo. Matt is alone, and also without a jacket. He folds his goose-fleshed arms across his chest and says, 'Sadie couldn't make it ... think she's got food poisoning.'

'Poor dear. How devastating that she won't be joining us this morning,' Ginger says, a wicked grin spread across her face.

'A lost opportunity to feed her to the lions,' mutters Queenie.

I say nothing because an awkward sensation is burning in my chest whenever I look in Matt's direction. I can't seem to help focusing in on his flexed biceps, and imagining the chest they lead to. My eyes stray lower, propelled by a force of their own.

Come on, Jess! He's young, far too young for the likes of me ... Time for coffee, and a nice home-made rusk.

I help myself to the abundant spread of early-morning snacks that have been laid out. There are mouth-melting rusks, an assortment of fruit, and hot coffee in stylishly rustic enamel mugs, sweetened with just the right amount of condensed milk. Now and then the air is pierced by the call of an exotic bird I can't name.

We sip the steaming coffee in silence and then, one by one, start laughing.

'Hilary bloody Mantel,' I say. 'Bet my husband's stuck-up lover idolises her.' Just saying it causes a jolt in my stomach.

Queenie reaches over and squeezes my hand just as a game-drive vehicle, Charl in the driver's seat, roars through my sudden melancholy: 'Come on, everyone, let's go see some wildlife!'

Queenie huddles up front with him, and Ginger and James take the front seat, leaving me and Matt one seat behind.

There's a gaping space between my thighs and his. I imagine things that make me flush. No, I need to think of unhappy things … Donald Trump putting his toupee on his head in the morning, climate change, my Gut Microbiome after the gluten-filled rusks.

Ginger whips out a pair of binoculars and a game-sighting checklist. Of course she's eager, I smile to myself – she spent an entire marriage not being able to go to a game reserve. 'Zebra, impala, waterbuck,' she says calmly.

'Giraffe!' says Matt. 'My favourite.'

Sooo bloody young, I think to myself. Young enough to still have a favourite animal.

Up front, I can hear Queenie gasp. 'This is something, this is all really quite something,' she says.

I squirm with a sudden realisation of how privileged I am, that a weekend in the bush has always just felt, well, normal.

I turn to Matt. 'Hey, what would you have said if it really *had* been Marian Keyes at that table?'

He breaks out in an impish grin. 'I would have fanboyed, I suppose. Said something about how I've read all her books multiple times and quote them at random. You?'

The air is amber, my cheeks rosy. Nothing like the crisp, early-morning breeze on your face during a game drive with a motley crew of new friends. I think of the five-strong pile of Marian Keyes novels teetering next to my bed. To be honest, I don't know what I'd have said to her. I certainly don't care about the investor event any more.

'Um, I think I'd just push Queenie's writing into her hands.'

We turn towards Queenie and Charl, who are laughing quietly at the front of the car, heads touching. 'She's really got something special.'

'Yeah.' Matt smiles. 'She really does.'

All six of us fall into a happy silence as we speed past impala, wart-hogs and riotous clumps of zebra. At a high clearing, we stop briefly to enjoy another flask of coffee, muffins and the last of the sunrise.

It's when I turn back to get my jacket from the back of the truck that I spot another game-viewing vehicle in the distance. And there, beneath a perfectly angled safari hat and a pair of Gucci sunglasses, I spot a flash of sleek dark hair. Perfect skin.

Marian!

I have to act. But I can't let Charl think we're a bunch of crazed stalk-ers – especially after last night.

'Guys. *Guys!* A herd of buffalo!'

'Shit, really?' Charl springs into action, scooping up the thermos flasks. He gallantly holds out a hand and pulls Queenie up next to him. The rest of us tumble in ungracefully, pulling the blankets around us tight against the cold.

Charl checks we're all seated while simultaneously pumping on the accelerator to release a plume of diesel fumes. 'Come on, let's go!'

We rumble down the koppie at speed, dust flying behind us. Deep, deep and deeper still into the thickening veld. Matt cranes his neck. Ginger and James adjust their binoculars.

Queenie frowns. 'Are you sure you saw something, Jess?'

'Let's go this way,' says Charl, moving in the complete opposite direc-tion of the other game vehicle.

'*No!*' I shout way too passionately. 'They're down there, to the right. Right by ... that other car over there,' I venture.

'Oh, that's Tshepo – he's the best at tracking. I'll give him a buzz on my walkie-talkie to see what they've found.'

'*NO!*' I shout again, and this time everyone in the car stares at me, wide-eyed. 'Sorry, I'm just super-excited. Love me a big, thick buffalo ... herd. Love their ... long horns. Um, let's not waste any time – just drive!'

'Okay then,' says Charl. 'Get ready for a real four-by-four experience!' He accelerates, kicking up even more dust and speeds in the direction of the other car.

As the vehicle bounces and bumps us all over the place, Queenie grins lustily. Ginger clutches James's leg with one hand and her fabulous straw hat with the other. Matt bumps up right against me.

And just like that, we're there, wedged so close to the other vehicle they can probably smell Ginger's overwhelming perfume.

'Er ... the buffalo?' Queenie asks hopefully.

Of course there are none. There's just a dried-up watering hole with a bored marabou stork picking at his nether regions.

In the car next to us, besides the driver, there are just two passengers. One handsome man with greying hair and a woman with long black hair and a celestial aura who's looking the other way.

'Matt ... *Matt!*' I whisper, but he's craning his neck to see the phantom buffalo herd.

And before I can say anything more, the car revs, the driver throws a casual wave and they drive away.

Ginger

Poor Jess. She was so disappointed by Marian Keyes turning out to be Hilary Mantel that she's started seeing Marian lookalikes everywhere. First, there was that insane drive through the bush because she insisted she saw buffalo, but in fact had seen a car with a lady with nice hair and a grey-haired man. Only the lady turned out to be about eighteen and the grey-haired man ('It's Himself, I'm telling you, it's Himself,' Jess had yelled at their backs as they drove off) was actually a grey-haired woman, probably the teenager's mother. The poor things waved at us, but you could see that they were confused by a safari vehicle full of people looking at them like they were the game.

Then it happened again when we stopped for a mid-morning brunch. (None of this self-catering, fry-your-own-eggs stuff – no, there was a full-on table set out on a ridge in the bush.) In the distance we could see a river and between us and the riverbank was a herd of impala and zebra. Charl made our breakfast with the help of a chap who'd already been there to set up. I could tell Queenie was completely impressed by Charl's skills with a skillet although I'm sure he has other skills too. Thinking about it, so does James … It's nice to see a man in the kitchen, even if the 'kitchen' isn't a kitchen so to speak.

But anyhow, we were all standing around sipping on champagne and orange juice when suddenly Jess went very still.

'Are you okay, love?' I said.

'Shhh,' she hissed. 'They're there.'

Matt swung around. 'Who?' Maybe he was scared it was Sadie.

'Shut up!' she said, which made Matt's face fall.

And then she inexplicably dropped to the ground, muttering that she'd seen Marian and this time it was for real. Another group of people were there, shielded by a clump of acacia trees, and it would seem that Jess was convinced that Marian was included in their number. In her smart, expensive clothes, Jess leopard-crawled through the veld to spy on them.

We hissed at her to come back but she was determined. And we didn't want to shout after her, especially if it turned out to be Hilary Mantel again, because she no doubt already thought we were as mad as a box of African snakes.

Jess looked quite sheepish, not to mention messy, when she came back.

'Not her,' she muttered. 'The one with the dark hair was an Italian man.' And then she looked like she might cry so we gave her another glass of champagne.

I couldn't help noticing how transfixed Matt was by the missing button on her now rather scruffy shirt and how he assured her it was an easy mistake to make, which it wasn't, because none of the rest of us had made it. I was about to tell her so when James squeezed my thigh, which lit up all the bits of me that had been lit up last night, and suddenly I couldn't look at anyone and I nearly choked on my croissant.

Once I'd caught my breath, I reminded everybody that we actually had a better plan to meet Marian. There was still the writing competition and we might actually win a trip to meet Marian in her own home in Ireland. As legitimate competition winners. 'And not like a group of star-crazed stalkers,' I added, with a pointed look at Jess, who blushed. But that might be because Matt was sitting almost on her lap by that point.

I smiled. 'If only ...' I said. 'If only there was someone among us who could write well.'

Then we all turned and stared at Queenie, but she was staring at Charl so she didn't notice. I cleared my throat. 'Sadly, I have no writing talent. None *at all*,' I said, which isn't quite true because I once won a poetry prize at the church Easter fête when I was eleven, but that's another story. 'Do *you*, Jess?'

'No. No. None. What about *you*, Matt?' Jess yelled pointedly, which made Matt flinch because he was basically sitting right on top of her. That Sadie would have had a heart attack, but luckily she was back at the lodge vomiting her guts out.

'Nope. Practically dyslexic,' said Matt, glancing down Jess's cleavage. Then we all looked at Queenie again.

'What about *you*, Queenie,' I said. 'Can *you* write a winning story and help us meet Marian Keyes in person?'

'Me?' said Queenie.

We all nodded, even James, even Charl. Everything was about to come together.

Among the members of this trusted circle of fans, Queenie would reveal her heretofore secret writing talent and see that she held the key to all our dreams.

'Oh God, no,' she said.

Matt

I expected Ginger to launch into all the reasons why Queenie was the perfect choice for writing the winning short story. How we knew for sure that she could write because we'd been stalking her on the Internet, reading her stories without her knowing, *discussing her writing* behind her back and relying on the fact that she'd choose us as her plus-three for the all-expenses paid trip to Ireland to meet Marian over anyone else in her life, including Charl the hot game ranger.

Of course that sounds creepy and patronising AF, so I was relieved when she said nothing. Relieved and then confused because it's not in Ginger's nature to say nothing. Ginger likes to call a spade a shovel. I thought perhaps James had had a softening effect, that Ginger had suddenly learnt the art of diplomacy, but no.

The reason Ginger was quiet was because Sadie's food poisoning was not in fact food poisoning. It was a stomach bug and it hit Ginger like a ton of bricks.

'I feel ...' Ginger didn't even get the chance to say 'sick' before she started retching and James, being the amazing and attentive gent he is, pulled off his bush hat just in time for Ginger to throw up in it. Which she did. More than once.

And yes, there were diced carrots in it despite the fact that Ginger hadn't eaten carrots.

The sour smell of the puke hits me, which gets my stomach going. My mouth fills with saliva and I stagger away and retch into a nearby spiky aloe bush, hoping like hell that I don't get attacked by a lurking leopard. Chance would be a fine thing; you hardly ever get to see leopards in the bush. Still, that kind of ends the conversation about creative writing as we all climb back into the vehicle, Ginger holding the ice bucket in case she needs to puke again, and it's a slightly miserable trip back to the reception area.

I'm feeling decidedly green around the gills and a bit down as I trudge back along the wooden walkway to our rondavel. Not even the glittering lizards basking in the sun can cheer me up. I'm expecting to find Sadie still lying in bed. But she isn't. She's sitting on the bed, fully dressed.

'Someone's feeling better,' I say feigning cheer.

'I'm sorry, Mattie.'

I notice her bag next to her, which seems to be packed.

'Sorry for what?'

She doesn't get a chance to answer because just then there's a knock at the door.

'I'll get it,' she says, but I'm too quick and I open the door to none other than Johnny-the-asshole.

'Johnny?' I'm now confused, nervous *and* guilty. Am I expected to fight over Sadie?

Are we going to spray each other with Doom at dawn? Mud wrestle in the crocodile enclosure? What's the protocol in these situations?

He slaps me on the back and comes in.

'Mate,' is all he says to me, then he wraps his arms around Sadie and nearly puts his tongue down her throat, which seems foolhardy under the circumstances. 'Feeling any better, princess? You gonna manage the trip home?'

'I've taken Imodium and Valoid so both ends should be okay.'

'That's a relief. Don't want you puking or shitting in the new BM.'

'BM as in bowel movement?' Yes, yes, I know I'm being completely childish, but I feel like I'm just getting down to Johnny's level, speaking to him in a language he understands.

'Ha! You're funny, mate. Nah. New car. M4 convertible. Cost a bomb.' He wants me to ask him how much, but I won't. Mainly because I already googled it and I know it costs around two mill.

It dawns on me that Sadie must've called him to fetch her and I feel a wave of something I can't quite identify wash over me.

'Sorry to mess up your fake-date weekend, mate,' he says to me with fake sincerity in his fake British accent (he grew up in Boksburg). 'I hope your mum feels better soon, yeah?'

Like she has a cold … How does he even know about Mom's cancer? 'Thanks, *mate*. Feel better, Sadie,' I say stiffly.

'I'm sorry, Mattie, but I don't think you'll miss me.' She tries to catch my eye, but I'm focusing on a point between her and Johnny-the-asshole, which probably makes me look like I'm on the spectrum but it's better than having to actually see her face.

'Mate, I've never heard of a bloke being in a bookclub. You sure you haven't got a vagina?' He laughs and that's when I hit him.

No, I don't.

I want to. Badly. But I don't.

Because clearly that's what Sadie wants. She wants me to fight Johnny for her, like this is some American romcom. Sadly for her, I've watched a fair number of them and I'm not going to fall into that trap.

'Actually Johnny, I *do* have a vagina. I was born with both male and female genitalia.'

Johnny's laugh falters; his Neanderthal brow creases. 'Really? So can you, like, finger …?'

'Matt's just teasing,' Sadie quickly tells Johnny, seeing the distaste on my face. 'Let's go.'

I see her waiting for me to pick up her bag. I don't. Instead I say, 'Have a safe trip back.'

'I'll message you …' says Sadie, still trying to catch my eye.

'No need,' I say cheerily.

She falters and then turns to Johnny. 'Won't you take my bags to the car? I need to speak to Matt quick.' When he looks confused by the instruction, she mouths, '*About his mom*,' as if speaking to a hearing-impaired child. 'You know. Cancer? Boobs?'

I'm sure he can talk about tits all day – it's the 'cancer' that sends him running with the bags to the car.

'I am sorry about this, Mattie. But you were having fun with your bookclub. Plus, that old woman is mean …'

'Ginger is not mean.'

'… and you have to admit that Jess is all over you.'

'She isn't.' But I feel a tiny thrill. *Is Jess all over me?* I kind of want to ask Sadie what she thinks, but it doesn't feel appropriate to discuss another woman with the person you shagged less than twenty-four hours ago. 'No, it's fine, really. If you want to go home, you must. No need to explain.'

'You're cross with me.' She wants me to be cross with her. Not today, Satan.

'Not at all. You'd better go. You know what the traffic's like when you hit Joburg.'

Sadie frowns. 'It's Saturday morning, I don't think there'll be much traffic …'

'Hey, why take the risk?' I reply.

'Okay, well … bye, Mattie.' And that's that. She's out of here.

When she's gone, I sit down and try to work out what I'm feeling. I'm not nauseous any more so hopefully I don't have the dreaded bug – I think I was just grossed out by Ginger's rather enthusiastic puking. I still think Johnny's an asshole, so no change there.

But I'm not sad about Sadie going. In fact, I'm … relieved. Having her here wasn't fun at all. (Well, apart from the sex, which was a bit fun.) But it occurs to me that I'm not even sure if I like her very much as a person. Funny that she thinks Ginger is mean – talk about projection! And that stuff about Jess? I feel a warm, fuzzy glow …

Although Jess did have sex with a guy in a toilet so her standards aren't exactly high.

The warm fuzzy glow disappears.

I decide to take a nice long shower to clear my head – there's an outside shower in a little private courtyard. It's open to the sky, but enclosed with sticks and the water runs straight into a garden with ferns and mossy rocks. There's also complimentary shower gel and some exfoliation stuff that kind of stings as you rub it in, but as you rinse it makes your skin as soft as a newborn baby. Well, if a newborn baby wasn't hairy.

For a moment I feel a pang that Sadie isn't here to experience my baby-skin softness, but then I think of the bliss of sleeping on my own in that nice big bed without her snoring.

What I do feel sad about is having to break the news to Mom that we're actually not an item, that I'm as sadly single as I ever was. I know Mom's going to be disappointed … and that's what gives me the idea.

'Let me get this straight. You want me to write a short story so we can win a competition to meet Marian so that you can surprise your mom?' She's whispering because we don't want to disturb the animals.

'Yep, that's pretty much it.' I'm sitting with Queenie on the viewing deck, sipping on a very nice gin and tonic and watching the animals gathering at the watering hole as if they've all received invitations to a cocktail party. The zebras are already there – Charl calls them disco donkeys – tails swishing, tossing their manes and keeping an eye out for the crocs that might enjoy a bit of zebra carpaccio for supper. I watch three giraffes loping over, simultaneously clumsy and graceful as I wait to see if the emotional blackmail that failed to work on Sadie will work on Queenie.

'But the prize is only for the writer and three people—'

'I've thought about that,' I quickly interject. 'I'll pay for my mom's flight and accommodation, and I'm sure they'll let her tag along to see Marian and if not, she can take my place.'

'Wow. You've really thought this through.' She wrinkles up her nose, 'You smell nice by the way. Is that the sandalwood, lemongrass and lavender exfoliation gel?'

'It is.'

'It's amazing. I think I could get used to this life ...' Her brow creases. 'But what makes you think I can *write*? I mean, working in a library is hardly the same as being a writer.'

'I can just tell,' I say.

'From *what*?' she asks more than a touch suspiciously.

Oh boy.

'From your messages and your emails and the way you talk ...' I lie glibly. 'You're a born storyteller.' Then I go in for the kill. 'And ... you're our only hope. None of the rest of us can write. And I really, *really* want to meet Marian. It's bucket-list stuff. And –' I feel my throat constricting '– and it might be Mom's last chance.' As I say it, I realise I'm not bullshitting. If Mom doesn't get treatment, she will die and even if she does get treatment, it might just delay the inevitable. She still might die.

It all suddenly hits me and the tears start trickling down my face and before I know it, I'm crying properly. And I want the ground to open up and swallow me because once I've started, I can't stop.

Mom is dying.

Queenie

I put my arms around him as he cries.

I've never shown anyone who knows me anything I've written. Well, that's not completely true. It'd be better to say that apart from Pa, I've never *willingly* shown anyone who knows me anything I've written. In high school we had to do those creative-writing essays in English and I'd hand in my work and Mrs Abrahams was always kind and gave me a good mark. That was enough for me, because it was the process I enjoyed. I could lose an entire afternoon to crafting an essay and what's that thing they say? That you know you're doing your soul's work when time ceases to exist? But then one day Mrs Abrahams made me read my essay out loud to the class. The whole friggen class. Of course it had to be the essay about the girl who liked the boy who didn't like her back, and everyone thought I was writing about Sean Petersen. Which I wasn't, but that story followed me around for the whole year, and Sean Petersen's girlfriend, Samantha Hendricks, started calling me 'The Writer' every time she saw me. She'd memorised some of the lines in my story and she'd shout them out as I walked by, which made everyone laugh. And let me just say that there is nothing worse than your own words being used to taunt you.

After that I made sure not to write anything that would get me noticed by Mrs Abrahams, but of course that didn't stop me from writing in secret. I had to then, and I still do: writing keeps my brain from overflowing. It's practically medicinal. But since then, I haven't shown my writing to anyone I know because when I even think about it, I get a tangible feeling of anxiety that starts in my stomach and ends up making my heart pound hard in my chest.

And then last year one of the library patrons asked about writing groups. I did some research for her and found one online. She didn't join it in the end – I think she started pottery instead because the library desk has since been flooded with misshapen pencil holders – but not knowing anyone in the group appealed to me, so I began to send some of my own stories to them. Just for the fun of it. It felt like a safe space, far from the Samantha Hendrickses of the world. No one says if you're good or bad – it's simply a place to get writing prompts and to send the story off to. It's enough for me that someone is reading it – I don't actually want to look a reader in the eye.

And I could think of nothing worse than those eyes belonging to Jess, Matt and Ginger.

All three of them have been dropping hints that I should write something for the competition and I've been quite good at pretending not to hear. Ginger was the most direct and I would have vomited on the spot if she hadn't beat me to it. But how to ignore Matt when he's sitting right here in front of me crying about his mom?

I repeat his words like a fool and try to buy time.

'You want me to write a short story so we can get to meet Marian so that you can surprise your mom?'

Jeez, no pressure – just scribble some words and win an international writing competition that will make all our dreams come true.

I can't do it. I can't write something that will win.

And why are they even on at me? I don't for a minute believe what Matt says about my writing in emails and on chats. Has Jess found my online writing group? I mean, if she could find my name on Pornhub, a little writing group with dodgy privacy settings can't be too difficult.

I don't know how I feel about that.

I take another sip of my gin and tonic.

On the one hand, if they've seen what I've written and they think it's good enough to win a competition, that's pretty great. On the other hand, it means they've been talking about me behind my back, which is pretty shit. High school all over again. And why would Jess tell me about Pornhub but not about what she'd seen on the writing group? I'm sure she's no

Samantha Hendricks, but I still don't get it. I'm not out there googling *her* name. And is she checking up on Ginger and Matt too? Or just me?

I just don't get it: why is Jess so interested in me? Am I her little 'Save the Poor Brown Girl' project? Is that why she offered to fly me to Joburg as well? If that's her jam, she can push right off.

I want to rage about Jess but I'm confused. She has been so kind to me, but not just to me, I see it in the way she deals with everyone. I like her. I don't want to believe that there is anything ulterior in the way she behaves towards me; I want to believe that it's all a misunderstanding. And surely Ginger would've told me if Jess was not being straight with me? I trust Ginger. But the thing that softens my heart the most is sitting right in front of me – Matt is a friend who is probably facing the biggest crisis of his life so far. I can't ignore him. I know what it's like and I know I would've done anything to make Ma happy while she was getting treatment.

I tighten my arms around Matt.

'Yes, okay, I'll do it.' Even as I say the words, I panic and my heart starts to pound – what the hell am I promising? 'I mean, I'll try to write a short story, but I don't think I'm good enough. And I don't have one single idea for a story – aren't writers supposed to have this endless supply of stories they can just pull out?'

I can see Matt is trying to get himself together, but the more he tries to stop crying, the more his tears flow. Poor guy. From what he's said about his family, I gather he hasn't had a chance to show his true feelings. Such pressure on men to keep it all in. Kevin – the lying, cheating, porno bastard – would've branded him a wuss or something ruder.

'You're going to win. I *know* you're going to win,' Matt says, swallowing the last of his tears as I release my arms from around him. He quickly wipes his face as he sees Charl walking across the deck towards us and takes a slow, steadying breath. 'Um … maybe you don't have to write something completely new. I'm sure you've already got something you could work on? Just an idea.'

So they *do* know about my online writing …

'Hey,' Charl says with that smile that has me wanting to run back to my room with him. 'Don't mean to interrupt –' he eyes Matt '– but I didn't think you'd want to miss the action.' He points to the watering hole.

Right there in front of us, so close it feels like I could touch them, is a herd of elephants! I count three adults and two babies at the water's edge. I stare in silence as Matt grabs his phone and starts recording. Charl sits down next to me on the lounger and drapes his arm around my shoulders, but I'm so mesmerised I'm hardly aware of it.

'And that's the top of a hippo's back peeking out the water,' Charl whispers. 'If you're quiet, you might be able to hear it breathing.'

'I thought it was just a rock!' I say, clutching at his arm and forgetting to be quiet. I know I must seem ridiculous to those who've been to the game reserve zillions of times, but I can't help myself – a bloody hippo and I thought it was a rock!

Then it hits me.

This. *This* is what I've been missing in my life.

It's not just Charl – though he's lovely and sexy and exciting and I'm starting to feel that I may want to keep him around for a bit longer than a holiday – and it's not just the game reserve and all the animals I've seen in real life for the first time. It's not even the hippo 'rock'.

It's the feeling of being alive.

Right now I could've been at home in Kensington lying in a ball on my bed worrying about Esmeralda. Instead, I took a risk to do something crazy and now I'm *literally* having the experience of a lifetime. In these past two days I've lived more than I have in years. I don't *want* to go back to working in the library, staying at home and zooming Zumba. I'm tired of being on guard for Esmeralda.

I want to do something bigger. Take bigger chances.

So I'm going to pretend to be a writer and I'm going to write the best damn short story I can. I don't think I'm going to win, but so what, I'm going to try.

I turn to Matt, who's still recording the waterhole scene. He smiles and swings round his camera to face me and Charl.

'And here we have Charl, game ranger extraordinaire, who arrived out of nowhere to show us this incredible scene right here, at our feet,' he says in a rather good David Attenborough impersonation. 'On his arm, the other half of this power couple is none other than Queenie, The Writer, who is going to win a writing competition and get all her super-cool new friends to meet Marian Keyes.'

'The Writer'.

Matt laughs, but it feels like Samantha Hendricks has time-travelled from high school all the way to the Pilanesberg. I want to smack the phone out of his hand.

Charl must feel me stiffen. 'You alright?'

Matt still has his phone trained on us.

'I'm fine,' I say. I have a smile stuck on my face but inside I am boiling. I turn to Charl. 'I told Matt I'd try to write a short story for a competition we all want to win. But before I show any of them a single word, I want to know why he and Ginger and Jess have been stalking me on the Internet. First on Pornhub and now on my online writing group. What exactly is the deal, Matt?'

I see the guilt on his face as he drops his phone. It tumbles to the ground, connecting with the wood right on its corner, and cracks.

'Shit,' says Matt as he bends to pick it up, his eyes fixed on the shattered screen.

Jess

A vicious storm is blowing through the game lodge, scattering napkins and abandoned champagne flutes. The dining area is shuttered up from the wind, but cicadas smash up against the window glass, trying to get to the light inside.

The atmosphere inside is chilly too. Queenie is huddled next to Charl, speaking to him in an agitated whisper. He looks perplexed but calm – applaudable for a man who met the raging woman he's now shielding just over forty-eight hours ago.

If I could just explain why I searched her name, if I could just show her how much I've grown to admire her …

Desperately, I grab Charl's arm. 'Sorry, Charl? Could you—'

'Don't touch him!' growls Queenie.

A few other heads in the dining room turn.

'I was just trying to—'

She stands in place, eyes fixed on me. Like a lioness steeling itself for the kill.

'Trying to *what*, Jess?' More eyes on us. 'Trying to schtupp him in the bathroom like that random guy at Tashas?'

Complete silence at the other tables now. Everyone is staring.

My cheeks are hot. I'm mortified. I fiddle with the bottom of my shirt, only for my top button to pop loose. One more wrong move and our captive audience will get a taste of what was on the menu at Tashas that day.

I look down. What I need is to start making small, slow steps to my rondavel, where I'll be able to crack open the mini bar, down a sherry and pretend this weekend, this friendship, this bloody bookclub, never happened. The only good thing in my life besides my kids, destroyed. I glare at Jess and Charl and turn on my heels to leave.

'Uh, Jess? Is that you, darling?'

I smell her before I see her. Sue Adamson. And the nauseatingly sweet wall of scent that is Thierry Mugler Angel.

As I meet her eyes, my head begins to pound. 'Sue.'

An old friend from Joe's circle. Very wealthy. Very appropriate at all times.

'Is everything okay over here?' Sue flutters a hand in Queenie's direction, her painted lips upturned.

'Yes, sorry for the, uh, disturbance.'

'Really?' she ponders. 'I thought I heard something about Tashas?'

'Just a little joke, Sue. Just this thing ... I do ... *we* do – I mean ... I do with *Joe*! Ha! He pretends ... to, uh, be a stranger – you know, to spice things up a little and he's *always* had a thing for Hyde Park. You'd swear they're pumping pheromones through the air vents ... ha ha!'

Sue is beginning to look ill.

'I haven't seen Joe in a while actually, darling.' A coolness comes over her. 'Please do tell him to give us a ring when he has a moment? Nigel has some, well, fairly *urgent* matters to discuss with him.'

Now it's my turn to feel ill. Nigel is an anchor investor in the fund. The non-existent, Ponzi-scheme bloody fund.

'Yes, yes, of course. Bye, Sue.'

'Take care.'

I turn in slow motion, cheeks burning, then sprint to my room and curl up on the bed. Everything is a complete disaster. The horrible fight with Queenie is unresolved. Our family is broke, my cheating husband will be arrested at any moment and my bookclub – the one joy I had, the one tenuous grasp I had on my flailing life – is about to be ripped apart.

What can I possibly say to Queenie? I didn't google her for any other reason than I was curious and have a loose relationship with personal boundaries. Maybe her age had something to do with it too – she reminds me of me, before I resigned myself to a life of hollow privilege.

A message beeps on my phone.

My heart leaps, thinking it's Queenie apologising for the outburst and wanting to chat, but it's Joe. It's a picture of both girls beaming over thick slabs of chocolate cake with scoops of ice cream. Goddammit, so much sugar – and now he's the favourite bloody parent too!

Sobs break free from my aching chest.

When I lift my head, the pristine white hotel pillow is stained with a smear of my mascara. *Way to go, Jess.*

I pull open the minibar fridge, but it's been cleaned out already. By me. I'll have to go to the bar. I throw on a shawl, smear on some red lipstick and pull my hair into a bun. I open the door a creak and scan the wooden walkway that runs between each of our rondavels.

There is only one path, so if I cross paths with Queenie I'll have to make a run for it. The path is lamp-lit and quiet except for the faint chirping of crickets and the purring call of a nightjar. I look up. The stars are brighter here and I catch my breath with the beauty of it. I almost forget about my furtive mission for more alcohol. I creep past Queenie and Charl's rondavel. One step, two steps. Just when I think I am safe, I come face to face with Ginger and Matt. Matt's done something with his hair. Showered maybe? It looks adorable.

'Sorry for getting you into trouble with Queenie, Matt. And sorry about your phone.'

'It's okay. Maybe it's the universe telling me to go offline.'

'Suppose so,' I say.

The two are blocking my path. They look sheepish. 'What's up?' I try.

'Oh, nothing. Just coming to check on you, that's all,' says Ginger. Matt gives her a nudge. 'Ouch, Matthew – that's my bad hip!'

'Sorry, sorry. We, uh, actually wanted to ask you something, Jess. Queenie is mad at *all* of us, not just you. Charl has whisked her off for a night in the private tented camp to help calm the situation.'

'I feel awful about all of this,' offers Ginger. 'We should have never kept secrets from Queenie or just expected her to bang out a piece of writing to get us to Ireland.' She looks back at Matt.

'So,' he says, 'we had a gin and a think. Queenie's got the writing chops, but she's nervous about coming up with the actual story. We realised that the way we met and became friends –' he waves his hand around vaguely '– is pretty unusual. So we were thinking …'

Ginger

Listen, I'm not saying it's easy talking Queenie round at breakfast the next morning. God, but she's furious with everybody. (Except Charl.) She won't even sit with us; she sits down at a small table away from the rest of us, just her and Charl. But, you know, I was married to Roger for forty years and he wasn't an easy man. And my daughters aren't what you would call pushovers either. If someone is in a sulk, I'm your womxn. God knows, I've spent years honing the skill.

So I go and sit down with them and I use what I think of as my 'Debbie technique' – apology and flattery.

'We are *so* sorry, Queenie,' I tell her and I don't have to fake it because I really am. 'The truth is, Jess looked you up because she admires you and wanted to know more about you. It's unforgivable and she's deeply ashamed and sorry. *Deeply.*'

'Why would she admire me, Ginger?' says Queenie. 'That's bullshit.'

'Because you are interesting and funny and kind and beautiful,' I say and am grateful that Charl nods vigorously. 'I *literally* do not know another person who'd have the balls to drive halfway across the country with a strange man she's just met – no offence, Charl – and get her formerly virtual friends to join her for a spontaneous weekend in an upmarket game reserve. And Jess, let's be honest, is a complete mess.'

'No, she's not,' says Queenie and I smile. This is exactly how I got Debbie to make friends with her frenemy in matric.

'Oh, she *really* is,' I say. 'She's a high-maintenance alcoholic who has sex with strangers in public toilets.'

Harsh, but also true.

'I thought you liked her, Ginger?' Queenie seems about to defend Jess. My job here is almost done.

'Oh, I *do* love her, Queenie,' I say. 'But just because I love her doesn't mean I can't see her problems. That's what friends do. And I love you and I can see that you're a great writer.'

'That's hardly the same thing,' Queenie says, but at least she's smiling.

'Well, Jess *is* sorry that she found things out about you behind your back, Queenie. And she's ashamed. And I'm sorry too because I was also part of it.'

'Anyway,' Queenie continues as if I haven't spoken, 'even if I *can* write, I don't have an actual story. That's where I always go wrong.'

'Well ...' I say. 'We understand that. And we've had an idea. We think you should write *our* story. It will be a winner, Queenie, you know it will. And that way, we'll all be in it together.'

'I suspect you've got lots of stories in you, don't you, Ginger?' Queenie's voice is softer now, more like the Queenie we know.

'I've had a tame life, Queenie,' I say sadly. 'I wish I'd been braver and done more and seen more.' I pause, thinking. 'But, you know, I see people and I watch. And mostly, I listen. I didn't get through all those years with Roger without a rich fantasy life.'

'You're terrible, Ginger. You're worse than the lot of us.'

Just like that, it's over. Queenie comes back to sit with the others and there's lots of hugging and apologising. So much apologising. It makes me think about my girls – maybe I haven't apologised to them enough over the years. Maybe I haven't explained enough, talked to them enough. Let them in.

As I'm thinking this, my cellphone rings and I see Lee-anne's name on the screen. For a moment I think about not answering – Lee-anne is so draining – but then I look at my friends and I think maybe their moms also find them draining, so I take the phone and walk away from the table.

'Hello, darling,' I say. 'How are you?'

'Mommy,' says Lee-anne and I can hear that she's sobbing. 'Mommy, you were right about Tex.'

I search my mind – what have I been right about? That she's a pain in the arse? But I've never actually *said* that.

'What's happened, darling?' I say. 'Are you okay?'

'She's left me, Mommy.'

'Oh, Lee-anne, my baby. Why?'

'Because of Harry Potter.' A fresh round of sobbing down the phone. I'm confused, I admit.

Lee-anne takes a moment to catch her breath. 'You know how we all hate JK Rowling now because she's a TERF?'

I hate the term TERF. I have no idea what it stands for and only a loose idea of what it actually means. It sounds like a gardening term to me, or the name of a particularly difficult exam. I know that this isn't the time to tell Lee-anne this. 'Shocking,' I say instead, hoping that I'm getting this right. 'Absolutely shocking.'

'Exactly,' says Lee-anne and I breathe a sigh of relief. 'And Tex knows where I stand on this.'

The whole fucking world knows where Lee-anne stands on this because she posts about it on Facebook and probably on all those other places I don't bother with. I know it's got something to do with transsexuals and when I've gone into the comments, it's often degenerated into a fight about public toilets. 'Rather wee at home; public toilets have germs,' I always want to comment. Well, I obviously can't say 'Rather wee at home' now.

'Right,' I say. 'Of course.'

'But she asked me to burn my *Harry Potter*s in a ritual ceremony and when I said I wasn't comfortable with that, she said *I* was a TERF!'

'Of course you're not, darling,' I say vehemently. If Lee-anne says she's not, then she's not. That's essentially what motherhood comes down to. 'And to ask you to burn your favourite books, darling, that's just terrible,' I say, hoping like hell that this is, indeed, the cause of the problem. I warm to my theme: 'I mean, the Nazis burnt books!'

'Exactly what I told her,' says Lee-anne and I feel rather proud of myself. 'And also, I know it's wrong, Mommy, but I still love *Harry Potter*. I can't help it.'

Well, obviously you do, I want to say. I mean, I hated Roger's Aunty Maeve, but I loved her chocolate cake and I ate it even though I wished the baker would drop down dead, which she eventually did, taking the recipe to her grave.

There's a lesson in there somewhere.

'It's okay,' I say. 'Tex should understand that.'

'Well, she left,' says Lee-anne. 'She packed up everything and then she wrote a note in lipstick on the bathroom mirror saying she can't be with a TERF.'

'Oh!' I say. 'Tex owns lipstick?' Tex once lectured me for a full twenty minutes on how make-up is the ammunition of the patriarchy.

There's a pause.

'She used mine, obviously,' says Lee-anne and then we're both laughing. 'Mommy,' says Lee-anne after we've finished. 'Where are you? I need you. Please come home.'

Matt

'She broke up with Lee-anne because of JK Rowling?'

We're having sundowners on the viewing deck because it is the most gorgeous evening. There is a line of pink where the sun has dipped below the horizon and behind us the sky is deepening to an indigo speckled with stars. Charl has managed to organise for us to stay an extra night at no extra charge so we're all having fancy gin and tonics to celebrate. Jess gulps her gin, which is filled with berries the exact deep-pink shade as her lips.

Stop it, you horndog. Stop. It.

'Not exactly. It was because she wouldn't burn her *Harry Potter*s and because she's a TERF, whatever that stands for,' says Ginger explaining the whole Lee-anne and Tex saga to us.

'Burn her *Harry Potters*? Like we're still in the apartheid era?' Jess looks horrified.

'A TERF is a trans-exclusionary radical feminist,' I say, trying to be helpful.

'Excuse my French but What. The. Fuck?' exclaims Ginger. 'Yes, actually burn books,' she says to Jess, multitasking in a way I can only dream of.

I explain to Ginger as clearly as possible what a TERF is and that some feminists are not happy with the transgender rights movement, which they think is trying to exclude women. We then move on to discussing what each letter in LGBTQIAP+ stands for.

'You know, I always used to confuse bisexuality with bestiality until Lee-anne told me, "Bisexuality good, bestiality bad. That's all you need to know, Mom."' Ginger cackles and we all join in.

'Words to live by, really,' says Jess.

We laugh until the tears run down our faces. When we're at the hiccup-ing, wiping-our-eyes stage, Ginger looks at her watch.

'Lee-anne's going to be here any minute –' (yes, rather than leave to go home, Ginger very sensibly got Lee-anne to join us for our last night) '– and we still haven't done any brainstorming. We need to make a start be-cause all she'll want to do when she gets here is analyse the whole Tex saga to death. I hope you've got strong stomachs because she'll probably talk about her sex life. Whenever I object, she tells me I'm being homophobic, but I tell her, "I'm not homophobic, I'm just your mother. I don't care who you shag—"'

'As long as it's not Fido,' I interject.

'Yes. And also, I don't want to hear about it. I mean, *she* doesn't want to hear how James and I went for round three last night without Viagra.'

'Wow. You go, girl.' Jess high-fives her.

'Point is, we're not going to get a word in edgewise. You know, you should talk to her, Matthew. Be good practice for you – like when those student hairdressers give people the most appalling haircuts and dye their perfectly good hair purple.'

'Thanks, Ginger,' I say.

'So now. How do we begin this story? What do we do first?'

Our eyes inevitably swivel to Queenie, who starts shaking her head. 'No. Uh uh. I told you I—'

'Come now, Queenie,' Ginger says firmly. 'You must have *some* ideas.'

'Well, I guess it's a good idea to explore, you know, *why* we each want-ed to meet Marian—'

'Exactly how much do you think you'll have to say about our actual lives?' Jess looks so worried I want to take her hand and promise to make everything better. Instead I give myself a stern lecture about not rescuing people.

'We could be a *version* of ourselves? This *is* fiction so we can be any-thing we want to be. I want to be a famous author that goes to literary fes-tivals and meets other international authors ...' Queenie looks dreamily into the distance.

'I want to be a famous author too!' exclaims Ginger. 'I could be a

BEBB author if we need some diversity?'

'BBBEE,' I say.

'That's what I said—'

'No. There *is* such a thing as cultural appropriation, you know. So better just to be ourselves.'

'But won't it get boring?' asks Ginger. 'I mean, who wants to hear about all the stupid things I've been up to? I don't want to give Lee-anne anything else she can accuse me of. I'm so sick of being called a boomer.'

'Maybe we don't have to be *ourselves*-ourselves,' says Jess, raising her hand to order another gin.

Is she drinking too much or am I just noticing because of my dad? She's very jumpy and her phone hasn't stopped pinging since we sat down. She put it on silent, but I notice she can't stop checking it. That's the one blessing about breaking my phone – I haven't heard from Mom or Micky or Sadie. For the next eighteen hours or so I can just bury my head in the sand and pretend that the rest of the world doesn't exist.

'I'm going to invite Marian for dinner,' says Ginger. 'I mean, not in real life – in the story. I want to cook my famous melanzane.'

'From what I remember when I worked in PR,' Jess pipes up, 'the publishing house will arrange dinners and invite local authors or they'll do these expensive dinners at a fancy restaurant and the author will be there, but it's not like you'd get to know her. There'd be nothing to stop you from inviting her to your house though.'

'And if anyone would have the vooma to invite Marian to dinner, it'd be you, Ginger,' says Queenie, smiling.

'True. You know I once invited Nelson Mandela to dinner?'

We're all agog.

'Did he come?'

'No, but he sent me a very nice letter saying no thanks. It was probably written by that Zelda woman, but still. Oh! Lee-anne, over here!'

Ginger starts waving.

Queenie

Reality sucks.

This is the third day I've been home and still everything irritates me. Every. Single. Thing.

I suppose it's normal to have a bit of post-holiday blues but this feels extreme, like I was soaring free as a bird, just getting used to seeing the world from a whole new perspective and now I've crash-landed face first into hard earth. I don't know where to go next. I'm trying to remind myself that I should just go with it; after all, you never know what is around the corner. Look at last week. Thursday started off as a horrible day because of Kevin and the trauma on the Prom, but it led to me meeting Charl and for the first time in a very long time I did something crazy and just went away with him. I stopped imagining and took a chance and I ended up having the kind of adventure I've always wanted.

And it didn't just impact me. The more I think about it, the trip to the Pilanesberg was a turning point for all four of us in the MK club. We met in real life and had so much fun together but we also had our first fight. We saw the best and the worst of each other – and it brought us closer in a way that messages and Zooms never would have. That breakfast on Sunday where Ginger apologised! It reminded me so much of what Ma used to tell me and Jennifer: that a good relationship is not one where there is no fighting, but one where you can have a good fight and then know how to meet each other again, learn to apologise and to accept an apology, and then to move on. That's exactly what happened when Jess joined us and we all talked and hugged and cried and Matt ate all the shortbread and then we were okay.

I miss Ma. She would've liked that I was taking risks and making new friends. Living.

I wonder what Lee-anne thought of her mother when she arrived with her own tears to add to ours. I got the sense she expected Ginger to drop everything and to leave us and James, and it made me think that that is how Ginger usually is with her daughters; I know it's a thing that mothers do. I always liked seeing Ma with her friends – she became more of a person, more than how I saw her as a ma. Her jokes became a bit ruder, her laughs a bit louder, she was less careful about me when her friends were around. I think she became more herself and I loved seeing that side of her. I loved seeing how her friends enjoyed her too; somehow it made her more special to me. I felt so lucky to have her when I saw how others valued her too. That's *my* funny, clever, smart mother. If you ask me, Lee-anne could do with seeing Ginger as a whole person.

I wish we could've stayed longer and had a few more days together but unwelcome as it was, Monday morning still came and we all had to go back to our lives. 'Next stop, Ireland!' we joked with each other as we said our goodbyes. I can't imagine winning the writing competition but if I do, that would be the trip of a lifetime. Imagine travelling overseas with Ginger, Matt and Jess. Only thing that worries me is that I wish Jennifer could come along too. How would I leave her behind? Seems anyways silly to think about that now, counting my chickens before they hatch.

I do still feel bad about Jennifer though.

She was so happy to see me at the airport, but I've been so miserable and I know that now she's also wishing I'd stayed away longer. This morning she shouted, 'Get out of your pyjamas!' and then slammed the front door so hard the glass panes rattled.

I can't blame her. I know I'm behaving like a child who's had a new toy taken away from her. I can't help it. Every time I think about the Pilanesberg, I want to stamp my feet. Now I'm back here in my room in Kensington with only Esmeralda and the bullshit Pornhub situation to look forward to. I know Jennifer is hurt, and the frustration makes me want to punch a wall.

And there's Charl, obviously.

He saw me behave like a brat and I still can't believe he didn't feed me to the lions. That was seriously a low point when I lost it with Jess, but Charl took it in his stride. We've been WhatsApping non-stop. He's talking about his next trip to Cape Town.

But what's the point? If Kevin's taught me anything it's that I can't do a long-distance relationship.

I decide to take Jennifer's advice; maybe something other than pyjamas will improve my mood.

'Yeah right,' I say out loud after I get out the shower. I can't even dress myself without getting mad. All my clothes are either too bright or too dark, too tight or too loose, too much or too little – like I am friggen Goldilocks. Let's not even talk about the hair.

Not that I need to get properly dressed anyway. When I got back from the Pilanesberg I extended my leave to this week too. Esmeralda was so happy not to have to deal with me at the library she couldn't keep the relief out of her voice when I called to ask her. I'm betting she doesn't know what to do about me and the Pornhub thing. Just as well. If I can get on Jennifer's nerves, I'll likely get Esmeralda to burst into flames just by looking at me. I can't afford that, especially now. I've blown my savings. I seriously need my job, or a lottery win.

Tomorrow I'll have to go back to work. For today it's good enough that I've had a shower. I put my gown back on.

I tried to explain it all to Faheema on the phone yesterday, but it didn't come out right. I blabbed about how I loved being away from Cape Town and how fantastic Charl is and how close I feel to the MK club and about me writing the short story. She actually said, 'Hang on – who are you? You're in the bush for the blink of an eye and you know these people for three minutes and now your life here is shit? You couldn't have told *me* about writing stories or about Kevin and Pornhub?'

I'd forgotten I hadn't told her about the Pornhub thing and I tried telling her that my stories have been a secret from everyone, but that the MK club had made me start to feel normal about writing – and admittedly only after a huge false start. Faheema wasn't having any of it. I felt even worse when she said that Zayn had dealt with a similar porno case for a client, and she could ask him to sort it out for me.

'I'm sure he'll help you deal with the fallout at work too, unless one of your new friends is also a lawyer,' she'd said with a bite in her voice. I tried to make her feel better by saying that she was my oldest friend and obviously I'd never forget her, but that made it sound like I was trying to break up with her.

So I've been sending her messages to try to explain but now she's ignoring me, which she's never done before.

Jennifer has no sympathy either – she's also angry that I hadn't told her about Kevin and Pornhub. So now I've got great friends and a hot guy a thousand-odd kilometres away, but my best friend and my sister right here won't talk to me. What a balls-up.

All I can do is hope Faheema and Jennifer don't see what I've written for the competition.

I can't believe I actually wrote it. All four thousand words of it in longhand on the plane. I'd planned to start writing on my laptop when I got home, but everyone's ideas were swimming in my head getting me so worked up that I bought a notebook at the airport and started writing the minute I could put down my tray. I didn't even care that I had the middle seat. At first I just wanted to put the ideas on paper because I was afraid I'd forget, but then these whole sentences started coming out. I did exactly as Ginger suggested: I wrote the story of how we met and why we wanted to meet Marian. I didn't mean to, but I wrote about Kevin and the Pornhub story and how the members of the MK club were the only people I felt I could talk to about it. I was careful not to say anything explicit about Jess's struggles with her husband, or Ginger with her daughters, or Matt with his mom. I also didn't use Kevin's real name in the story – I wanted to, that would serve him right – but I thought about the woman in that video. If Kevin's phone was stolen and the clip was posted by the thief, then she's been even more violated than I have. I mean, my contact details were public – but her whole punani is out there. And I don't want to be responsible for any more people looking at it. I know I shouldn't, but I even feel a little sorry for Kevin. I checked this morning and that video is still up. I'm hoping Zayn's lawyer's letter will have more success than I've had.

I also need to send the story to everyone; Ginger's been asking. But I'm scared. What if they hate it? What if it doesn't live up to their expectations? I'm slightly embarrassed too. I've never written anything so personal, or so sentimental, since high school. I know the story is supposed to be about how we all want to meet Marian Keyes and how we plot and plan to get to her. I even reveal Ginger as the mastermind with a melanzane dinner invitation up her sleeve, but somehow I have ended up writing about how we went from being strangers peering at each other's profile pictures to real-life friends who support each other through some pretty out-there moments.

I wrote about how meeting them online reminded me that the virtual world can help us make connections that otherwise simply would not happen, and it's not all horror, like when my Facebook was hacked last year, or nasty, like with Pornhub. I ended the story by saying that if it doesn't win the competition and get us to Marian, I will feel like I've let everyone down, but a part of me will still feel like I've won something amazing. I've made great friends, been on a proper game-reserve adventure and have been pushed to write in a way I've never done before.

Maybe I even met a guy.

I don't know if the others will like that ending – it seems so selfish – especially when I think of Matt's reasons for wanting to meet Marian. But the thing is, it's true.

I finished it as the plane touched down and I was satisfied.

Thinking about the story makes me feel a little better about being back home in Kensington.

I sit down on my bed in my gown and pull my laptop closer. Some last edits then I'll submit it this afternoon, I promise myself.

But before I can change a single word, the doorbell goes. I ignore it – Jennifer has a key and Faheema never misses work for anything.

Another ring.

I consider going to see who it is but I'm in my dressing gown.

The bell goes again. This time the person holds it down so that one long ring echoes in the house. What the hell?

The security gate rattles as it's shaken.

'Queenie, Queenie! I know you're here! The library said you were. Open up! I'm not leaving.'

Kevin.

Jess

The story arrives in our inboxes in the morning, prefaced by Queenie saying, 'Ugh, you're going to hate it.'

'It's a first draft,' says Ginger, on our newly christened WhatsApp group, created courtesy of Lee-anne. Apart from her pocket-calling the group last night and then sending us a voice note of what sounded like clinking cutlery with an extremely loud episode of a brooding British TV show in the background, this mode of communication has suited us all just fine. We even have our own profile picture – it's of the four of us sitting at dinner at the game lodge, with Marian crudely photoshopped in. Poor woman, if she knew everything that was going on, she'd think we needed some serious psychiatric intervention.

'Don't be so hard on yourself, Queenie,' I type.

'I can't wait to read it!!!' says Matthew.

The exclamation points concern me. Didn't somebody once say that more than one exclamation point is a mark of madness? Well, with Matt I worry it's a sign he's trying a little too hard to be chipper. I know his mom is waiting for the results of more tests. I make a note to message him privately a little later. Not that I need reminding. My brain keeps snagging on him when I'm not looking.

But on to the draft.

I read it once, guffawing into my hand. Then read it again and feel a bit weepy at the end. It's just perfect and Queenie is now officially my new favourite author (after Marian Keyes). Which is just in time as I'm about to finish my last Marian Keyes novel.

'You bloody did it!' I message the group.

Queenie sends a line of blush emojis. Then: 'K, guys. Gotta go. Have pining ex-boyf to get rid of and hot game ranger threatening to surprise me here in Cape Town.'

'Remember,' types Ginger, 'a woman can juggle as many men as she likes, as long as they never cross paths.'

More blush emojis and a reddening of my cheeks in real life. A feeling unfolds in my chest, one that compels me to shoot a message to Matt. It's lust, but boredom too. With the girls at school, a whole morning stretches ahead of me.

'Hey – you doing anything?'

Matt is typing. 'Um … nothing in particular?'

'Want to hang out?'

'Is Ginger coming?'

'She can't make it,' I lie.

He sends his address, which is about fifteen minutes from my house, and the gate code.

I pop a codeine pill, for no other reason than my nerves are bristling and the colours outside seem too bright. I open the fridge and wash it down with a glug of some lacklustre dry white. My car has run out of petrol and I doubt the petrol card is working so I take Joe's 'special occasions' BMW convertible.

I roll down the top and breathe in the balmy Joburg spring air.

The GPS leads me deep into the leafy parks to a rambling old house where Matt is already waiting at the gate. His shirt is buttoned up one too many. He grins sheepishly as I pull over.

'Whoa! That's quite a ride!'

'Thanks. It's an RWP.'

He raises an eyebrow.

'Rejected-Wife Privilege.'

'Got it.'

He's not himself, I can tell. His cheeks are flushed and as we drive away, he keeps looking back at his house.

'So,' I start. 'Queenie's story's good, hey?'

'Oh yeah, prize-winning material. We're going to win this thing, I know it.'

'Then you can meet Marian and take your mom along.'

He looks away.

We drive through streets lined with plane trees, their leaves just start-ing to turn.

'You want to talk about it?'

'Not really. I mean not *yet*. The news is very fresh. I just wish I could go back to when things were simple, you know?'

I'm not good in situations like these. Why sit with pain when there are a wonderful variety of substances to numb uncomfortable feelings? But Matt's different – he looks desperately sad, but wears it comfortably.

'Maybe I could take you somewhere that reminds you of easier times?'

He perks up, but then shakes his head. 'No, it's silly.'

'Tell me!'

'Okay, okay – Mom used to take us to the zoo.' He smiles. 'I was ob-sessed with tigers and she used to lug us all the way to the top of the hill so I could spot one. I had a matching tiger tracksuit and everything.'

I laugh. 'That must have won you friends at school.'

He looks at me strangely, too lost in his thoughts to catch the sarcasm. 'Actually, quite the opposite.'

If the security up front think it's strange that two adults are visiting the zoo in the middle of a workday, they don't let on. Matt, emboldened now, leads us up the hill towards the tiger enclosure.

'Thanks for this, Jess. This feels really good, actually! I needed to get out of that house.' He looks at me with wide brown eyes. Something about the gaze pulls me in. I'm dizzy. Shit, that combination of pills is something I usually only indulge in around bedtime. It's no surprise that I trip over a stone, grazing both my knees and tearing my bohemian silk skirt.

Matt takes my hand and pulls me back up. A warmth spreads over me.

He doesn't let go.

We reach the top of the hill, red-faced and breathy.

'It's over there,' he says, pointing to a thick cluster of bamboo shoots. 'This was my favourite bit, knowing that the tigers were just a few steps away.'

We approach the enclosure still as cats, until a big sign looms into view: *New tiger enclosure currently under construction.*

Behind the glass is a mess of rubble and pulled-out shrubbery.

'Ah, I'm sorry, Matt. They must be somewhere else now, maybe next to the other big cats?'

'Wait a second,' he says, pulling my hand.

He kisses me. Deeply. Urgently tugs at my skirt. We push open the door to the enclosure and run inside, giggling. *Tigers were here!*

He kisses my neck, pushes a hand up my shirt. I'm surprised at the force of his attraction, turned on by it.

'Matt!'

'I need you, Jess.'

I hoist myself up on a big cement feeding trough and pull him towards me. 'I've wanted this for a while—'

'I've wanted it too, Jess. I think you're just beautiful. When we're all together in the bookclub, I can't take my eyes off you.'

He nibbles my lip gently and kisses me lustily. He's gentle, with an underlying strength.

'I need you, right now.' My voice is hoarse.

He slips off my panties with an impressive one-handed move. Funny, he's more experienced than I thought he was. A voice in my head warns me that we're friends, this means something, it should be special, but I can't stop myself. I tilt my hips onto him with a sigh that turns deeper and that builds into a scream.

'Well, look at you,' I say when it's done. 'Look at *you*.'

It was good, very good in fact, but I already feel like I've tainted a good thing.

That's the problem with 'no strings attached sex'; it has a tendency to be a trap made out of the strings. Hundreds of them. Next comes the shame hangover. First Tashas, now this? My new friends might see it as a pattern. Worse, they might think it's all I am.

This can't be all I have to contribute to the world. This can't be the only way to feel. The novels I have binged over the past few months flash through my mind, story after story of people overcoming their circumstances, sometimes even overcoming the worst in themselves. Right now I feel more bad than good.

I take a deep breath and wonder, *What would a character in a Marian Keyes novel do?*

Ginger

Lee-anne has hardly got out of bed.

She's been squatting in my spare room, even though she's got a perfectly good flat of her own. Tex has moved out and Lee-anne is too scared to go home and check whether the *Harry Potter* books – full collection, signed – are still there. She's convinced Tex has destroyed them. I've told her I could go for her and check. And then hopefully, if the books are okay, she can go home. And if they're not, maybe I can find some online and quietly replace them and *then* she'll go home.

Because having her around is not fun.

Firstly, and possibly most importantly, James can't stay the night. And after what happened when we went to the game reserve with my Marian friends, I want him to stay the night. Every night. I mean, I'm not saying that we're going to have wild sex *every* night – neither of us is in the first flush of youth – but I like his body next to me in the bed. It's been a revelation because I hated Roger's presence in my bed. He snorted and snored and farted and I always felt like the bed was full of little flakes of his skin because he struggled with terrible dryness, you know. James has on occasion snorted and when he has had a few drinks he snores and that last night on the holiday, he farted. But only once. And somehow I didn't mind. I actually thought it was quite funny.

The second problem is that Lee-anne's a bloody misery. Until this morning, she *literally* wouldn't get out of bed. I had to take her meals and persuade her to wash. Frankly, I went through enough of this drama when the two of them were in their teens, thank you very much. I've earned my stripes and now it's *my* time to live.

196

But then, of course, Debbie visits. They close the door and talk for hours, which is fine because it gives me a break. Then Debbie emerges and wanders around my house criticising everything. My furniture is too soft, apparently, and I may not be able to stand up as I get older, she tells me. My floors are too slippery and I might break my hip. I don't have smoke alarms so I'll probably leave something on the stove and burn the house down. That is if my sub-standard alarm system doesn't allow intruders into the house first, in which case, according to Debbie, I will be brutally tortured, raped and left for dead. She says 'Left for dead' with great relish.

Anyhow, after I read Queenie's story, I decided it would be just the thing to cheer Lee-anne up, especially since she met everyone up in the Pilanesberg and seems to think she is now part of the group. I've had to keep it very hush-hush that we have a new WhatsApp group or she'll want to be part of it. So I left her with Queenie's writing, and that was an hour ago, and she's just emerged from her room fully dressed and washed and made us both a cup of tea.

Well, I can hardly believe it.

'You guys are going to win this competition, you know,' she says over the tea.

'It's very good, isn't it?' I say. Because it is.

'Excellent,' says Lee-anne. 'You can be really proud of what you and your friends have done. Anyhow, I need to go and check on the flat. See if that bitch burnt my books. Water the plants. I'll call later.'

And with that, she leaves. I mean, I'm not holding my breath because she didn't take her stuff, but I have a sneaking suspicion she'll be back for it soon.

And I think it's all thanks to Queenie's tale.

Just as well Lee-anne has left, because this afternoon the doorbell rings and there's Jess standing on my doorstep.

Now the thing about Jess is that she always looks lovely. Groomed and, well, expensive.

But today she looks like a complete wreck. She's been crying, obviously, because there are tracks of mascara down her cheeks. And her hair is kind of wild – like she's just had sex in a tiger's enclosure or something. She's completely out of it – drunk or stoned or something – but she still managed to remember that we'd all shared our addresses when we'd filled in the competition form. She'd looked up the email and found me. That's how badly she wanted my help, I think.

'Come in,' I say, and she kind of falls through the door and into my arms. It's strange how I mind this sort of drama less when it's not my daughters – you'd think it would be the other way around.

I sit her down at the kitchen table and make her a strong cup of coffee. Luckily I bought a cake (and some shortbread) yesterday to try to tempt Lee-anne out of bed, so I cut Jess a huge slice of that (and have one myself, of course). And then I say, 'So, tell me.'

And she does. And can you believe it, she *did* have sex in a tiger enclosure! What are the chances? With Matt, which I think is a good thing because God knows there have been vibes. But now Jess is horrified by what she has done. Does he think she's a slut, she asks, because she *knows* she *is* a slut.

'Well,' I say, 'one man in Tashas and Matt at the zoo hardly qualifies you as a slut. My friend Gwen slept with a different man every Thursday, regular as clockwork, and nobody judged her for that.'

Jess looks at me, or I think she does, because her eyes are a bit squint from whatever she's taken. 'So you don't think I have a problem and Matt hates me?' she says.

I sigh.

'Oh, honey,' I say. 'You *do* have a problem. But it's not Matt. It's time for us to talk about how much you drink and all the pills you take. *That's* the problem.' Although Matt is probably also struggling with all of this, I think. Poor boy. Maybe I need to visit him, see how he's doing. After all, we all have each other's addresses now.

For a moment I think Jess is going to stand up and walk out.

But then she lays her head on the table and cries and cries and cries.

Matt

'You *followed* me?' I say, a little bit shell-shocked as I unlock the door and we go inside. I'm really regretting ever giving her the code to our gate.

Hand on hip, Sadie is utterly unrepentant. 'I didn't mean to. I was just popping around to say hi and then I saw you go off with *her*. Got anything to eat?' She opens the fridge and starts digging around.

Good luck, I think. My fridge is as arid as the Kalahari. Sadie finds a block of cheese, unwraps it, sniffs it and takes a bite. Yes. Straight out of the cheese.

'Oh, so you followed me *by accident*?' I nod as if I'm considering this. 'I can see how that would happen. And don't do that!' I point to the cheese. 'Cut a slice if you want some.'

She ignores me and takes another bite.

'Don't be so ...' Sadie makes a face and a gesture with her hand that I think means 'asshole'.

'So *what*? You realise you're behaving like a stalker?'

'And you're behaving like a man-whore. I saw you, Mattie. At the zoo, for fuck's sake! Little kids could've seen you. Been scarred for life.'

'There were no little kids around and *I'm* a man-whore? Kind of rich coming from you, Sadie. Jumping from your boyfriend's bed into mine and then back again.'

'I *knew* that's what this was about. You're so jealous!'

'Not any more.' As I say the words, I realise they're true.

'Why? Because now you're in love with Jess?'

I think about this. 'She's a lot nicer to me than you are – which I'm kind of enjoying. Plus, she's sexy as hell.'

I have to admit that the way Sadie's face falls gives me a lot of pleasure. And we're so busy arguing that we don't hear the light knock at the door.

'Are you too busy to come try the shortbread I've just made?' In the doorway, lit by sunlight streaming through the window, Mom looks ethereal. Is it my imagination or has she got thinner? 'Hello, Sadie – didn't realise you were here, darling.'

Sadie gives a little sob and rushes out the cottage, taking my block of cheese with her. Mom looks stunned.

'Don't worry, Mom – that's got nothing to do with your shortbread.'

'Oh, I hope you haven't been horrible to her, Mattie. Go after her! Say you're sorry …'

Of course I've chickened out of telling her that Sadie and I have never, in fact, been a proper couple. The friends-with-benefits conversation isn't really one I want to have with my mother, but the time to be honest is now upon us.

I pat the chair next to me. 'Come sit, Mom.'

She looks worried as she sits down next to me. I take her hand. It isn't my imagination. She has lost weight.

'I feel like you're about to tell me bad news, Mattie.'

'Depends how you look at it, I guess.'

I don't even try to choose my words carefully; there isn't really any nice way of saying this.

'Mom, Sadie and I were never actually an item. Yes, we had sex –' I go red as I say this '– but that was mainly because she was having a rough time with Johnny.'

'And going away with you to that game reserve?'

'I was kind of hoping if we pretended to be a thing, it would become a thing. Turned out the opposite.'

'What happened?'

'Sadie wasn't the complete focus of my attention so she called Johnny to fetch her.'

'She was probably feeling neglected …'

'No, Mom. She literally needs to be the centre of attention all the time and she uses shock tactics to get it. As soon as I stopped caring, she wanted me back. And when I went out with someone else, she followed me.'

Frowning, Mom shakes her head like she's trying to get her thoughts in order. 'Why did you pretend to be going out with her in the first place?'

'Well, firstly, I didn't want you to think I was some kind of man-whore, sleeping with her and ditching her. And, secondly, because … well …' I confess I'm struggling here.

Realisation dawns on her face. 'You did it for *me*?'

I nod, feeling close to tears.

'Oh, Mattie.' Mom pulls me into a hug.

'But before I start sounding like some kind of Madiba figure, let me add that I did have a massive crush on Sadie so it wasn't like it was a hardship.'

'And this other girl you went out with?'

I'm hoping we can sort of gloss over that bit, but Mom's too sharp. And although she is open-minded, I'm not sure how open-minded she'll be about my relationship with a mother of two who's probably ten years older than me and not actually divorced yet.

'I'm not sure we could really describe her as a girl. She's more of a woman … Older than—'

'Yoo hoo!' At this point, Ginger arrives and saves me from further interrogation.

'Hope you don't mind me just walking in but a nice man called William opened the gate for me. Also asked me if I knew Jesus. I *did* know a Spanish guy called Jesus once. Amazing dancer, amazing everything really; it was almost a religious experience.'

Relieved, I leap to my feet and envelop her in a bear hug.

She pats me on the back. 'I just popped in to bring you some shortbread, love. I saw how you were tucking into it at the lodge.' She produces a Tupperware.

'I'll put on the kettle. Mom, this is Ginger … er …'

Mom is gazing at Ginger with decided distaste. My heart sinks.

'Er, Ginger, Mom's *also* made shortbread, but you can never have too much—'

'Oh, I didn't bake this.' Ginger laughs airily, but I get the feeling she's lying to make Mom feel better. 'I got it at that lovely home industries down the road. I didn't want to bake in front of Lee-anne in case she made me make it vegan and gluten-free. It just isn't the same without butter and proper white flour that's been bleached and stripped of every nutrient it ever possessed.'

Ginger and I cackle, but Mom doesn't even crack a smile. *Who'd have thought she'd be so possessive about shortbread?*

'And how are *you* feeling?' Ginger sits down next to Mom and pats her hand. 'When are you starting treatment? Or have you started already?'

'You *told* her?' Mom looks properly pissed off.

'I'm sorry, Mom … I didn't realise it was a secret?' I'm confused – Mom isn't usually like this. 'And to be honest, Mom, I've needed the support of my friends too.'

'And suddenly you have *a lot* of friends, don't you?'

Oh Jesus. 'Mom, no! I'm not sleeping with *Ginger*!'

'Hell, no.' Ginger guffaws and I'm a tiny bit insulted. 'No offence, Mattie – you're lovely and so handsome, lovely eyes and lovely …' Her eyes move down to my butt. 'But you're no James.' She turns to my mother. 'No, the one he's sleeping with is Jess!'

Why the actual fuckitty fuck …?

'She *told* you?' I close my eyes and attempt to manifest an alien ship to come and suck me up. I don't even care if an anal probe is involved.

'She only told *me* because she was upset *you* might think she was a total slut.'

I open my eyes. 'God, no. Why would she think that?'

'Maybe it was the whole spontaneous bonk-in-the-tiger-enclosure thing but she now thinks it was a rebound shag-and-release situation.'

'A bonk in a tiger enclosure? I am a Friend of the Zoo, Matthew,' Mom says icily.

'I guess Matt is too.' Ginger winks at me. Mom does not look amused.

'Um, could we maybe not discuss this in front of my mom?'

'Why not?' Mom says tartly. 'You've apparently discussed my cancer with everyone.' Then she turns to Ginger. 'And for your information, I'm not having treatment.'

Ginger nods thoughtfully. 'Mattie said so. Which I think is a great pity.' *Someone kill me now.*

'Oh really? Have you *had* stage four breast cancer? Is *your* body riddled with it?'

For once Ginger's at a loss for words.

'I didn't think so. So perhaps you shouldn't talk about things you know nothing about.' My mother whips around and eyeballs me. 'And getting your friends here to lecture me and leaving books about it lying around is neither subtle *nor* helpful!'

I admit I did leave a copy of *This Charming Man* next to her bed to remind her of the journo character's aunt who had treatment for breast cancer *and* a copy of *Lucy Sullivan is Getting Married* because I thought the alcoholic dad might make her think a bit about her own relationship.

I don't know what to say so it's fortunate that Ginger's silence doesn't last long.

'No. I haven't been in your situation and Mattie didn't ask me to come over and speak to you, but maybe it's a good thing I'm here. I nursed my mother through cancer and one of my biggest regrets is that she didn't have treatment. She said she wanted a *good* death.'

'And did she have that? A good death?' Mom demands.

'Ish. I mean, death's a bit like childbirth; there is no fun way of doing it. And good death or not, she still died too soon. I miss her every day and I don't want Mattie to go through that.' Ginger pats my hand. 'I know how much you mean to him.'

Mom just stares at her.

'Helloooooo!'

And I shit you not, Jess comes rushing in. Yes, I am an idiot and I need to stop giving people the code to our gate.

'I know you might not want to see me, Matt—' She stops short when she sees Ginger and Mom. 'Sorry, I didn't know you had guests.'

'Don't tell me you also brought shortbread,' Ginger says.

'I did, actually.' They both cackle, but Mom doesn't seem to find this funny either. 'I just stopped by to tell you I did it,' Jess starts babbling.

Ginger looks shocked. 'You surely didn't bake it yourself?'

'Don't be ridiculous; I got this from that little home-industry shop. No, I thought about what you said, Ginger, about the booze and the pills and the sex with strange men.' She smiles at me. 'Not you, Mattie. The dude from the loo at Tashas—'

Where is that alien ship?

'Plus, I made an appointment to see an addiction counsellor and—'

'Well done!' Ginger says with a huge smile.

'Thank you, Ginger. And *then*, I submitted our short story!' Jess is beaming.

'You mean *Queenie's* short story,' says Ginger.

'Well, I *wanted* to tell her,' says Jess. 'You know, in case she got angry with me again. I even tried to phone her before I submitted it, but I couldn't get hold of her so I just sent it in anyway.'

I'm trying to make hand gestures to get them both to shut up. They've clearly forgotten this whole thing is supposed to be a surprise for my mom.

'Matthew,' Mom asks icily. 'Who exactly is Queenie? And have you been sleeping with her too?'

Jess's smile fades and she stares accusingly at me.

Fucking shortbread.

Queenie

'Why are you all being so awkward?' I ask ten minutes into the conversation when I can't stand it any more. At first I thought it was just the Wi-Fi that was making everyone so stuttery over the WhatsApp group call, but then I realise that their silences are definitely getting longer. This chat is starting to feel like a one-woman show and I haven't even got to the part about Kevin yet. 'What the hell is going on?'

'Well …' Ginger lets out a sigh when neither Jess nor Matt say anything. 'Fine, I'll tell her. I think it's mostly my fault anyhow. It all started so innocently, but at the end of the day there was just too much shortbread. See, *I* bought some and took it to Matt's house and then Jess arrived with *her* shortbread and his mum was there and *she* thought he was into everyone's shortbread including yours, Queenie, even though I said it was only Jess's he was really into …'

'What?' I am totally confused, but both Matt and Jess are laughing. Possibly hysterically. 'I hate shortbread. Too crumbly.'

'Oh no, if it's crumbly you're not doing it right,' Ginger says seriously, which sets off the others again.

'Oh my God, Ginger, just tell her,' Matt splutters, wiping his eyes on his sleeve. 'If Mom knows then Queenie obviously should. But the short version please.'

'Yes, and without the confectionery,' says Jess, face buried in her hands. 'Remember I'm doing this without a single drink or pill in my body.'

'Very well.' Ginger is brisk. 'Queenie, here's what you need to know: Jess and Matt did the monkey business in the tiger enclosure at the zoo. Sadie saw it and was so upset she took a bite right out of Matt's cheese – I mean, what kind of person does that? Any rate, Matt has finally come to his senses about that girl so he told her off and she left. But then Matt's mum and me and Jess arrived at Matt's house – all of us with shortbread – and I spilled about him and Jess and that we all know about his mum's cancer, and she was rather upset about that. What's your mum's name anyhow, Matt?' Ginger peers into her camera, presumably at where Matt's face is on her screen. 'I can't very well keep calling her "Matt's mum"; I feel like I'm back at school! You know, when my girls were little, it—'

'Okay,' I say, trying to remain calm while excluding any visuals from my mind. 'Matt and Jess. In the tiger enclosure. No wonder you two are so quiet.'

I'm not surprised – anyone with two eyes in their head could see they were into each other at the game reserve. Good riddance to horrid Sadie too. I am a little worried though – what does this mean for the four of us as friends? Won't it be awkward? I hope not. I'm not ready to lose them, especially with Faheema and Jennifer still angry with me.

'Don't worry, Queenie,' Jess says. 'We're not going to let it stuff up our Marian group. Me and Matt are okay. Mostly.'

I see Matt nodding along although he looks a bit jumpy so that could just be the Wi-Fi again.

'Ginger also did an intervention and told me the booze and the pills have to go. So I've got an addiction counsellor. I'm even wondering if I should start getting my Gut Microbiome back under control.'

I have a feeling she didn't mean to say that part out loud.

'Biome schmiome,' Ginger cuts in. 'Kick the drink and drugs, but eat all the shortbread!'

'Yes, Ginger.' Jess laughs as she takes a sip from her tea cup.

'So how is your mum now, Matt? Other than shocked that you've got a Mrs Jones,' I ask. 'Sorry, Jess – couldn't help myself,' I say as Jess snorts the tea out her nose. I feel better after what she's said about the group, but I want to hear Matt's voice so I can judge for myself if he really is okay. He hasn't said much.

'I think she's a bit rattled, to be honest,' he says, face tight and voice sombre. 'She doesn't want to think about her son having sex with anyone, obvs. But she's dealing with it. The real thing is that Ginger talked to her about having cancer treatment and something Ginger said must have got to her. I don't want to push her, you know, but it's not like she has all the time in the world to make up her mind. At least she's not talking about the kind of funeral she wants any more. That must be a good sign.'

'She'll say when she's ready,' Ginger says kindly, her soothing voice the verbal equivalent of the hug we all want to give Matt. 'Right, Queenie, now you know it all. That's what's happening. What's the deal down there in Cape Town?'

'I wish I could say Cape Town was living up to its reputation as Slaap-stad,' I say, rolling my eyes, 'but things are a little mad here at the moment.'

I almost don't know how to start, except that it has to be with Kevin since he's the source of all the madness.

'I told you Kevin arrived out of the blue? I didn't even know he was in South Africa, and there he pitches up rattling the gate at my house, screaming at the top of his lungs for me to let him in. Me in my gown, nogal. I promised myself I'd look like a million bucks the next time he saw me but there I was – no broeks, hair still dripping from the shower. I made him wait outside while I got dressed. I didn't want to be alone in the house with him – Kevin could always sweet talk me ... So we ended up having a chat in the garden.'

'Sounds very civilised?' Jess says.

'"Civilised" is not quite right. It was, how can I say this ... it was sur-real. Watching Kevin go through all the stages, I felt like I was having an out-of-body experience. First, he was super remorseful; all the apologies you can imagine. You know –' I make quote signs with my fingers – '"*she didn't mean anything to me – it was a once-off, it's never happened before, it will never happen again,*" that kind of thing. Honestly, he seemed more upset that he'd been caught than that he'd actually cheated. I wasn't buy-ing any of it and I told him so. Then he got angry when I said I didn't want to carry on as we were, that I didn't want to carry on at all. He wanted me to be "grateful" that he'd come all the way to Cape Town to apologise, but then he let slip that his contract hadn't been renewed and he was waiting to hear about a new job. That Pornhub clip must have got him into trouble at work too. Anyway, what he was really trying to do was get me to agree to him living with me in Cape Town. Can you believe it?'

'The audacity!' Ginger says it so loudly that I stop talking for a second.

'It gets worse. He grilled me about Charl, demanded to know how long it's been going on and if Charl is the real reason I won't take him back. Then – like a bad movie – he went into a rage and the idiot actually rammed his hand into the garden wall.'

Simultaneously, Jess, Ginger and Matt erupt:

'How does he know about Charl?'

'Punching a wall is totally unacceptable.'

'That must've been scary.'

Jess leans in so her face fills her corner of my screen. 'You think that's the reason Kevin wants you back? People always want what they can't have.'

'I just kept thinking how bladdy ridiculous he is to have such a tantrum when he was the cheat in the first place. He calmed down when he saw his own blood on his knuckles – the man has a weak stomach – and then the crying started. I think you're right, Jess – Kevin only made a comeback because he got jealous. He told me he'd seen Charl and me together on Facebook. Remember that day we saw the animals at the waterhole? I posted a selfie of us on my page.'

'Time to unfriend Kevin?' asks Matt.

'Oh believe me, the minute I booted Kevin from my garden, that's exactly what I did. And that's when I saw that he had posted an old photo of the two of us – and tagged me on it – and written this whole story about how much he loves me and is never letting me go. He even said it was time to make an honest woman of me. Which, of course, Charl saw ...'

What the fuck. When did my life turn into a bad romcom?

'... so now I'm on the phone to Charl trying to make sure he knows it's not true because I really don't want to mess that up before it's even properly started ...'

I let the last of the air in my chest rush out in one hard breath.

'... and in the middle of all this, I'm worrying about my job because I think they're going to fire me over the Pornhub thing.'

I don't mean to be this dramatic, but the sob pulses out of my throat before I have time to stop it.

Matt, Ginger and Jess are quiet. That's the awkward thing about video calls compared to real life: no one knows when it's their turn to talk, especially when someone is crying.

Jess reacts first.

'Oh, Queenie, it's going to be okay. Charl seems like a reasonable guy and someone who loves animals is bound to be kind. He'll understand about Kevin.'

'And James is convinced that Pornhub will take that clip down with a lawyer's letter. Then the library can't fire you,' Ginger says.

'Just block Kevin on Facebook, on your calls, everywhere. That guy is bad news,' Matt finishes.

Or so I think.

'You just stay positive. I've submitted your story and I just *know* we're going to win,' Jess says with a big smile on her face.

Oh my God.

My story has been submitted to the competition.

In two weeks' time we'll know if we are going to Ireland to meet Marian Keyes.

Jess

'Tea?' Matt offers, barely meeting my gaze.

'I'm great, thanks,' I say, scanning the tables at the restaurant. Why he's suggested Tashas Hyde Park is beyond me.

'I think you are great, Jess,' says Matt. 'Really great.'

Oh, honey, I think, *I've been through enough of these to know what's next.* Part of me wants to put a friend out of his misery, but the other part wants to enjoy the man squirm.

What can I say, we all have our kinks.

He swallows. 'I really like you and you're –' he blushes '– ridiculously good in bed.'

'Well, in zoo enclosure, technically,' I correct.

'Bu-ut ...' He's started talking faster now. 'Things are really complicated what with my mom and me staying at home to help care for her and the Marian thing and Sadie keeps calling and you're still married ...'

Poor darling, he looks distraught.

'Matt, Matt! Stop before you have an asthma attack. It's okay! I never expected this to be a *thing*.'

He looks shocked.

'It is actually possible for an adult woman to have no-strings-attached sex and not need to make it something it's not.'

'Oh.'

'I've been self-destructing ... You were a part of that.' I try to sound casual, cold even, but a lump rises in my throat.

'So are we ...?'

'Still friends? Of course.'

Men truly are tiresome no matter what age or whether they read Marian Keyes or not. Apparently men also seem to ride in on the same waves, like dolphins ... or plastic pollution because just then my phone buzzes with a WhatsApp from Joe.

'Coffee at Tashas? If you're free, that is?' it says.

Good timing on his part. He knows I have an hour until I have to pick Willow up from preschool. He doesn't have to say which Tashas – he knows I am a common fixture at Hyde Park Corner, as much a 'part of the furniture' as the shop managers and security guards.

I cringe and shift my seat so at least I don't have a direct line of sight to the bloody loo.

'Matt, listen, we're all good, but I actually need you to leave right now.'

'But we still need to talk—'

'Right. Now.'

He looks slightly shell-shocked as he slouches off into the depths of the shopping centre. Matt is so sweet and surprisingly skilled in bed/the tiger enclosure, but I sense that he's not ready to be anyone's Prince Charming just yet.

And that's when Joe lopes in from stage left.

He is looking simultaneously older yet somehow more attractive. I swallow. I hope Beverly understands what she's taken. What a strong, good man she has ... well, apart from the tendency towards fraud. He sits down and smiles at me with that rugged, lopsided grin that always made me go weak at the knees.

'Gotta love Tashas.'

'Don't we all,' I sigh, strongly considering breaking my tentative abstinence and ordering a whiskey off the menu.

He orders an Earl Grey tea and I silently turn up my nose at Beverly's influence.

'You must be wondering why I asked to see you,' he says, and I try to read his face for clues. 'I mean, it's been a while since we talked – well, about something other than the kids.'

'It's about the message I left Beverly, isn't it?'

'You never were the best singer.' He laughs. 'She found the whole thing quite ... "curious" is the word she used.'

This feels odd. We should be sitting at the table like we usually do, right up next to one another, hand in hand. I've never stopped loving Joe, I realise with a jolt. It's just that life, and bloody Beverly, got in our way.

'I'm so sorry. I lost myself for a moment there,' I say. 'You're looking good ... better.' I swallow. Why do I feel on the brink of tears?

'I have something to tell you,' he says.

I brace myself for the speech: *It's time to split our redundant assets and raging debt—*

'I behaved rashly after the news of my, uh, financial indiscretions came out, and I think I've given you the wrong impression. I was so ashamed about what happened, I couldn't face you or the kids so I went to stay in the empty cottage at Beverly's house to do some soul-searching and decide on my next course of action.'

A cottage. At Beverly's house?

'I thought you were ...' I make a crude gesture.

'Oh God, no. No! Beverly is married. To Barbara. You might know of her – she's a celebrated literary-fiction writer.'

'Of course she is.'

'Quite sombre themes, really. I struggled to read it.'

There's a tautness in the air. He's too far away; I don't know how to talk to him without touching him. I can't hold it in any longer. I run around the table and hug him.

'Joe. I've fucked up so much. I thought you'd left me and I have a problem ... with drinking. You know how I hadn't touched alcohol since my twenties? Well, I'd forgotten it's because my relationship with it gets warped, really fast.'

He looks genuinely heartbroken. 'Oh, Jess ... I wish I could have been there for you.'

'I haven't been myself for a while.'

'I don't think I let you be yourself,' he says gently. 'I was so consumed by my own life that I wasn't the husband you needed.'

I shake my head. 'I need to take responsibility for my addiction, for all my self-destructive behaviour, really. I always thought you were standing in the way of my career, but I made every decision of the past few years myself.'

'I need to take responsibility for my mistakes with the fund.'

My thoughts turn to my dream of getting Marian to speak at the fundraiser. 'I had an idea of how to help you …'

He raises his hand. 'No. I need to face this on my own. Life might be a bit shit for a while, but it's going to be fine in the end.' He looks down at my phone, which is flashing with notifications. 'Looks like you're wanted.'

A message from Queenie: 'Guys! Marian Keyes just followed me on Twitter!!!'

Epilogue

Ginger

I'm not really sure how I'm going to explain it all to Sybil Portley-Smythe. I am, after all, cancelling bookclub to go to the vow-renewal ceremony of the man who robbed her of her life savings. And yes, he's worked out a repayment plan with the court and everybody might get their money back in the end because he is actually an awfully clever businessman, but still – Sybil's not going to be thrilled.

I didn't see that part coming, I must say. When Jess came off the booze, pills and sex mania to go to therapy, I knew things would change for her. I kind of knew that dear, sweet Matt would find himself alone again, tiger-enclosure sex or not. But I didn't see the part where it turned out that Jess's husband was not as big a wanker as everyone had thought, and that they're now going to renew their vows.

Joe wants them to do it before we all go off to Ireland. To be honest, if he knew what had happened with her and Matt, I doubt he'd be letting her come to Ireland. But he doesn't and he won't, providing everyone keeps their mouths closed.

I thought Matt might find it hard to come to the ceremony, but he's so delighted by how well his mother is after having treatment that he's practically bullet-proof. He wanted to bring his mum along to the renewal ceremony as his date, but after the shortbread debacle we're not sure she can keep the secret. So he's bringing a nice girl he met in the frozen-goods aisle at Woolworths instead.

When we got the news that Queenie won the competition, it was like a light went on in her head and she realised what she was capable of.

First, she got a restraining order against Kevin, who'd become a problem, turning up at all hours and punching things and then singing love songs to her from the road. Queenie's neighbours were pretty understanding until Kevin sang that song about walking all those miles just to be the man who woke up next to Queenie. I believe it was around then that someone threw a shoe at him and let out their dogs. Everybody's happier now that he's shut up.

Especially Charl. Queenie's all coy about that and says things like, 'Ag man, we're taking it slowly,' but mark my words, there'll be wedding bells by the end of next year. I'm hoping that Queenie will move up to Joburg to be near him so we can all be together to watch her writing career shoot through the roof – which is exactly what's been happening since she beat the 768 other entrants in the Marian Keyes short-story competition.

So now Queenie's come up to Joburg for Jess's renewal ceremony and to meet an agent who's flown in from London just to meet her. She told the agent that we'd all be in Ireland next week anyway, but he wasn't having any of it. Said he wanted to get to her first. Apparently this is unheard of. Unless of course Marian Keyes has said something …

I can't lie – we're all still so excited about meeting Marian. It's been our fantasy for so long. And now that we're actually getting to go to her house, we're pinching ourselves! But at the same time, somewhere along the line, she's become part of the backstory. What we're really excited about is the four of us having another adventure together.

In other words, if Marian cancelled for some reason, we'd be sad, but we'd be okay. Which I guess brings me to my own life.

Lee-anne moved out permanently, thank God. She's back in her little flat with her plants and her *Harry Potters* (unharmed) and no sign of that awful Tex. She's met someone new and she hasn't introduced us yet – says she's taking it day by day. But she doesn't shout at me any more when I say woman instead of womxn, so I think this could be the womxn for her.

Debbie's another one who's changed. She's dropped the whole old-age home argument and that's thanks to James. All that talk about me breaking my hip and getting raped and falling over a stray cat and what-ever else ended after just one lunch with him. I think maybe she saw me through his eyes. Because he just thinks I'm the bee's knees. And there's something about James; nobody, not even Debbie, would suggest sending *him* to a frail-care facility.

'He's actually quite sexy, Mom,' Debbie said after she'd met him. 'As Marian Keyes would say, he's a bit of a ride.'

'Hands off, young lady. That ride's all mine.'

Well, for a moment she was shocked but then we were laughing and I knew that actually, my girls are my world. Even if they are a massive pain in the bee-hind.

When the four of us get back from Ireland, James is going to move in with me. Don't tell the others, but he asked me to marry him. But I thought back to Roger and marriage and everything it entails and I decided I'd prefer to live in dreadful sin. I explained this to James and he said that as long as he can spend the rest of his days with me, he doesn't care if there's a ring or not.

I said that was fine, he could spend all the rest of his days with me, except for next week. Next week, my friends and I are going to Ireland to meet a famous writer. But the week after, well, then we can begin working the future.

And we will. All of us.

Matt

She's so pretty ...

Marian, I mean. Not Jess.

You thought I meant Jess, right? Well, obvs Jess is sexy as hell but she's also very married. Going to the vow-renewal ceremony of someone you've recently shagged when they're not renewing their vows to you went surprisingly okay, by the way. I was really dreading it because I would be lying if I said I didn't still have feelings for Jess. I didn't take things further with her (or let's say, she kicked me to the kerb before I could even try to take things further) because I care too much about her and her life is complicated enough without me adding to it. I didn't want to spoil things for her so I took this girl I met at Woolies.

Sian? Shona? Shaz? Something like that. We'd both reached for the same packet of frozen peas, so no, it's not the start of a great romance. I literally had to take someone to make everybody feel less awkward and although bloody Sadie was clamouring to come, I've finally got her out of my system.

Well, almost. Just to be sure and because Sadie's nagging was driving me nuts, I first spoke to Ginger about maybe bringing Sadie to the ceremony and Ginger said, 'Matthew, are you *insane*? You know she's going to get drunk and have a catfight with Jess and then Joe will know that the two of you bumped uglies and that'll ruin both our trip *and* our bookclub.'

'Please don't say "bumped uglies". There was nothing ugly about it.'

'There is absolutely nothing pretty about penises or vaginas,' said Ginger.

'Beauty is in the eye of the beholder.'

We then had a very long argument about whether vaginas are pretty. 'They can be erotic, but not pretty,' said Ginger with finality.

So, back to Marian.

Her house is so stylish, lots of colour and a surprising amount of glass, plus pieces of furniture she's painted herself. And as for her, her pictures do not do her justice. Her skin is like porcelain. The girls can't stop exclaiming over it and talking about their own sun damage. Ginger shows her where she's had some sun spots burnt off and at one point Jess actually reaches out and strokes Marian's face. Yes. Strokes Marian Keyes' face. Which is like stroking the Queen's face. And then they all start talking about something called Sephora and I'm not sure where it is but Marian calls it her 'happy place' and Marian's so sweet to my mom and wants to know all about her treatment and she speaks about her own battle with depression. As it turns out, as soon as the organisers heard about the situation with my mom, they paid for her to come too so I didn't need to fork out and Marian had no issue with hosting an extra person. The whole day feels like a dream and when I finally get my chance with Marian, I just hug her and say, 'I love you.'

Yep. That husband of hers, Tony/Himself/whatever, better watch out. If he decides to leave for a bit like the guy in *The Break*, Marian is mine. I tell him as much. I like to think that maybe he feels a bit threatened, but it looks like he's trying not to laugh.

Marian doesn't laugh. She pats my face and says, 'Ah, Mattie, you're a ride, but I'm a bit old for you.' And before I can insist that she really, *really* isn't, Ginger grabs my hand and tells me to stop being a dick and to let Queenie have some time with Marian.

'At least I'm a handsome dick,' I say.

No, I don't – I'll only think of a clever line two weeks later when I'm picking up a new woman in Woolies. (Yes, Woolies is the new Tinder, didn't you know?) No, I just nod and allow Ginger to drag me off to where Mom is having a restorative cup of tea and pretending to eat something. The treatment is taking its toll. But at least she's getting treatment.

All we've got is this moment and as moments go, this one is pretty damn perfect.

Queenie

Meeting Marian Keyes last month was nothing like I imagined.

I thought we'd all be awe-struck and stumbling over our feet and that we'd have nothing real to say like when we were at the restaurant in the Pilanesberg. I was sure we'd make complete fools of ourselves with all the fangirling.

Who am I kidding?

It was exactly like that except that once we'd got over our mumbly selves and started actually talking, we couldn't stop. Meeting Marian was even better than I imagined. She didn't make us feel like fools – she was just so normal, and for a while it was as if we were simply meeting a friend for tea. The poor woman didn't even blink when Jess stroked her face! And she didn't mind that we each had brought a pile of her books and wanted various special dedications for all our family and friends. She just smiled and wrote lovely things.

I totally overdid it, I know, but I couldn't help gushing like a burst water pipe and telling Marian all the predictable things about how much she inspired me, how her books have a way of being relevant to ordinary life but also let me laugh and cry. All too obvious now when I think about it, but I find it easier to write how I feel rather than say it out loud. I might have embarrassed her, but in the end she simply said, 'Tankin yew so very much,' in that very lovely Irish accent.

I'll have to write an apology note.

I know everyone is expecting me to say that winning the Marian Keyes competition is the best thing that has ever happened to me. Well, obviously, it's been major – and it's brought some big changes. For instance, although I still feel a little awkward, I now don't feel like a complete fraud when someone calls me a writer. I even have an agent. Me! Queenie from Cape Town. Not that I'm going to be in Cape Town much longer. After I gave Esmeralda the set of signed Marian Keyes books for the library, I handed in my notice. I'm moving to Joburg. I want a new start in a new city with new adventures, and where better than a place where I already have friends and a brand-new boyfriend. I don't have a job yet, but Esmeralda said she'd give me a reference for wherever I want to go. She's been so nice; I'm not sure if it's because of all the Marian Keyes publicity or because Zayn finally sorted out the Pornhub thing.

I'm sad about moving away from Jennifer, but my adventures with the MK club seem to have given her a kick up the bum. When I eventually told her I was worried about not taking her along to meet Marian, she sprung her own surprise on me! She said she realised that she needed her own adventures, not just to hang on to mine. She and Faheema cooked up a plan to use Faheema's air miles to get to London and they got me to meet up with them after seeing Marian. Those few days with the two of them made my first overseas trip even more incredible, and since we've been back Jennifer's not only passed her driver's test, she's also bought herself a brand-new Polo. On top of that, she asked me to help sell some of Ma's old furniture because she's thinking of taking in a tenant and needs to free up space. And Faheema has promised to keep an eye out for her. I think those two are going to adopt each other like they always promised me they would. They said they'd come visit me in Joburg as soon as I'm set up.

So winning the Marian Keyes competition has definitely brought big changes. But was it the best thing that's ever happened to me?

No.

The best thing that's ever happened to me was taking the chance, answering Matt's message and joining the MK club. I didn't know it at the time, but doing that and meeting Matt, Jess and Ginger gave me the courage to start doing new things. We were four complete strangers who became friends and from them I learnt to *do*, not just to imagine. Without the feeling that taking a chance could be a good thing, I think Charl would have stayed just a nice guy who helped me on the promenade. Without them pushing me, I'm not sure when, if ever, I would have shared the stories I kept scribbling.

Knowing them pushed me to start doing. And starting right now, I am going to be doing it all.

Jess

A woman sitting in Tashas, drinking a glass of wine alone ... people turn and notice something like that. Except I'm not alone and I don't have a glass of wine in my hand, but a kola tonic and lemonade. Joe squeezes my hand – he knows it's still hard for me to be out celebrating while everybody else is drinking. And now that I'm back on the social circuit working as an account executive for Lindiwe's public relations firm, these occasions are cropping up even more.

It's okay though because I feel stronger now. I've started to learn that

life doesn't happen to me. I have agency and I have the power to be whoever I want to be.

'Gosh I love this drink! It makes me feel joyous and grown-up without
turning me into …' I want to say an 'alcohol-crazed sex maniac' but I happen to be sitting next to my two girls, who – despite any of my poor efforts
in raising them – are being utterly delightful and impressing the entire MK
bookclub. I don't have to finish the sentence in any case because Matt goes
as scarlet as Queenie's utterly exquisite red jumpsuit. She's in full glam
and turning heads because tonight she launched her debut novel at Hyde
Park Exclusive Books.

'I spotted the books editor from *The Sunday Times* as well as the en-
tertainment editor for *Johannesburg Review of Books*,' Ginger is saying
authoritatively.

'Mom says everyone who's someone on Twitter was here. She says your
launch was trending!' says Matt.

'You elderly millennials are so cute,' quips Hannah. 'You'll be taking
pictures of your food next!' I kick her under the table and she shrugs.

Tashas has had a revamp. It's now called Le Parc and is Frenchier than
ever. The music, thankfully, has also undergone a metamorphosis and has
changed to jaunty jazz. I lean back and take everything in. How far we
have all come, how I have changed since that lunch when I cracked open
my first Marian Keyes novel. The only people who haven't changed are the
old couple who eat every meal at the café. They're at the table right next
to ours, sharing a glorious puff of Neapolitan pizza.

Back to our table. Queenie is glowing, showing off her redone crown
tattoo on her foot and chatting excitedly about her favourite parts of the
launch and her plot for book two. Ginger and James are showing Willow
photographs of their gorgeous Afghan puppy, Dumbledore. Matt and Joe
are, surprisingly, getting on rather well and – I cringe – setting up a golf
date at the Parkview Golf Club in the near future. My heart is filled to
overflowing with gratitude. My eyes well up.

'You know, I think this is my dream dinner party. You know how people always ask that question – who would you invite to your dream dinner
party? Well, it's you guys. I don't need any celebrities at this table, not even

Marian! Just you.'

'Actually, now that you mention it,' Matt pipes up, 'there *is* another author I'm desperate to meet in person ...'

Ginger coughs up some tea. Queenie slaps his wrist. I begin to guffaw. Now everyone in the café truly is staring. At a motley crew that have no obvious similarities – except for an abundant, enduring, sometimes crazy-making love of books.

The End

About Marian Keyes

Marian Keyes is not, as it happens, a figment of our imagination. She is the inimitable Irish author of nineteen bestselling novels (and counting) and is beloved by fans all over the world. Marian is hilarious on Twitter and for many writers and readers of women's fiction (or should that be womxn's fiction?) she is an inspiration and an icon. When the four of us found out that Marian was coming to South Africa for the literary festivals, we were beside ourselves!

And when some of us realised we were interviewing her or even on panels with her, we got even more excited. We would become her best friends! We would invite her and her husband, Himself, to dinner! She would love us!

And then Covid hit. And the literary festivals were cancelled and we couldn't leave our houses and yes, we all cried.

But from that tragedy came the idea of writing a book together – just for fun – about four characters who wanted to meet Marian as badly as we did. We told Marian about our idea and she was gracious and charming about our madcap plan and about the updates we sent her along the way.

Chasing Marian is the result.

About the Authors

AMY HEYDENRYCH is based in Johannesburg with her husband and son. Her first two novels – *Shame on You* and *The Pact* – are thrillers that reflect the zeitgeist of our complex digital age where the line between reality and fiction blurs. She was named as one of the Top 200 Young South Africans and has a body of award-winning literary-fiction work including short stories and poems. By day, Amy works as a consultant for one of the world's largest strategic consulting and innovation firms.

(Photo © Rosanna Heydenrych)

QARNITA LOXTON was born in Cape Town, where she still lives with her family. She has practised as an attorney, studied psychology and worked as an executive coach. Her first novel, *Being Kari*, was longlisted for the 9mobile Prize for Literature in 2018 and shortlisted for the 2018 Herman Charles Bosman Prize. *Being Lily*, *Being Shelley* and *Being Dianne* followed, concluding the series. In 2021 Qarnita was awarded the Philida Literary Award for an oeuvre of literary excellence. (She does often need to spellcheck 'oeuvre' though.)

(Photo © Grethe Rosseaux)

PAMELA POWER has worked in the South African television industry making sh*t up for the last twenty years. She is the author of three previous novels and a director at https://goseedo.co.za, where she blogs about books, films and life. She has two kids, three needy cats and one husband and lives in Johannesburg. She should be editing scripts and finishing her next novel but she's too busy tweeting about #TheEstateOn3.
(Photo © Jane Thomas)

GAIL SCHIMMEL is an admitted attorney with four degrees to her name. She is currently the CEO of the Advertising Regulatory Board. Gail has published six novels, most recently *Never Tell A Lie* and *Two Months*. She lives in Johannesburg with her husband, two children, an ancient cat and two very naughty dogs.

(Photo © Nicolise Harding)

Acknowledgements

Amy: Guys, how are we going to do this?

Gail: All I know is that if we each write individual acknowledgements it will go on for another book. We need to be brief.

Pamela: I hate everyone and everything at this point. Is that brief enough?

Qarnita: Where are the emojis? Can you even say thank you properly without emojis?

Pamela: No.

Gail: Pamela! It's not your turn ...

Amy: Well, I'd like to thank Pan Macmillan and Andrea Nattrass for having faith in this madcap project.

Gail: You're saying that first because you think that Andrea might be watching us write on Google Docs. But yes, they're definitely number ONE on the list. And then Nicola Rijsdijk.

Pamela: Andrea is always watching us. Probably a good thing – imagine what we'd do if they didn't keep an eye on us? I'd be licking banners somewhere. Also, thank you, Jane Bowman (the last time she saw me I was on stage at Beefcakes in my underwear #truestory).

Qarnita: Now I've got stage fright, thanks for that. Are we all going to thank everyone? Or can your thanks be my thanks to Andrea and Nicola and Jane and marketing and sales and all at Pan Macmillan willing to take on a project with FOUR writers? Have to thank my husband and kids directly though – they are not into group chat. Also MUST thank my librarian friends, Nizam Bray especially.

Amy: I want to thank my family, who I love dearly, as well as all friends and acquaintances who definitely did NOT inspire any of the characters in this book.

Gail: This is what I am talking about. We can't thank everyone who didn't inspire the bloody book. We'll be here forever. Let's just thank the one person who DID inspire the book?

Pamela: MARIAN!!! Thank you, thank you, thank you, lovely Marian.

231

(Also everyone at Pan Macmillan – Terry, Andrea, Veronica, Eileen, Dee – my husband, Paul, and my kids, Liam and Ruby, my cats, Jinx, Poppy and Nigel, the SA bookish community, Twitter and Dr Richard Parry. All mistakes are ours – feel free to interrupt me at any point, Qarnita.)

Qarnita: I want to thank Marian for not blocking any of us on Twitter and especially for chatting to Gail, who screenshot all the chats so that we could all have a look and laugh hysterically with happiness at every response. Also, I did have a little lie-down when Marian followed us on Twitter.

Pamela: We all did!

Amy: I'd like to add my thanks to Tashas for a damn fine brunch and inspiring what might be one of the most awkward sex scenes in SA literature. Oh, and Hilary Mantel for not inspiring this book.

Gail: You know who we also really need to thank? Each other. Because that's what it came down to, didn't it?

Pamela: Why are you making me blub now???? Yes. All of you got me through Covid …

Qarnita: Pam, do you want to say more or still blubbing?

Pamela: Still blubbing.

Qarnita: Fine, will take the gap. Oh no, I can see Gail hovering in my sentence!!

Gail: Dammit guys! In order! We have to stay in order! Must I be the head girl till the very end??

Pamela: Yes.

Amy: Yes, I'm awaiting my punishment.

Qarnita: Okay, sorry, whose turn is it now? Is that how you spell 'whose'? And there is Amy on about whips again.

Gail: That's it. I'm calling this group to order. Our thanks to everyone and our love to each other and that is that.

Pamela: Love you guys.

Qarnita: But I also wanted to say Thank You to the three of you from my own damn name. I admire you so much. This project was huge fun and unexpected and really just the best. Helped get me through the whole

Covid world. Love you all! (Is Gail still waiting for order?)

Amy: Reading the next instalment of this book each week got me through the darkest lockdown days. Thank you for bringing joy to my life and thank you to everyone who picks up this book and passes it on to their friends. I hope you feel the joy with which this book was written.

xxxx